Maurizio de Giovanni lives and works in Naples. He is the author [illegible] a bestselling series of 1930s crime novels starring Inspector [illegible] [illegible]claim[illegible] [illegible]fully translated into sev[illegible] [illegible] [illegible]aptation is under way. [illegible] a new crime series set in present-day Naples; it was a bestseller in Italy and won the Giorgio Scerbanenco Prize for Best Crime Thriller of 2012.

Praise for *The Crocodile*

'This novel is a perfect killing machine of flesh, bone, blood and cartilage. The story of the Crocodile will make you tremble to your very soul' Donato Carrisi, internationally bestselling author of *The Whisperer*

The Naples we are plunged into in de Giovanni's vivid and astringent novel is a phantasmagoric place, and it is the acute sense of locale that transforms the piece (imaginatively translated from the Italian by Antony Shugaar) from standard police procedural into something rich and strange' Barry Forshaw, *Financial Times*

'De Giovanni manages to conjure up the terrifying darkness at the heart of a serial killer in this chilling procedural' *Publishers Weekly*

'Intriguing . . . De Giovanni's tale is fast-paced' Julian Fleming, *Sunday Business Post*

'Engaging and emotional, *The Crocodile* is a memorable take on revenge' *S[illegible] [illegible]erald*

THE CROCODILE

Maurizio de Giovanni

Translated from Italian by
Antony Shugaar

ABACUS

First published in Great Britain in 2013 by Abacus
This paperback edition published in 2014 by Abacus
First published in Italy with the title *Il metodo del coccodrillo* in 2012
by Arnoldo Mondadori Editore

A CIP catalogue record for this book
is available from the British Library.

ISBN 978-0-349-13889-3

Typeset in Sabon by M Rules
Printed and bound in Great Britain by
Clays Ltd, St Ives plc

Papers used by Abacus are from well-managed forests
and other responsible sources.

FSC
www.fsc.org
MIX
Paper from
responsible sources
FSC® C104740

Abacus
An imprint of
Little, Brown Book Group
100 Victoria Embankment
London EC4Y 0DY

An Hachette UK Company
www.hachette.co.uk

www.littlebrown.co.uk

To Luigi Alfredo Ricciardi, and
the souls in darkness

Hush a bye baby,
Oh, I'll give you a star.
Sleep pretty baby,
It's the brightest by far.
Hush a bye, hush a bye,
Now do you want the world?
For the sweet love of God,
Go to sleep, darling girl.

THE CROCODILE

Prologue

Death comes in on track three at 8.14 in the morning, seven minutes behind schedule.

He blends in with the commuters, jostled by backpacks and briefcases, suitcases wheeled and otherwise, none of them able to sense the icy chill of his breath.

Death walks hesitantly, protecting himself from the haste of others. Now he stands in the vast concourse of the train station, surrounded by shouting children and the odour of defrosting pastries from the snack shops. He takes a look around, wipes away a tear from behind the left lens of his glasses with a quick motion, whereupon his tissue returns to its place in the breast pocket of his jacket.

He identifies the exit, from the noise and flow of the crowd, amid all the brand new shops. He no longer recognises the place: everything is different after all these years. He's planned out everything to the smallest detail. This search for the exit will prove to be his one and only moment of hesitation.

No one notices him. A young man leans against a column smoking a cigarette; he runs his gaze over and past him as if he were transparent. It's a clinical once-over look: nothing worth stealing, his down-at-heel shoes and unfashionable suit speaking as eloquently as the photosensitive lenses and the dark necktie. The young man's eyes slide past him, coming to a halt on the half-open handbag dangling from the shoulder of a woman gesticulating frantically as she talks into her mobile phone. No one else sees Death as he moves warily through the atrium of the train station.

Now he's outdoors. Humidity, the smell of exhaust. It has just stopped raining and the pavement is slippery with oozing muck. A shaft of sunlight breaks through and Death squints in the sudden glare, wiping away another tear. He looks around and spots the taxi rank. He trudges along, his feet dragging.

He climbs into a battered vehicle. The interior stinks of stale smoke, the seat sags listlessly. He murmurs an address to the driver, who repeats it loudly in confirmation as he jerks the car into motion and pulls into the stream of traffic without a glance behind him. No one honks their horn.

Death has come to town.

Chapter 1

Sergeant Luciano Giuffrè rubbed his face with both hands, pushing his glasses on to his forehead as he massaged his eyes.

'Signora, this is getting us nowhere. We have to come to some kind of understanding. We can't have you coming in here and wasting our time. We have urgent work to do. So would you tell me exactly what happened?'

The woman compressed her lips, shooting a sidelong glance at the neighbouring desk.

'Signor Captain, don't talk so loud. I don't want *him* hearing things that are none of his business.'

Giuffrè raised both arms in a gesture of helplessness.

'Listen, lady – for the last time, I'm not the station captain. I'm only a lowly sergeant with the hard luck to be assigned to this desk, where I'm in charge of taking crime reports. And *he* isn't eavesdropping on things that are none of his business. He's Inspector Lojacono, and he has the same job I do. But, as you can see, he's been luckier than me. For some reason, no one seems to want to file their complaints with *him*.'

The man sitting at the other desk showed no sign of having heard Giuffrè's tirade. He kept his eyes on the computer screen and his hand on the mouse, seemingly lost in thought.

The woman, a middle-aged, working-class matron with a small purse clutched in her plump hands, made a great show of ignoring him.

'What can I tell you? Customers always go to the salesmen they trust.'

'What do you mean by talking about salesmen, signora? Now you're going to make me lose my temper! Really, how dare you? This is a police station: show some respect! Customers, salesmen, where do you think you are – a butcher's shop? Now, either you tell me immediately, in the next two minutes, exactly what happened, or I'll have an officer show you out of here. Ready?'

The woman blinked her eyes rapidly.

'Forgive me, Signor Captain. I must be a little tense this morning. What you need to know is that the woman downstairs has started taking in cats again. And now she has three, you understand? Three.'

Giuffrè sat staring at her.

'OK, and what are we supposed to do about it?'

The woman leaned forward and muttered under her breath,

'These cats meow.'

'Oh, Jesus, of course they meow – they're cats. And there's no law against cats meowing.'

'Then you're determined not to understand me – those cats

meow and they stink. I leaned over the balcony and I said to her, perfectly sweetly, I said: "Listen, you miserable good-for-nothing, will you get it through your thick skull once and for all that you need to move out of this building, you and your filthy creatures."'

Giuffrè shook his head.

'Damn, it's a good thing you said it sweetly. And what did she say to you?'

The woman straightened her back against the chair, to underscore the depth of her indignation.

'She told me to go fuck myself.'

Giuffrè nodded, agreeing with the spirit if not the letter of the cat-owner's sentiments. 'Well?'

The woman opened her piggish eyes wide.

'Well, now I want to file a criminal complaint, Signor Captain. You need to haul her in here and slap her in a cell, her and the cats she keeps. I want to report her for aggravated incitement to self-fucking.'

Giuffrè didn't know whether to laugh or cry.

'Signora, there are no cells in here, I'm not the station captain, and as far as I know, there's no law against telling someone to go fuck themselves. Moreover, it strikes me that you called the woman downstairs a "miserable good-for-nothing" first, am I right? Listen to me, why don't you go home, try to keep your temper under wraps, and remember that a couple of cats never hurt anybody – they even catch mice. Go on, now. Please stop wasting our time.'

The woman got to her feet, rigid with disgust.

'So that's what we get for paying our taxes, is it? I always say to my husband he shouldn't declare half of the merchandise he sells. Have a nice day.'

And she stormed out.

Giuffrè took off his thick-lensed glasses and slammed them down on to his desk.

'I have to ask what I did wrong in a previous life to deserve this job. In a city where the first thing we do every morning is go out and count the dead bodies in the streets, how on earth could a woman like that decide to come into the police station to file a complaint against another woman who told her to go fuck herself? And the law says she has every right to do so, might I add? Does such a thing strike you as conceivable?'

The occupant of the neighbouring desk glanced away from the monitor for a brief moment. His face had vaguely Asian features: dark, almond-shaped eyes, high cheekbones and shapely, fleshy lips. Tousled, unkempt locks of hair dangled over his forehead. He was a little over forty, but sharp creases at the sides of his mouth and eyes spoke of much older sorrows and joys.

'Oh, come on, Giuffrè. That's just part of the general nonsense. You need something to do if you want to make the time go by in here, don't you?'

The sergeant shoved his glasses back on to the bridge of his nose, feigning astonishment. He was a very expressive little man whose every word was accompanied by an analogous gesture, as if the person listening were deaf.

'Oh, and what do we have here? Has Inspector Lojacono woken up from his beauty sleep? What would you like now –

a cup of coffee and a pastry? Or would you rather I bring you your morning newspaper, so you can read up on what the nation did while you were slumbering?'

Lojacono gave a half-smile.

'I can't help it if everyone who comes in here takes one look at me and then makes a beeline for your desk. You heard the fat lady, didn't you? Customers develop a certain loyalty to their favourite salesmen.'

Giuffrè drew himself up to his full five foot five inches.

'You realise that you're stuck in the same leaky boat as me, don't you? Or do you think you're just passing through here? You know what everyone else calls this office? They call it the loony bin. So what do you think, that they're singling me out?'

Lojacono looked indifferent.

'What the hell do I care? They can call this shithole whatever they like. I'm more disgusted with it than they ever will be.'

Lojacono turned back to his monitor, where there was a time and a date, right under the game of cards that he played obsessively against the computer. April 10, 2012. Ten months and a few days. That's how long he'd been sitting there. In hell.

Chapter 2

The girl at the reception desk had a pair of earphones blaring out Beyoncé at full volume – after all, for four hundred fucking euros a month, under the table and with no benefits, what did those bastards even expect? On the other hand, the way things were these days, an easy job at the front desk of a small ten-room hotel in Posillipo, where she could get a little studying in on the side, wasn't the sort of thing you'd put out with the rubbish. So damn boring, though.

She looked up and jumped in her seat. There was a man standing right in front of her, gazing at her across the counter.

'I'm sorry, I didn't hear you come in. How can I help you?'

The first impression she had was of an old man. If she'd looked a little more closely, behind the antiquated suit of indeterminate colour, behind the dark tie, behind the glasses with photosensitive lenses (God, how many years had it been since she'd seen a pair like that? Her grandfather wore those!), maybe she'd have revised her guess downward a couple of years. But with her final exam in public finance bearing down on her and Beyoncé howling out of the earphones dangling around her neck, the anonymous, invisible client standing before her needed to be taken care of and dismissed as quickly as possible.

'I have a reservation for a room, I think room seven. But could you check? Thanks.'

Even his voice was nondescript, little more than a whisper. The man dug a paper tissue out of his breast pocket and quickly dabbed at his left eye. The girl assumed he had some allergy.

'Yes, here's the reservation. Room nine has become available, though, if you're interested. You can get a glimpse of the water from the window, while room seven is on the street. If you like we can—'

The old man broke in politely.

'No, thanks. I'd rather confirm room seven, if it's all the same to you. It might not be as noisy, and I'm here to get some rest. You do have a key to the downstairs door in case I stay out . . . late, don't you? I read on your website that you offer that option, since there's no night clerk.'

He's here to get some rest, but he wants a key for the front door so he can stay out late. Filthy old pig.

'Of course, here you are, this key is for the night entry door and this one is the room key. How long will you be staying with us?'

A question she'd tossed in as an afterthought, a formality. The old man seemed to be thinking hard, trying to come up with the answer, his watery gaze wandering behind the lenses, a deep crease furrowing his forehead under the sparse white hair.

'I'm not sure. A month or so, maybe less. In any case, not long.'

'Whatever you prefer. Here's your ID back. Have a pleasant stay.'

And Beyoncé rose in her ears again, the soundtrack to public finance.

Room number seven. Carefully selected from the hotel floor plan, studied obsessively on the internet. The single bed pushed against the wall, the bathroom with the shower and no bidet, the armoire with squeaky door hinges. A writing desk, a chair, a bedside table. Perfect. Perfect in every way.

The old man put his suitcase on the bed, unzipped it, and quickly checked its contents. Then he took off his jacket and carefully hung it up in the armoire, moved the writing desk over in front of the window and raised the roller blind halfway. He looked across the narrow private street and nodded in satisfaction, then loosened his tie and sat down. He examined the pen and the stationery bearing the hotel's pretentious coat-of-arms, glanced at the window again, and started writing.

There were a few items of clothing in the suitcase. And a pistol.

Chapter 3

Lojacono checked his watch, for the hundredth time. He decided that 11.58 was the latest he could push it, especially because Giuffrè had finally left his desk. He picked up the phone and dialled the number.

'Hello?' said Sonia on the other end of the line.

In Lojacono's mind, the deep sound of her voice triggered a succession of images that he hastily scrubbed out of existence as soon as they materialised: laughter, a soft breast, the sweet taste of her lips. All part of the distant past.

'Ciao, it's me.'

'Ciao, you piece of shit. What the fuck do *you* want?'

Lojacono smiled bitterly.

'I'm so happy to hear your voice too, my darling.'

The woman raised her voice.

'Go ahead, joke about it while you're at it. After the shame you've brought down upon us – on me and on your daughter. Only now are we finally able to leave the house, a full year after it happened. You coward. And you're not supposed to call us; even the lawyer said that you're not allowed. All you're allowed to do is send us the money, understood?'

The inspector ran his hand over his eyes. Suddenly he just lacked the strength.

'Please, Sonia. You know that I send the money, punctually. I'm giving you practically every penny I make, and you can't even begin to imagine what a shitty life I'm living here. There's no need for you to weigh in too.'

The woman burst into a long chorus of laughter that had nothing cheerful about it.

'No need for me to weigh in? Do you have even the faintest idea of what you've done? If you'd been a successful mobster, at least, there's no doubt that we'd be respected now if nothing else, Marinella and I, instead of having everyone, even our relatives, turn their backs on us. And we're forced to live here, where nobody knows us, as if we were a couple of thieves or whores. You son of a bitch.'

Son of a bitch. How little it takes to become a son of a bitch.

'Anyway, I wanted to know how you were doing. And I wanted to talk to Marinella.'

Sonia lashed out, angrily.

'Forget it. Just forget it. She doesn't want to talk to you, and it's my duty to protect her from you. She's only fifteen, and you've already destroyed her social life. Stop trying to get in touch with her. She has a different mobile number now.'

Lojacono pounded the desktop hard with his hand, making pens and paper clips jump into the air.

'Goddamn it to hell, she's my daughter! And I haven't

heard the sound of her voice in ten months! No judge on earth can tell a father he has to be dead to his daughter!'

Sonia's voice turned as chilly as a knife blade.

'Well, you should have thought before handing information over to the Mafia, without taking so much as a penny in exchange. You're a turd, and if some poor girl has a turd for a father, no one can force her to pay the price for the rest of her life. Just send us the money and leave us be.'

Lojacono found himself muttering incoherent words into the silent receiver, and when an embarrassed Giuffrè came back into the room, he stood up abruptly and went outside.

He'd known him: Di Fede, Alfonso. They'd even attended school together, a couple of grades in elementary school, before Alfonso started herding sheep like the rest of his family. Lojacono remembered him as an oversized, silent, fierce-eyed boy. He never opened a book; well aware of what fate had in store for him, evidently.

Of course, he'd followed the man's career from a distance, so similar to so many others: the most ferocious and loyal get promoted, ratcheting upward rank by rank – the same as it is in the police, come to think of it. Arrested and released a couple of times, only to vanish into the fields between Gela and Canicattì, another courier with his sleeves rolled up, busily delivering messages and, when so ordered, death.

They'd never crossed paths. Di Fede hadn't been one of the scattered few that they managed to round up on those scorching hot summer nights when they raided houses built in open violation of planning regulations, in out of the way parts of town, bursting into barren rooms littered with wine bottles and dirty magazines, where men sat deciding the fate of who-knows-who, who-knows-where.

But in the end, someone did manage to lay hands on him, in Germany of all places. And during the long interrogation sessions that finally led him to turn state's witness, what had emerged? His name, the name of Inspector Lojacono, Giuseppe, of the Agrigento major case squad, a golden boy with a glittering career ahead of him. The career might have been gilded, but unfortunately the golden boy lacked political protection.

Yes, said state's witness Di Fede, Alfonso, that's right: Lojacono tipped us off, of course he did. He was how we knew everything the major case squad was going to do before they did it. We knew where it was safe to go and where it wasn't. Can I have another espresso now?

Who could say where his name had come up, from what nook or cranny of Di Fede's memory, prompted by what need to cover up someone else's involvement? In the sleepless nights spent staring at the bedroom ceiling that followed his immediate suspension, Lojacono had puzzled over that one a thousand times.

The effect on his own life, and on Sonia and Marinella's lives, had been devastating. No one was willing to speak to them now – some out of fear that the informant's account was true, others out of fear that it wasn't. As long as the matter remained in doubt, everyone kept their distance, and there the three of them were left, in the middle of nowhere.

He'd read the uncertainty in his wife's and daughter's eyes

immediately. Not that he'd expected unwavering support. He'd seen this sort of thing happen far too often: he knew how rare it was, outside of books and movies, for families to remain steadfast allies in bad times as well as good. But he had hoped he'd at least be given an opportunity to explain, to defend his good name.

It would have been so much better if there'd actually been a trial. In that case, he would have had a chance to demolish the absurd accusation, revealing it for what it was – little more than vicious slander. But it was the very fact that there was no evidence that led to a dismissal of charges, meaning no lawyers, no courtroom hearings.

Advisability: that had been the operative term. No disciplinary measures, merely a matter of advisability. Of course, there was a case file; in some dimly lit room somewhere, there was a folder with his name on it full of documents: copies of reports, interviews, judgments. Fragments, relics of a policeman's life, a life spent in one of the most complicated places on earth. Everything taken apart and archived, for reasons of 'advisability'.

'You have to understand, Lojacono,' the chief of police had told him, 'I'm doing it for the good of the squad; I need your co-workers to feel safe. And for the good of your family, it's not in anyone's interest for you to stay here. You're too exposed. A question of advisability.'

It had been deemed advisable to move Sonia and Marinella to Palermo. Why run the risk of extortion, or worse? There were families whose members had been killed at the hands of Di Fede and his men; no one could say what some hothead might decide to do to someone who had collaborated with them.

Marinella had been forced to change schools, lose all her best friends, even the little boy who liked her. Terrible things, at her age. The last thing he had heard in her voice was hatred.

The coffee up here was good. At least that was something.

The transfer had been advisable, of course. Far enough to put him out of play, but not far enough to make it look like a punishment, for something he might or might not have done, for something that couldn't be proven, one way or another. Naples, San Gaetano police station, in the flabby belly of a city that was decomposing. Evidently they couldn't find anything worse, at least nothing that was readily available.

The inspector had welcomed him in a meeting in his office. 'You understand, Lojacono, given the situation, that it's not advisable to put you in charge of investigations.' Advisable, not advisable, he'd mused as he listened. 'So I'll have to ask you not to get involved in anything that smacks of investigation.'

'Then what will I be doing?' he'd asked.

'Don't worry about that, you won't be asked to do anything. Check in with the Crime Reports Office, and once you're there you can do what you like: read books, write your memoirs. Just stay there and don't worry. It won't last long, I can promise you that.'

Ten months. Enough to make you lose your mind. Phone call after phone call, in a desperate and unsuccessful attempt to talk to his daughter. From his hometown, from his home office, came only deafening silence. Suspended in time and space, sitting at an empty desk, playing poker against the computer, with no one to keep him company but Giuffrè, another outcast, a one-time driver for a member of parliament, and so on the staff but in bureaucratic purdah, assigned to take down the deranged complaints of crazy old women, as he had that morning.

I shouldn't think badly of Giuffrè, he told himself. After all, he's the only one willing to talk to me.

Chapter 4

Sweetheart, my darling,

I'm here. At last. I'm breathing your air. Perhaps, even as I write, here in this room, there might be a little left – air that once flowed into your lungs and then out again.

The last few months were endless. She took so long to die, and in the end every breath she took was a desperate death rattle. I sat up all night at her bedside, hoping that noise would come to an end, that I'd finally be free. God, it took her for ever.

She had become my prison. She wasted away in the bed, slowly, imperceptibly. No one came to see us after a while; the very sight of her was intolerable. A shipwreck of life.

Not me. I never let myself go. I had you, my darling.

The thought of you sustained me every second of the day; the idea that I could see you again, hold you again in my arms – that idea lifted me up and carried me away from my despair. You saved me, my darling. Your smile, your beauty, your blonde hair. The warmth of your hands on my face. I could feel you at night, in my half-waking state punctuated by that endless death rattle. I saw you with the eyes of my desire, like a lighthouse in the night, like a house in a tempest.

Sweetheart, my darling.

The sound of your name murmured in the silence gave me the strength it took to stay by her side right up to the end. Because I knew there was still a chance I could hold you close to me again.

I never wasted a second, you know that, right? I organised everything.

I learned how to surf the internet. People say that it's hard for a man my age, but it wasn't difficult at all. You're smiling, aren't you, my darling? You're thinking that nothing could be as hard as these years I've lived without you. That's right, that's exactly how it is. Nothing is as hard as that.

It's incredible how easy it is to organise everything. All you need is the time, and I had nothing but time. Then, your letters told me everything I needed to know. How many times I read them and re-read them, my darling. Spreading them out before me like relics, taking care not to get them dirty, not to tear them. Touched only by your fingers and mine. No one else's.

Your letters told me everything I needed to know: names, dates. And the computer did the rest. While she was struggling for death and waiting to die, I was finding addresses, locations and timetables. You know you can find anything on the web, my darling. Anything. All you need is patience and determination; and you know how patient I can be.

It won't be long now. And I'll have finally done what needs doing if I hope to wrap you in my arms again, to stay with you, this time for good, without obstacles. It won't be long.

I never had time to tell her, you know. And maybe I wouldn't have, even if I had had the time. Why give her an extra cause for concern, or even a cause for sorrow? You know how emotional she could be.

Finally, I'm ready now. And I'm eager to get to work, immediately. Starting tonight, the hunt is on.

Chapter 5

Mirko is smoking in front of the mirror. He's checking his hair; he has a brand new mohawk. He likes it. Nothing overstated, he knows it's not a good idea to stand out in people's memories; he's smart, he thinks about this kind of thing, he's not a child any more. He's sixteen years old now.

He can still feel the thrill that ran through his body a month ago, when Antonio first approached him. Antonio: a living legend to all the kids in the neighbourhood. Antonio, who dates all the prettiest girls around. Antonio, who two years ago was a *scazzottiello* like the rest of them, just another punk kid playing football late at night in the Galleria, but now he's got an enormous motorcycle with chrome-plated exhaust pipes that makes the shop windows rattle when it goes by.

So Antonio comes over to him, while he's sitting on the wall with his friends talking about girls, and says to him: '*Guagliò*, come here, I want to talk to you.'

Mirko can still remember the look on his friends' faces:

surprise, envy, even concern. And the sound of his heart pounding in his ears as he broke away from his group and walked towards his destiny.

Antonio had locked arms with him. The way he would with a friend, with a peer. And he had told Mirko that he struck him as better than the others, smarter, wider awake. That he'd seen him on his motor scooter, and that he'd made a good impression. 'You're not the kind of guy that's going to pull *strunzate*; you're not a fuck-up,' he'd said to him. 'You're chilled, you just hang. That's what we like. That's what you need to be one of my guys.'

'One of your guys?' Mirko had asked, and his voice had barely squeaked out of his mouth.

Antonio had put Mirko to the test. One beep on his mobile phone and Mirko came running. He'd carried a few packages around the city; one time, he even had a passenger, a young guy he'd never seen before, and he'd taken him from one neighbourhood to another on the far side of town. Then, finally, Antonio had assigned him a couple of street vendors, black African immigrants who peddled CDs, and told him to make sure they didn't pull a fast one, like pretending the police had confiscated their merchandise.

For the past few days now, though, he was finally working for real. He'd pull up outside the rich kids' school, up in the nice part of town, and sit there on his scooter, off to one side. When school finished, he'd mingle with the students, and someone would approach him with a folded banknote in their hand; they'd shake hands, and he'd palm him a baggie. Just another kid surrounded by kids like him.

Dressed like them, with a scooter just like theirs. It was easy, so easy.

And Mirko had received, directly from Antonio's hands, two fifty-euro notes. 'But you need to be careful,' Antonio had told him.

Mirko looks at himself in the mirror again, suddenly slightly worried: this mohawk isn't too showy, is it? It's not like someone's going to recognise him, is it? Some sharp-eyed high school teacher who doesn't know enough to mind his own fucking business?

Then he thinks it over and remembers that some of those idiots who were so eager to give him their money have hair exactly like his, and that calms him down.

For no good reason, his thoughts go to the blonde. He'd noticed her immediately, among all the other airheads, outside the school. Mamma mia, she was a real beauty! She looked like an angel, and when she laid her eyes on him he felt even punier than when Antonio first called him over. And she had smiled at him – at him, of all people. She must have taken him for someone else, but for whatever reason, she'd smiled at him.

Mirko takes a look around. Of course, if the blonde saw where he lives, what a shitty home he has, he could imagine how she'd laugh. But that doesn't mean she necessarily has to know, does it?

He touches the pocket where he keeps the hundred euros. He doesn't want to break the notes, but he has to buy petrol for his scooter. Maybe it's time to take a stroll through Mamma's handbag.

He smiles into the mirror, cigarette in his mouth, one eye half-closed. Mamma. Who always tells him that 'it's you and me alone against the world'. Who gives him everything she has, and has done so as long as he can remember. Mamma, who works and does nothing else, who hasn't even ever had a man. Who's never gone out to the movies, never eaten in a restaurant. But who keeps that hovel clean and sweet-smelling, for her boy.

I'm not a boy any more, Mamma. Let me do what I need to, and I'll take care of you now. I'll bring money home, Mamma. And I'll take you out to dinner and a movie every night from now on.

I wonder if the blonde likes guys with mohawks, he thinks as he looks at himself in the mirror. Anyway, who cares what she likes?

Chapter 6

Letizia's trattoria had become fashionable. People came from Vomero, Posillipo and Chiaia to eat there, leaving their cars in parking garages on the edge of the quarter, where they'd be safe from the rapacious eyes of car thieves.

One day, a newspaper had published a highly flattering review by a food writer, and everything changed. Letizia often wondered when it was that the man had come in, just one more anonymous diner, and taken his seat at the red-and-white checked table, sampling the 'sublime red onion-tomato sauce' and the 'fantastic ragù meat loaf, a sensory delight', as he had described his meal. Actually, she was glad that she hadn't known at the time; she was proud of the fact that the reviewer hadn't been given any special treatment.

Since the man was an authority in his field, famous for his all-guns-blazing takedowns of pretentious high-end restaurants, the favourable review spelled the beginning of an unstoppable rise in the tiny trattoria's popularity. The phone rang non-stop and reservations poured in. Letizia could perfectly well have raised prices sharply, expanded the dining room, to the disadvantage of the kitchen or the wine cellar, made more tables available to her ravenous clientele, and even hired a couple of waiters; but it would no longer be her trattoria if she had.

She liked taking orders herself, moving around in the dining room, chatting with the diners. She felt that a little personal interaction, without presuming on her customers' good nature, helped her to understand what people preferred so that she could encourage them with some advice or a suggestion. Dining is meant to involve conversation: if you don't want to talk, go stand at the counter in a panino place.

Letizia herself, as the reviewer had written, was one of the reasons it was worth climbing the dark, damp alley: 'a dark good-looking woman, all smiles and personality, with a ready wit and a contagious laugh'. What the man couldn't have known was that behind that laughter was an iron personality, forged by profound sorrow and a great deal of hard work.

She never talked about her husband, who had died many years ago; some said in a car crash, others said after a brief illness. She hadn't had children and no one knew of any subsequent relationships, even though a great many men had been attracted by her lovely smile and generous bosom. She had her trattoria to run and at this point in her life – well past forty – she wanted no distractions.

Just before the article and the sudden rush for reservations that followed, she had noticed one regular customer. He always sat at the corner table, the one that was least visible, the table no one else wanted because it was right under the television set and close to the front door. He never took off his overcoat, he never had anything to read, he never had company for dinner. He always asked for the special, which he ate quickly; but then he'd linger, drinking wine, downing one glass after another, methodically, without enjoyment, as if he were taking medicine. Letizia watched him curiously, sympathetically. He had an odd face. It looked as if it had been carved out of hardwood, high cheekbones, black almond-shaped eyes. In her mind, she called him 'the Chinese'. She wished she could talk to him. Her sociable nature made her want to break the silence that isolated him from the rest of the world like a transparent veil, but she sensed that the equilibrium between them was fragile and that, after a few one-syllable replies, he might very well stop coming to eat there.

She'd impulsively started reserving the table for him. Even when there was a queue outside, with customers standing out on the pavement in the pouring rain, patiently waiting their turn under their umbrellas, the corner table sat empty, awaiting its silent occupant. And sure enough, he would show up, hair rumpled, overcoat creased, and take a seat under the television. For Letizia it had become something to look forward to, so much so that for him the prices, which had remained the same even though the trattoria was increasingly popular, were actually slightly discounted.

One night the Chinese fell asleep, shoulders against the wall, wineglass in hand. There was a dolorous expression on his face as he chased after some terrible, unimaginable dream.

Two couples, sitting at the next table, started elbowing each other and sniggering. One of the girls intentionally dropped a fork to see him wake up with a jerk. But he went on sleeping his sleep of despair. Letizia felt a stab of sympathy in her heart and went over, sitting down at his table to protect his rest. Without opening his eyes, he murmured,

'Forgive me, I have a headache. I'll get up in a minute and free up the table for you.'

'Don't worry, you can stay as long as you like. I'll bring you a couple of aspirin. You'll see, you'll feel better right away.'

Without opening his eyes, he smiled a crooked smile and said,

'The headache I have isn't something you can cure with aspirin. But thanks all the same. Maybe another glass of wine, and the bill.'

From that night on, whenever the trattoria was almost empty, Letizia developed the habit of sitting at the corner table to eat her dinner, instead of eating in the kitchen.

One word after another, night after night, 'the Chinese' turned into Inspector Giuseppe Lojacono, known to the friends and family he no longer had as Peppuccio, from Montallegro, a village in the province of Agrigento; and his sad story emerged in the images glimpsed at the bottom of glasses full of red wine, including his ruined marriage and his daughter's voice, the sound of which he was starting to forget.

Night after night, Letizia had become a door through which Lojacono spied on a city that was very different from the way he'd first imagined it: mistrustful, damp and dark, increasingly hidden and far less decipherable than he had thought. Everyone eager to avoid trouble of any kind, everyone keeping their nose out of other people's business, ready to take to their heels. A city that ran through your fingers, turning to liquid, or suddenly evaporating.

Even though Lojacono himself came from a place whose ways were, at best, difficult to fathom, he wondered exactly where the delicate balance point lay between this city and those entrusted with its governance. He saw his fellow policemen venture out and return, conclude complex operations and undertake others, with no clear objective, while all around them illicit trafficking bubbled along like a stew pot, endlessly. Shaking his head, he told Letizia that it was like a system, a net that had no visible means of support. It wasn't clear how the thing stood up.

Letizia smiled and gave a shrug. She replied that perhaps everyone was just doing their best, against impossible odds, to remain standing. And maybe that was all that kept the city upright, because deep down the place was empty, both physically and morally.

When she said that, he smiled that odd smile of his, that smile she liked so much, and raised a glass to that dark city and to her own luminous laughter.

Chapter 7

The old man walks along, hugging the wall.

His feet drag a little, his worn-out shoes grazing the wet and uneven paving stones. He's cautious, eyes on the ground to make sure he doesn't trip and fall. Every so often he reaches a hand into his pocket, pulls a tissue out and dries his left eye, dabbing under the lens of his glasses.

The old man makes his way slowly. When he comes to a junction he stops and looks first in one direction, then the other, waiting for howling scooters piled high with people, two or three on each, to zip by.

The old man walks along, hugging the wall, and no one sees him. He's like a breath of wind, like a rat in the shadows. Who should bother to glance at him, no different from so many others like him, phantoms that populate the city of shadows?

Every so often the old man crosses paths with someone: a woman bent double with the burden of years, a black man with a shopping bag on his shoulder, a man whose face bears the marks of the blows fate has dealt him. He turns his gaze away and so do they, because death is ugly to look upon, as is death's harbinger.

The old man walks along, hugging the wall, and no one sees him. He passes by the windows of the *bassi*, the miserable shopfront hovel flats, but he doesn't look inside, he doesn't glance at the poverty. And the poverty doesn't look up at him.

The old man walks and the street rises before him, but despite the climb his pace does not slacken. He knows that if he keeps moving constantly, no one will wonder who he is, the way they would if he were to stop and look up. No one sees those who walk in silence, head down, clearly beset by thoughts and problems; no one wants to run the risk of sharing thoughts and problems, even if it entails nothing more than exchanging a glance.

The old man walks, bending his back in an effort to look even older. Old age is a heavy burden, and no one wants that burden for themselves. Old age seems like a contagious disease; it prompts disgust, and so others shun it.

The old man knows how to pass unobserved. In fact, he's invisible, hugging the wall, diligently yielding to others, careful not to become an obstacle to anything, to anyone. Only a sleeping dog raises its muzzle and twitches an ear at his passage, sensing the whiff of death that wafts around him; but the dog thinks it must be dreaming, and falls back into slumber.

The old man walks, searching for a specific address. He reaches it and comes to a halt. He looks for the darkest shadows, he studies a main street door. He sees a motor scooter, he compares the licence plate with a number in his memory. He withdraws into a corner stinking of stale piss and braces himself to wait. Patiently.

The old man knows how to wait.

Chapter 8

Giada is stretched out on the sofa in the living room, talking on the phone with Allegra, as usual. As usual she still has her shoes on. She'd really catch it if her mother could see her; Mamma would start up with the usual litany. But Mamma's not home, so who the hell cares?

'And what did you tell her?'

Allegra laughs. She's sophisticated even when she laughs. That's the way Allegra is, always perfectly poised, well mannered, meticulous; her delicate features, her neatly coiffed hair, well groomed and well dressed. But Giada knows her well, they've been friends for ever; she knows what a sewer of filth that pouty pink mouth can turn into.

'You can probably guess. I told her that if she doesn't watch out I'll pop those fake overblown tits of hers, and that if she keeps playing the slut with Christian I'll tell everyone I know that her mother caught syphilis from the Sri Lankan houseboy they hired.'

Giada lurches on the couch.

'Have you lost your mind? Did her mother really ... No way!'

'Of course not. But everyone would believe me; they all know that Marzia's mother is a slut. And for that matter, like mother like daughter. Better to be cautious, don't you think?'

'Still, if you ask me, you took it too far. Wouldn't it have been a better idea just to tell Christian that you didn't like the way the girl was looking at him?'

Allegra snorts.

'Oh, sure, and give him the satisfaction of thinking he's so important? Darling, you really don't have a clue how to deal with men. You're fourteen – when are you going to come to your senses?'

Giada silently grimaces into the phone; her friend never misses a chance to lord it over her just because she's a year older.

'I ... I don't feel ready, those hands on my body, those sticky mouths ... Gross. And after all, you're into enough filth for the two of us, so in statistical terms we're right on schedule.'

Her friend sniggers.

'You don't know what you're missing, girl. There's nothing like a good healthy fuck to get you over your hang-ups. You think too much, Gia'. If I had your blonde hair and blue eyes, I'd be famous all over town. And you don't even have a father or brothers to answer to: you've got a dream situation! By the way, did your dad ever send you your birthday present from the States?'

There's nothing on earth that annoys Giada more than

talking about her father. Allegra knows that perfectly well, and she prods her intentionally. But Giada decides not to give her the satisfaction, for once.

'He sent me money, of course. He's such a pig. Just think, an envelope with a thousand dollars in cash and a note. That arsehole doesn't even realise dollars are worthless these days. It's been three years since I last talked to him, and I don't even want to talk to him now.'

'Sure, I don't blame you, who cares about him? Still, with that money you could finally get your own scooter, couldn't you? Without having to say a thing to your mother.'

At the thought of her mother, Giada instinctively takes her shoes off the sofa.

'You know, it's not a money thing. In fact, my grandparents told me that if I go and see them, they'll give me a thousand euros. I could pay for it no problem. It's only that my mum's afraid; she says the streets are full of potholes, people don't know how to drive. She just doesn't want me to.'

Her friend laughs complacently.

'Gia, you're the last woman left on earth who's afraid to displease her mammina dearest. You know, you need to grow up. At your age, there's no way you can still not be smoking, not having sex, and doing whatever your mamma tells you. Carry on like this, I'll be ashamed to be seen with you.'

Giada joins in the laughter.

'If you didn't have me, who would you boast to about all the crap you pull? You know for sure that sooner or later I'll make up my mind. Maybe sooner rather than later. But I at least want it to be with a boy I like. Do I have your permission to go with someone I like, at least?'

'You're too picky. There's no one you like, but everyone's dying to take you out. Gianmarco, for instance – he's so buff, I'd take him to bed in a minute, except for the fact that he's best friends with Christian. He's asked me for your number twice already, and I reckon I'm going to go ahead and give it to him, just to get him crossed off the list.'

Giada objects,

'No, oh my god, the last thing I need is a conceited jerk like him. The other day I saw a boy, outside of school . . . I've never seen him before. Maybe if I see him again I'll give him my number.'

'There you go, at last! Good girl. You get started and you'll see how much fun it is; you'll start trying different flavours, just like ice cream. Which, now that I think about it, is a pretty good metaphor.'

In spite of herself, Giada bursts out laughing.

'You really are an incredible slut. What a pathetic choice I made when I picked you as my best friend!'

'Oh, come on, without me you'd die of boredom, living your solitary life with Mammina dearest. Oh, go fuck yourself, why don't you. I've got to get dressed; Christian'll be here any minute. I bought a push-up bra that's going to drive him out of his mind and forget about that tart's silicone tits. Of course, if I had your breasts . . .'

'Well, maybe I'll lend them to you; you'd make better use of them than I do. Screw you, we'll talk later on.'

Chapter 9

Sweetheart, my darling,

I found the boy. It wasn't hard; the address was correct. First I had a taxi take me past there, then I went back on foot.

You should have seen what that place looked like. In the middle of the city, one building crammed up against another, without a breath of air. I don't know how these people live, without even so much as a glimpse of blue sky. Where we're from it's different, you remember? Fresh air, the smell of the soil; and then there are the seasons – snow in the winter, red leaves in autumn. In this city, if you ask me, nobody even knows what time of year it is: they go from summer to winter, and that's all they know. Why you ever chose to leave our town is beyond me.

Anyway, the location is perfect. There's a little corner nook, you should see it, like it was custom built for the purpose. I even slipped into it last night. I fit like a glove, you know I'm not big; I've even lost weight. In perfect shape, you'd say.

So, I wedged myself in and waited. I'd identified the scooter, there was no mistaking it, it was the same licence plate number. I didn't even have long to wait: an hour later he came out whistling a tune, unlocked it, unchained it, got on and took off, without a helmet. Think of that.

He's not a bad-looking kid, maybe a bit muscle-bound. He had a funny haircut; maybe that's why he didn't wear a helmet. How ridiculous is that, risking your life so you don't mess up your hair. Of course, how funny is it for me to be saying that, eh?

Forgive me, my darling, but I feel slightly giddy today. I've waited so long, I've thought so much about it, and now that I'm here, I can hardly wait.

I'm taking care of the details. I stopped by one of those African street vendors; he was selling counterfeit designer bags. They spread them out on a white sheet on the pavement, and when the police go by you should see them. They grab all four corners with all the merchandise inside and go running down the alleys. But of course you already know all these things. Anyway, as you can imagine I needed a large bag, something to put the essentials in, something at least a yard long, capable of carrying a couple pounds' weight, more or less.

I thought to myself: if I buy a decent quality bag, someone will probably snatch it, and then where will I be? Can you imagine that: a mugger taking everything, after more than ten years of painstaking planning? So I'll get a cheap, shabby-looking bag that's unlikely to tempt any bag snatchers. I looked and looked and I finally found the perfect one, and I pretended to haggle on the price, just to be inconspicuous, and I even saved five euros. If you'd been there, you would have laughed till tears came to your eyes.

How I miss you, my darling. At every moment of the day, the only thing that keeps me going is the thought that every step I take brings me a little closer to when I'll see you again. At last.

So everything's ready. Tonight it begins. I'm so excited, I can hardly wait. Tonight it begins at last.

Chapter 10

Eleonora walks along, hugging the wall, and no one sees her.

She's clutching a crumpled ball of paper in her hand and she's crying. Not sobbing, her face isn't twisted in a grimace, but tears roll freely down her cheeks.

Passers-by look away in embarrassment. Tears scare people.

The sun strikes her at intervals, wounding her with its light, and her stomach knots in spasms. Eleonora stops in a corner and struggles to suppress the retching.

Pregnant, she thinks. It says so right here. I'm pregnant. Of course I would feel like vomiting, wouldn't I?

But Eleonora knows it's not because she's pregnant that she feels her heart racing crazily in her chest. It's because she doesn't know how he'll react.

She's in love, she's head over heels in love. He's the man she's waited for all these years, while her girlfriends were describing the qualities of their boyfriends: the Prince Charming who chose to smile at her, of all the girls. A man to show off to everyone else, a man on whose arm she could feel like a woman, fulfilled, natural. The man she wants with her for the rest of her life.

Eleonora wipes her mouth with a tissue and looks up in time to catch the disapproving glare of a woman who thinks she must be on drugs.

Disapproval. How will his family react, when presented with the news? She has no doubts about the strength of his love: he'd never lie to her. But she also knows how he dotes on his father, and how strict the old man can be. They've talked about him a thousand times, and a thousand times she has dreamed of the moment when she'd finally meet him. But in those dreams, she was never introduced holding this crumpled ball of paper in her hand.

Pregnant. Six weeks pregnant. She tries to tally up the time, to remember, but every single instant of love with him is marvellous, every single instant is worthy of being branded into her memory.

Now what'll happen, Eleonora wonders. How can I tell him? And what will he say when I do? What will we do, the two of us? We're still at school, there's a long road ahead of us. I don't want to force him to change his plans, his ambitions; and I have dreams of my own. I can't throw Mamma and Papa's sacrifices to the wind.

In front of her eyes float the images of her parents. What will she say to them? Another spasm, another surge of retching.

Eleonora walks along, hugging the wall, and no one sees her.

Chapter 11

Mirko is happy, or at least he thinks he is. He can't think of anything that could dim the glow of this moment.

He spent the evening with his long-time friends, who by now consider him something on the order of a minor god. At a certain point, he even pulled out one of the two fifty-euro notes, with feigned distraction, to make them think that it had plenty of company in his wallet, and said, '*Guagliu*', this round is on me. This is for all the times you guys stood me beers, when I didn't have a cent to my name.' So cool! And a couple of them have even had their hair cut in a mohawk, just like his. In short, he feels important.

And Antonio gave him a hug when he brought back the money from selling the baggies. He pinched Mirko on the cheek and told him, 'Bravo, *guagliuncie*'. You did good, believe me.' And he said it right in front of two guys from another neighbourhood, guys Mirko knows by sight but understands are in business with Antonio. Those guys looked at him and nodded their heads affirmatively, with serious faces. In other words, the next time they see him, they'll know him; they might even say hello to him.

Everything that occurs to him tonight makes him smile. Outside the rich kids' school that morning he saw the blonde girl again. Always surrounded by her girlfriends. One of them, a cute brunette, even came over to buy a baggie, but he'd already sold everything he had. Too bad, because maybe he would have given it to her and kicked in the ten euros for Antonio himself, in exchange for the blonde girl's name, or even her mobile number.

He decides that when things start spinning along at full capacity, the first thing he'll do is trade in his motor scooter and get a real motorcycle instead. He's seen the blonde taking the bus home from school, or getting in her girlfriend's micro car, one of those tiny unlicensed cars. So if he shows up outside the school on a real motorbike, maybe not like the one Antonio rides, but one at least as good as the bikes those idiots he goes to school with ride, then she'd really have no option but to accept a ride home from him. Then he'd know where she lives.

But first, Mirko thinks as he climbs the road homeward, he'll need to do something for his mother. A man, if he's a real man, has to pay his debts before anything else. And his mother brought him up, making sure he had everything he needed. He hadn't been forced to steal, he'd never pulled any of the bullshit that other kids in the quarter got up to, because his mother, even if she was single, made sure that his every whim was satisfied.

So now, Mamma, the first lot of money is for you. I'll take

you out to the movies, and then to dinner in a restaurant. And then maybe I'll get you some new clothes. A flowered dress, like the ones you used to look at wide-eyed in the shop windows on the Via Toledo, when you used to come and pick me up from school.

By now he's almost home, he's in the courtyard. He props his motor scooter in its usual place. He looks up: the window is illuminated. Never once has he come home to find her asleep, even if he stays out as late as he has tonight. But tonight is special, Mamma. Because so many different things have happened, all of them wonderful. Now let me lock the chain on the scooter, and I'll hurry upstairs to tell you all about it.

Tonight it begins.

Chapter 12

Lojacono didn't really mind much when they asked him to stay on for the night shift. He could spend his sleepless night gazing up at the police station ceiling or at the ceiling of his studio flat. What difference did it make?

Usually they'd keep him out of whatever was happening, to avoid the risk that he might be involved, however marginally, in some ongoing investigation; at most they'd send him out for a street brawl or a mugging – small-time stuff. At least that way they got some use out of him; he was still a non-commissioned officer after all, even if he was an extra officer over the allotted staff. A day-tripper, as he'd heard Giuffrè call him, ironically. A day-tripper, on duty at the loony bin.

But once everyone had left except the night watch, the San Gaetano police station turned into a place that was almost half decent. The silence, the lights turned off, the whistling of someone down the hallway. If places have a soul, Lojacono thought to himself, that soul comes out at night.

Giuffrè told him that his willingness to work night shifts baffled him. If they fucked you over, shipping you out to a place where there's nothing for you to do except play poker against your computer, and taking everything you owned away from you, why didn't you pay them back in kind? Look after your own interests and refuse to go out of your way to help.

The little man with a pot-belly and bottle-bottom glasses had a point. For that matter, that's how he behaved, calling in sick regularly and doing no more than the bare minimum. Lojacono felt sure that the station captain had never even seen Giuffrè; he literally succeeded in becoming invisible when he needed to.

As the night dragged on in a silence torn apart only by the occasional roar of an engine struggling uphill, Lojacono, drifting between nodding off and full wakefulness, thought about Marinella. He wondered how things were going for her, life in the new city. She was a smart girl, a bit introverted, perhaps. He hoped that she'd managed to make new friends, good ones. If so, maybe, as time went by, she might set aside the resentment she felt for him. Who could say? She might eventually want to talk to him.

On the other hand, he was afraid that she might start running with a bad crowd, fall into the clutches of some bad guy. He didn't think his wife had a tight enough grip on her; Marinella was smart, but she was still only a child.

He wondered whether he might not be the classic father who couldn't stop thinking of his daughter as a little girl. A terrible trap to fall into. He remembered his last conversation with Sonia, the woman's violent verbal barrage against him. He understood now that the relationship was over and done with, that there was no way to rebuild their old love, after so much hatred. He discovered, as he lay on the fold-out bed they had for those on night shifts, analysing himself, that he wasn't especially torn up over the fact; emotions are born, live, grow old, and die, just like people. But the way he missed Marinella was an open bloody wound, and it showed no signs of healing.

He hadn't had any difficulty procuring his daughter's new mobile phone number – he was a cop, after all. But he'd never had the nerve to call her. It struck him as an intrusion into the girl's life, trespassing somehow. But he missed her; it killed him how much he missed her.

Sleep turned his worries into a dream. He saw his daughter in a nightclub, cheerful and pretty. He watched as she drank and took a pill her girlfriend gave her. He watched as she got into a car with a boy whose face, in the dream, was obscured. The car took off at speed, hurtling into the night. He tried to call out to her, to warn her of the danger, but his voice caught in his throat. He watched as the car took a curve at insane speed. He saw a lorry coming around the bend from the opposite direction.

He found himself sitting bolt upright on the bed, eyes wide open, as the office phone rang and rang.

Chapter 13

The place was pretty close by, the courtyard of an old building about half a mile from the police station. Lojacono had grabbed a uniform jacket from the locker room and climbed into the police car, recruiting a sleepy young policeman as his driver. The phone call had come in anonymously, a woman's voice going on about a dead body.

There was a small crowd standing outside the half-open front door, a dozen or so silent onlookers. The inspector ran his gaze over the windows of the adjoining flats, a couple of them lit up, a few others wide open with curious faces watching the drama unfold. The silence was unreal: it seemed like a film set, right before the cameras began to roll.

They stopped the car at the mouth of the street, top lights flashing, to keep people from coming in or out. They walked up the street and into the courtyard.

The scene that met their eyes was illuminated by a lamp, which hung from a pair of crossed cables running over the centre of the courtyard and swung lazily in the breeze. To call it a courtyard was perhaps overstating the case: it was really nothing but an airshaft bringing light to the building's suffocating windows. On one side was a heap of rubble, beams, bricks and a couple of bags of cement; on the other, a few parked scooters. Near the last scooter in the line, almost up against the wall, sprawled the body of a boy, face down. A short distance away, one woman held another in her arms; the two of them were sitting on a step. The older of the two, dishevelled and wearing a dressing gown, was murmuring words, perhaps a prayer, with her arms wrapped around the second woman's shoulders, who was younger and wore an incongruous pair of pink flannel pyjamas.

The woman's face was a terrible sight. She couldn't be much over forty, and she was skinny, her chestnut hair gathered in an elastic band; her face was collapsing into a silent scream, her mouth wide open, a streamer of drool at either side, eyes staring wide in immense pain and sorrow, her neck straining in a spasm. She was emitting no sound at all, except for a faint hiss. Lojacono couldn't take his eyes off that face, the very picture of madness, of a one-way journey into the abyss. With a stab of grief, he felt as if he'd plunged back into the dream he was having when the call came in, and he understood without a shadow of a doubt that this was the boy's mother.

The drizzle had ceased, there was a little watery mud on the pavement that the rain had washed out of the construction site. Lojacono made his way over to the prone body, careful not to step on any potential evidence. He squatted down next to the corpse.

He saw the bullet hole in the back of the neck, at the base of the hairline, recently trimmed and shaved in keeping with the latest style. It was a small, sharply defined hole; some very small calibre, in his opinion. The boy's hand still held the scooter keys: he hadn't even had a chance to lock the chain. The padlock dangled from the rear wheel. The inspector looked up and noticed that there was a narrow gap next to the street door, a dark opening left over from some renovation work done decades ago. His gaze returned to the ground and he saw the bullet casing. Just one. He pulled out his handkerchief and picked it up.

The sound of sirens split the night, and a second police car arrived, closely followed by a third. Suddenly the courtyard was full of cops.

Chapter 14

Lojacono had had only one conversation with Di Vincenzo, the captain of the San Gaetano police station, on the day he arrived. He remembered a man who was ill at ease, who kept tapping his fingers on a closed binder on the paper-piled desk in front of him. Marked on the cover was one word: 'Lojacono'.

The man he saw now was a completely different person, collar unbuttoned, tie askew. His brow was furrowed, his voice was deep and confident, and he had the imperious air of someone who's used to handling situations with unruffled competence.

He waved the three cops following him towards the two women, the corpse and the entrance into the courtyard. Then he walked over to the inspector.

'Lojacono, what are you doing here? Explain yourself. I thought we had an understanding that you wouldn't get involved in any investigations.'

'Captain, I was on duty. If you want to get mad at

somebody, how about the guys who aren't willing to work the night shift? It's certainly not my idea of fun.'

Di Vincenzo blinked rapidly. He wasn't used to that kind of answer, but he had to admit that the logic was flawless. Just as he was trying to come up with a retort, a young woman walked up to him and spoke to him abruptly.

'All right, Di Vincenzo, what do we know? Who's the deceased? And who was the first person on the scene?'

She'd asked the last question with her eyes focused on Lojacono, who was a good eight inches taller than her; but the woman's face, fine-drawn features, and especially her large dark eyes, emanated absolute authority.

Di Vincenzo hissed,

'Dottoressa Piras, Assistant Public Prosecutor. This is Inspector Lojacono. He took the call, but we got here immediately after him, so I was ordering him to head back to the police station.'

The woman never took her eyes off Lojacono's face.

'Not before he tells us exactly what he saw. I think we can all agree that the first responder has the most important information. Who's the deceased?'

Lojacono registered the Sardinian accent and the impeccable business suit that sheathed the public prosecutor's svelte, petite body. Either she was still awake when the call came in or else she was the world's fastest woman at getting dressed and made up.

'To tell the truth, we had in fact just arrived, dottoressa. We haven't even had time to talk to the two women over there, who must have close ties to the victim.'

Piras nodded.

'Sicilian, eh? A new arrival. Well then, if you don't have any information for us, please follow the station captain's orders and head back to the station.'

Di Vincenzo couldn't wait to confirm the order.

'That's right, Lojacono. Back to the station.'

Without taking his eyes off Piras's face, Lojacono held out the tissue to Di Vincenzo.

'At your orders, Captain. In any case, this is the cartridge that was found close to the corpse, over by that nook next to the street door. A .22, if I'm not mistaken. There's only one bullet hole, in the back of the boy's head. I'd guess the shot was fired at point blank range, while the victim was padlocking the chain around the scooter, the one that's lying still open on the vehicle's rear wheel.'

Di Vincenzo had an unhealthy-looking red splotch on his neck.

'If we need any further information we'll be glad to ask you to step in to do the job of the medical examiner and forensics, thank you, Lojacono. Now if you'd be so kind as to get out of my crime scene, you'd be doing me a favour.'

The inspector turned on his heel and moved off without saying goodbye. Then he murmured, audibly,

'And don't forget about the tissues.'

He started walking again, but he hadn't gone a yard before Piras said, in a loud voice,

'Just one minute! What do you mean by "the tissues"?'

Lojacono stopped and without turning around said,

'In the nook by the door, you can see it from here, there's

a little pile of rubbish, drenched with rain. On top of the pile there are three used tissues, clearly deposited more recently than the junk underneath. It seems evident to me that the murderer dropped them there, because that's where I found the shell and because that's the only direction you could fire from if you wanted to kill someone who was parking their scooter right there. Now if you'll forgive me, dottoressa, I've been ordered out of here.'

And, with his hands in his pockets, he walked away from the scene of the crime.

Behind him, in the silence, the hiss that came from Mirko's mother's voiceless scream.

Chapter 15

Donato shuts his book; he can't seem to concentrate. Might as well put on some music, stretch out on the bed, and let the mind go where it will.

This isn't normal, for him. Generally speaking, he's the kind of guy who doesn't give up, especially when a final exam is impending. He's methodical, precise, attends classes, attends extra seminars, reads the textbook cover to cover, goes over it again with highlighters, coloured pencils, and a cross-referenced extended study session with his class notes. Outcome: the highest possible score – 30, or 30 *cum laude*.

Method, Donato muses, can stand in for passion. Passion, as Papa has always told him, isn't anywhere near as fundamental as people like to say when it comes to work. Work is work. Work is hard labour. It's a string of daily tasks, repeating themselves endlessly, interlocking one with another like the links of a chain. What matters is precision, commitment and, of course, success. Passion, Donato my boy, should be relegated to other compartments of your life.

That's why he's never had the slightest doubt about what courses to take, what department to choose, what major and speciality to focus on. Once passion has been excluded from the criteria to be considered, everything else can absolutely be planned out and optimised. With the father that he has – moreover, a father who can guide him, direct him, aid him and even, in the end, place him – it would have been ridiculous to think of any other choice.

For instance, Donato liked to draw. And he even had a certain talent for it: he was good at capturing colour and light and shapes and transferring them, in his own personal way, to the blank sheet of paper. But that's no profession, and he was forced to come to terms with that fact very early on. Papa says that Mamma liked to draw too. But Donato never found anything, in the flat or in the trunks where they still keep her clothing and possessions. Even his memory of this tall, smiling woman has faded over the years, leaving only the image of the hospital bed from which a sort of skeleton covered with flesh waggles its fingers, waving a sad goodbye to him.

But he still has Papa. There's Papa who takes care of everything, and always has. There's Papa, whom he must never disappoint.

But then there's her too.

Donato met her at the university. Surrounded by a hundred other girls, she was different from all of them – beautiful and terrified, looking wildly around for someone to point her the way, with a sheet of paper clutched in one hand. On impulse he broke away from his little group and walked over to her, smiling, to ask if there was anything he could do to help. And that's when their eyes met. For the first time.

He'd read books and he'd seen dozens of films that focused on the importance of that first glance, and he'd never believed a word of it. It was all just literature. How on earth, he had always wondered, can someone understand what's inside another person from a single glance? Another person's past, tastes, memories? Their fantasies, their desires? After all, aren't all those things the basic building blocks of the love between two human beings?

But that single glance had been enough. More than enough. Everything was there, Donato thinks to himself as he looks at the ceiling, fingers knitted behind his head. Everything he'd ever need. And in the months that followed, his conviction was only reinforced. Donato wasn't distracted from his studies: not that. But now there's another hunger, another drive pushing him to wake up in the morning every day. Donato is in love.

Sure, he's had other girlfriends before; he's got a certain appeal and he knows it. But he's a serious young man, he doesn't like to fool around or waste time. Finding a young woman with the same ambitions for the future is a much rarer thing than you might think; and so, when he speaks with her, when he dreams with her, he feels as if he's found a mirror in which he can see a reflection of his better self.

It was natural to develop a certain closeness, it was natural to spend time alone together, it was natural to make love. Natural and wonderful, a symphony of the senses and the mind, the soul and the body. She burst inside him, with an even greater intensity than he had exploded inside of her.

He's never mentioned it to Papa. This is the one outstanding concern for Donato. Papa is too important to him: he was father, mother, mentor, guide, staff, and support – but never friend. Papa is stern, straight as an arrow, formal, and always crystal clear about the world: white is white and black is black. Perhaps a less than ideal sounding board for one's confidences and insecurities. Papa. What would Papa have to say about all this?

Donato hears his father's voice as if he were actually standing there, in his bedroom, looming over his bedside: Now is not the time. If you want to fool around a little, go ahead, but there'll be plenty of time later for serious relationships.

But now he's a man, not a sobbing child who's lost his mamma. A man who knows what he wants, who knows the importance of things and knows how to plan for the future; but also a man who wants love in his life, now that he's found it.

He also knows his father, and he knows that many of the objections that are sure to rain down on him will have to do with his studies, the importance of concentration. And so he's come up with a strategy: he'll take this exam, one of the most important ones of the whole course. He'll do better than usual: *summa cum laude*. He'll do so well that the professor, a friend of Papa's, will call him to offer his congratulations. Only then will he tell his father that he's in love – it will be unequivocal that not only did his love not distract him, it actually drove him to distinguish himself, to achieve the very highest level of excellence.

He knows his father, and he knows that his supremely rational nature can overcome prejudices and stubborn convictions; for that matter, it was his father who always told him that prejudice is merely a consecration of stupidity.

He knows his father, and he feels certain that he'll yield when confronted with an undeniable fact, that he won't stand in the way of his dreams.

His father and her. Donato can't imagine how they could be at odds, two people who both love the same young man so wholeheartedly. He's optimistic, and he can't help but think that way.

What if he were forced to make a decision tomorrow, just to imagine an unlikely situation? Donato feels a faint shiver of fear. The thought of living without her is impossible. But Papa, Papa is part of me and I'm part of him. It'd kill him if I ever turned my back on him. He always tells me that I'm his one reason for living.

Donato suddenly stands up from the bed. That's not the way it'll be, he tells himself. It'll all go well, I'll take the exam, I'll do exceptionally well, and the three of us will go out to dinner together. And we'll talk about the future.

So now, let's get started with this last revision session.

Chapter 16

Sweetheart, my darling,

What's that phrase they use in the movies? That's a wrap!

What a pity that I won't be able to see you until it's all over. I wish I could tell you in detail how things went. You would have been so proud of me. It all went according to plan, down to the tiniest detail. And even if it hadn't, I was ready to take care of unexpected developments. I could feel my mind whirring away like a well-oiled machine. Not that I was worried I might lack the courage, for instance, or suddenly panic – none of that. Ten years is a long time to spend thinking it over every day, picturing every single aspect. If there are doubts, you've resolved them by the time you're ready.

So I got there at ten o'clock. I reckoned that this was the perfect time, that there would be hardly anyone passing on the street at that time of night, and everyone would be watching television or eating dinner. In the previous few days I'd noticed that the last tenant to return home at night was always the same guy: he lives in a third-floor flat, and he always arrives on foot with a canvas bag. No idea what he does. Anyway, after nine-thirty no one uses the courtyard.

The boy always parks (or I should say 'used to park', shouldn't I, my darling?) his scooter in the same place, right in the corner, where the little nook is located. I have to admit that this was a bit of good luck. But no matter what, I figured it out: if you take care, if you walk with your head down, shuffling your feet, if you act like you're old and tired, then people look the other way. In other words, you become invisible. And invisible is what I've made myself, and that's what I intend to remain until the end. Good, isn't it?

So anyway, I wriggled into my little nook. It stank of piss and that was actually convenient too. If by some unlikely chance I was seen, I'd have pretended I was taking a leak. But no one saw me.

I stood there, waiting. It takes as long as it takes, haven't I always told you that?

Without haste, I screwed the tube on to the barrel of the gun. Everything fitted nicely into my counterfeit bag, even my packet of tissues. This eye is always weepy, but you know, I've grown used to it. The lady doctor back home told me, the last time I went in for a check-up, that it's a chronic condition by now and there's nothing that she can do. And anyway, what does it matter? I felt like laughing in her face on my way out of the clinic.

So what I did was I screwed the tube on to the gun, as I was telling you. It's simply spectacular, I've tried it lots of times at home, and what you hear is a sound like someone snapping their fingers. I've destroyed so many cushions, you can't even imagine. One time, towards the end, I even thought of using it on her, so that I wouldn't have to listen to her breath rattling away any more. But then how would I have been able to finish what I needed to do so that I could see you again?

I put on my reading glasses, because I reckoned that when I extended my arm he'd be about a foot away when he lowered his head to lock the chain. The night before I'd given it a try, and he didn't even sense the air from my hand. He was whistling a tune, all pleased with himself. I wonder why. He was happy yesterday too. At that age, my darling, everyone's happy; there's no other way to be.

I keep wandering off topic, but it's because I'm so happy myself. At last, I've begun.

I'd been ready and waiting for two hours by the time he got there. Completely ready. In fact, every so often I had to put the gun back into my bag because my arm was getting tired. I'd rehearsed every detail so many times in my head that when I did it, it was as if I was merely thinking it one more time. He dropped his keys, he had to pick them up and that gave me a little extra time, three or four seconds longer than it usually took him. I aimed, just think, right at the corner of the angle that the barber razored in to shape that ridiculous hairdo of his. Then I walked away from there, and I only came back after a small crowd had assembled to see what had happened.

Then the police came. First one car, then two more. People were elbowing each other and talking, and I was there, with my shoulder bag, listening in. You know, my darling, everyone detests the cops. They really hate them. And I didn't sense any pity in the crowd for the boy; all they were wondering was who he was, but everyone was happy that it hadn't happened to them. People are strange, that's for sure.

When the first car pulled up, two men got out, and I noticed one of them in particular. He moved slowly, unhurriedly, as if he were listening to a familiar piece of music. He went over to the nook and picked up something off the ground – I imagine the shell casing. Then he followed the same trajectory I had covered, looking at the ground as he went.

Don't you worry about me, my darling. No one was watching me, as usual. You know, I never would have thought it, but apparently this is a city that really minds its own business. And I took care to set my feet down on their sides, to scrape my shoes off thoroughly: there were no prints. Still, the policeman followed in exactly the same direction.

Then he looked up at the little crowd of people where I was standing, and luckily I didn't move. His eyes are narrow, you know, as if he were Chinese.

Then the others arrived, including a woman; I imagine she's the assistant prosecutor (but are prosecutors so young nowadays?). And they sent him away. That's good, I thought. He seemed like the only one there that could figure anything out.

So anyway, sweetheart, my darling, everything is proceeding according to plan. I'm really quite satisfied.

Now it's time to get started on the girl.

Chapter 17

'So, you've decided you want to be a cop after all, eh?' said Giuffrè. 'I heard you were a regular Serpico. And that you went head-to-head with none other than Di Vincenzo, himself, in person.'

Lojacono didn't even look up from the monitor. What a miserable hand: all low numbers in different suits. This time you're fucked, he thought to himself. This damned computer: it beat him systematically.

'I'm no Serpico. I happened to be here when a night-time emergency call came in, so I responded. And I reported what I saw.'

Giuffrè had no intention of letting it drop; he was like a dog with a bone. For once, he was the only guy in police headquarters to be speaking to the man of the hour, the subject of every conversation in the station.

'Listen, do you even know what they call you? The Montalbano of the loony bin. Doesn't seem like a good thing, letting other people make fun of you behind your back, does it? So why don't you tell me about your phenomenal hunches, and I'll teach them all a thing or two.'

'What hunches are you talking about, Giuffrè? Have you lost your mind? I saw a couple of tissues that weren't wet and I picked up a shell casing. Where's the guesswork in that? You go ahead and tell those morons that there's no Inspector Montalbano – and by the way he doesn't exist where I come from either – nor is there any loony bin. And tell them not to bust my balls, or I'll be busting theirs in return, and I'm not speaking metaphorically. You know what I want to know? Who the boy was.'

Giuffrè shrugged.

'Some kid named Lorusso, Mirko, aged sixteen or thereabouts. Only child, no father, mother works as a homecare nurse. A two-bit delinquent; he probably stole money from some Camorrista and was duly punished. *S'hanna 'mpara' 'a piccerille*, as we say here – a matter of teaching kids good manners.'

Lojacono had been dealt another terrible hand by his computer: a two of clubs, a three of diamonds, and a seven, a four and a nine of hearts.

'The Camorra has nothing to do with it. Whoever killed him had some other reason.'

Giuffrè shook his head in wonderment.

'Mamma mia, so you really do want to be a policeman when you grow up. Who are you now – Inspector Maigret? Come on, Sherlock, tell me how you know the Camorra has nothing to do with this.'

Lojacono finally tore his eyes away from the monitor, having lost once again.

'First: the .22. It's already an inaccurate and troublesome gun to start with, and you add the fact that he probably had a silencer on the thing because the courtyard is small and it echoes. Second: where the kid lives, with the risk of someone happening by and spoiling everything. Third: no easy escape route. A motorcycle or a car can't get out of there without being noticed: it's a blind alley. Wouldn't it have been much easier to ride up to the scooter on a fast bike, in any old place, and shoot three or four times to make sure? Which is the typical procedure when it comes to settling a score. Fourth: his age. Could such a young kid have done something serious enough to deserve this kind of death sentence? And if he had, why would he come home all relaxed and let himself be killed where they knew they could find him? I'll say it again: if you ask me, the Camorra has nothing to do with this.'

The sergeant sat there open-mouthed. Behind his thick lenses, his eyes looked enormous.

'And you thought all these things in the two minutes that you were there? And you didn't say anything to anyone?'

Lojacono shrugged his shoulders.

'No one asked me. They told me to get out of there as fast as I could, so I left. You know that orders are meant to be obeyed, don't you? After all, these are my own personal considerations, nothing more. But maybe you're right and I'm wrong. Maybe it's the Camorra settling some accounts.'

'Whatever the case, I really like the way you think. And I'll tell you what I'd like even more: if these dickheads would stop assuming that no one working in here has any idea what they're doing. And then there's Di Vincenzo, who really strikes me as the princess and the pea with all his haughtiness – I'd love to see how he cracks this case. Because fine, I understand this is a working-class neighbourhood, but up till now we haven't seen a lot of murders here. And a kid only makes it worse; people get upset about that. You'll see – they'll be breathing down his neck.'

Lojacono shook his head.

'It's the mother's tragedy. You should have seen her – she was all torn up. Now you say they were alone, and that helps me understand. She lost everything. Her whole life ended, in a split second, in that courtyard. She was the very picture of grief, the poor woman.'

Giuffrè went on with the thread of his thought.

'Good old Di Vincenzo has a tough piece of work on his hands with this prosecutor. Piras is a feisty young fighting hen, and he's not going to be able to manage her.'

Lojacono remembered the attractive young woman.

'Yes, I saw her. She showed up right away. Why, do you know her?'

'Sure I know her. When I was driving around that MP – he was a lawyer, you know – I met her a couple of times when we gave her a lift in the car. Dottoressa Laura Piras, from Cagliari, thirty or so. She's small, but quite the babe. Be warned, if she catches you looking at her tits – which are remarkable, as you no doubt saw for yourself – she's capable of ripping your eyes out of your head. She's determined, there's no stopping her, and she's on a career path that's pointing straight up. I bet you she'll have Di Vincenzo dancing a quickstep.'

'So is she married? Does she have children?'

Giuffrè started sniggering.

'Oh, what's this, now you've got the hots for Piras? So there's life in those trousers of yours. I'm glad to hear it! People who don't have any weakness of the flesh frankly scare me. Anyway, the answer is no. Even though everyone gives it a try, even the Honourable MP himself. I can't tell you what a fool she made him look, right in front of me, or I guess I should say right behind me because I was driving. She told him to keep his hand where it belonged or she'd rip it right off his wrist.'

Lojacono gave him a chilly glance.

'Don't get all excited, there's no weakness of the flesh. It's just that I assume that someone who has children has a better chance of understanding what it means to lose such a young boy. And I was hoping that she could understand it. That's all.'

'You're right about that. Even if my son's a big provolone of a lunkhead, and I sweat blood to send him to college, I still think of him first and always. And juvenile delinquent though he might have been, this kid was only sixteen years old. Oh Mother of God, the woman about the cats is here again. Let's see what's happened since last time. *Prego*, *Signo*'. Take a seat.'

Chapter 18

Allegra walks out of the front entrance of the school, sniggering,

'And the best thing is that no one can see me but him. God, it makes me laugh! Did you see the look on his face?'

Giada has long since learned that her girlfriend is capable of anything, but this latest thing is especially upsetting.

'Yes, but seriously, aren't you scared to do it? What if he gets pissed off and tells the principal or, even worse, your parents? Do you realise you could be excluded from every school in the city?'

Allegra stops and turns gracefully to look at her.

'Are you joking? There's no telling the trouble he'd get himself into. My word against his, but it would be simple to make him look like a dirty old fiend, which, by the way, is what he would be, if he only had the nerve to take a step forward. Believe me, I have him by the balls; there's nothing he can do.'

'This totally freaks me out. I don't understand how you

work up the nerve to do these things. I mean, even the thought of it: you take a seat in the front row, you slip off your panties, and you start swinging your legs open and shut. Isn't it kind of gross?'

Allegra blithely dispenses with her objections.

'But why should it be? First of all, I'm not letting him touch it, I'm just letting him look at it. And it kills me to watch him! First he turns red, then white, then he comes out in spots. Then he looks up, then to the side, everywhere but there; he starts babbling, then he takes a hundred quick glances at it, you know, he goes completely stupid, and he doesn't even understand the lecture on ancient Greek that he's supposed to be explaining to us. And when it's all said and done, have you seen my grades? Eight out of ten, as smooth as silk, and you know I never even bought the textbook.'

Giada shakes her head, laughing.

'You're going to get arrested sooner or later, I guarantee it. Leave aside the fact that you'll have him on your conscience. I mean, he's ancient, he must be at least fifty, and you're going to give him a heart attack. Plus he's a priest. You'll go straight to hell is what'll happen.'

Allegra dismisses her objections with a delicate gesture of her hand.

'Priest or no priest, he's a leering, drooling old man and he'll never have the courage to take action. The other day he even said to me: "Signorina, when you have time we should talk. You have need of spiritual comfort." Oh right, as if! I already know the kind of spiritual comfort he has in mind for me; you wouldn't catch me dead alone with him. Anyway, whatever, you want to come to my house? I'll give you a ride.'

'No way. The other day we came this close to dying in a car crash. Whenever I'm in the car, you talk to me instead of watching the road. No thanks. I'll take the bus.'

'All right, do what you want. If you insist on being a pathetic loser, be my guest. Go to hell, talk to you later.'

'Go to hell, see you later.'

Giada doesn't mind taking the bus; it's taller than the wall that runs alongside the road and she can take in the whole panorama on both sides of the hill. On one side, Nisida, the beach at Bagnoli that's gradually emerging from the ruins of the old factory that's being knocked down; and on the other side, the bright blue bay, criss-crossed by the wakes of boats. When all's said and done, she decides, this is a beautiful city. When viewed from a distance.

She has a fuzzy memory of a day when her father took her running down by the sea. She was small, and he'd pretend to leave her behind, then he'd stop and stand there, laughing. She treasures that memory, tucked away in a corner of her mind. She pulls it out every now and then, secretly, when she's alone.

She boards the bus and sits at the front, as usual. She thinks about her mother. Yesterday they had another fight and in the end, like always, her mother broke down in tears. You can't have an argument with her mother; before you know it, tears well up in her eyes, whatever you say, like turning on a tap. And she'll say: You're the only thing that matters in my life. The only thing.

Giada doesn't like that sense of responsibility. It keeps her from feeling free to have fun, like any ordinary kid her age. The thought of her mother, who practically lives only for her, paralyses her.

With her head resting on the filthy glass, she thinks back to the argument. She wants to stop going to violin lessons, she doesn't feel any particular aptitude, and that old bitch of a music teacher scheduled her lesson from eight to nine at night, so when she comes home the park is deserted and it kind of scares her. Her mother retorted that in that case she should be scared on Saturday nights too, when she comes home at midnight. And Giada shot back that everyone else in the world, on Saturdays, comes home at four in the morning, while she is the only one who has to be home by midnight, and anyway, at that time of night on a Saturday there are lots more people around than on a Wednesday night at nine o'clock. And then her mother said that if that bastard of a father of yours, instead of going to America with his girl-friend, had stayed here to be a father, he could have helped you with school. And then she broke down crying. As usual.

Recalling this, Giada sighs gently. She decides that she has a lot of life left to live, that she wants nothing more than to live it, and she doesn't understand why they won't just let her.

Almost her stop. She looks up. The bus is empty. No, wait, there's someone right at the back; an old man, maybe.

She stands up and gets ready to get off.

Chapter 19

Letizia flopped into a chair at Lojacono's table.

'Mamma mia, I'm shattered tonight. I really am turning into an old woman. There was a time when I bounced from one table to another like a young gazelle.'

The inspector smiled, giving her a wink.

'Ah, you look like a schoolgirl, you know. Come on, it's obvious that all the men who eat here must be interested in you, because if it was for the cooking . . .'

Letizia picked up a fork from the table and pretended to stab him with it.

'Hey, how dare you? Let me tell you, there's no better ragù anywhere in the city, which means anywhere on earth. And you know that perfectly well, since you eat it almost every night.'

Lojacono patted his belly.

'Of course I do, and take a look at what you're turning me into. When I first started coming here I was an athlete and now I look like a sixty-year-old captain of industry.'

Letizia blushed imperceptibly.

'No, no, I assure you, you look fine. You'd have to eat a lot more ragù than that. But listen, I heard you were there last week when they killed the son of that nurse, Luisa. Is that right? What happened exactly?'

'Yeah, I was on call that night. Such a pity; he was just a boy.'

Letizia shrugged.

'Sure, he was young, but they get started early here. I hear that he'd started to run with the wrong crowd, that . . . he was getting busy.'

'What do you mean, he was getting busy?'

'You know, easy money. Take something across town, a bit of petty drug-dealing. They recruit them early. They call them *muschilli* – gnats. And then, little by little, they ease them into the business. Who knows, he could easily have broken some rule without even realising it.'

Lojacono drank another sip of wine.

'I don't know about that. It strikes me as odd; it doesn't seem like a typical Mafia hit. They're arrogant, you know. When they teach someone a lesson, they want the lesson to be out there, for everyone to see. But what about the mother – can you tell me anything about her?'

Letizia extended her arms disconsolately.

'What can I say? I've known her practically for ever. She had this son, nobody seems to know who the father was, and she worked her fingers to the bone to bring him up right. She made sure he lacked for nothing. She worked for a while in some clinic somewhere and now she does home care, injections, IVs, stuff like that. There are times when she's out all night sitting up with some invalid, which means the boy hangs out, or I guess used to hang out, on the streets, getting to know all these little losers. That's the way the world works sometimes.'

Lojacono looked into the middle distance, lost in thought, before saying,

'There were tissues on the ground, right near where the boy was killed. A number of tissues, as if the person who used them had been there for a long time. Hours, for all we know. So a guy stands there, in the dark, in the pouring rain, for hours waiting for a kid to come home so he can shoot him in the head, one shot, small calibre pistol, a toy gun. A handgun you could carry in your pocket. That's no Camorrista, take it from me.'

Letizia listened, holding her breath.

'Tissues? You mean like paper tissues? Can't you test them for DNA? I saw a TV show the other night—'

Lojacono waved his hand dismissively.

'Forget about those TV shows, they're full of shit. Somebody finds a fingerprint and before you know it they have the murderer's horoscope. Giuffrè, a guy who works in the same office as me, saw the forensics report that the medical examiner sent in: lachrymal secretion. And cell flaking, which means that when he wiped the tears off his eye, little scraps of eyelid skin stuck to the tissue. They analysed everything, but all they were able to determine was the gender: male.'

Letizia was perplexed.

'What do you mean, tears? So the murderer was crying?'

'Not necessarily. Maybe he has a cold. It'd make perfect sense: all that time standing in one place in this wet chilly weather. Anyway, this is secret information – in theory not even I should know about it – so do me a favour and keep it to yourself. Still, I like the way they're moving fast. The prosecutor is young but she knows what she's doing. I saw her that night and she strikes me as one of those women who aren't satisfied with just being attractive but want to get out there and do something.'

Letizia got a hollow feeling in her stomach, but she remained expressionless.

'So you had a chance to determine that the lady prosecutor is attractive, did you? I hope you got her phone number. Maybe you'll both have a chance to talk the case over at your leisure . . . Why don't you bring her here for a nice intimate dinner?'

Lojacono burst out laughing.

'So you can poison the two of us? Don't be silly, you know I'm not the kind of guy who does that sort of thing.'

Letizia gave a hollow laugh, and poured herself a glass of wine.

Chapter 20

Eleonora sits motionless on the step. And she waits.

She knew it wasn't something she could tell him on the phone. These aren't things you can talk about at a distance. This is news that has to be delivered in flesh and blood, that needs to hover in the ambient air. This is news that has to fall into a familiar space, not hurtle through some unknown and undefined ether. This is news that must meet the eyes of the recipient, news that must resonate, giving an image of pupils, mouth, complexion, each and every slight change.

Eleonora didn't bring the sheet of paper with her. It struck her as pointless; harmful, actually. As if she needed a document as proof, certification of the fact.

This is hard news to deliver. You don't know whether it's good or bad news you're bringing. You'll only know it when you see his face, in the very instant that the word falls into the space between you and turns solid: either a rose or a stone, a note of music or a knife blade.

Eleonora trembles. A terrible fear has taken hold of her. She understands in some obscure way, because her woman's intuition tells her so clearly, that nothing will ever be the same as it was once she speaks to him. For better or for worse, nothing will ever be the same.

Eleonora dug deep over the last few nights, seeking the courage she would need. She hunted through the conversations, the stories, even the laughter that she'd shared with him for traces of that courage. For the first time, she felt older than him, as she studied his temperament, his character, wondering whether he'd be capable of handling the words she had to say to him, whether he could proudly present her to his family, the way she hoped.

As the endless hours of night tick past, it occurs to Eleonora that she doesn't really know him after all. She'd always believed that the only thing that mattered was their love, the love she glimpsed in his eyes when he saw her coming towards him, the love she felt in her own heart when she thought of him; but she really doesn't know him at all. What does he do when they're not together? What does he think, how does he pass the time, what are his fears? Perhaps that information could help her guess how he'll react. Information that she doesn't yet possess, and perhaps never will.

Eleonora runs a hand over her face. She couldn't stand to lose him. She tries to think positively, the way her father always told her to do: if you ask for trouble, trouble will answer. If you ask for good things, good things will come to you. Papa, how I wish you were here with me, right now. But instead, I also have the problem of how to break this news to you.

Suddenly, Eleonora has lost all faith. Suddenly, all the promises she was given, on the beach or in bed after making love, seem to be written on the wind. Everything she believed in, everything she relied upon, has melted away like the snow back home. Now she sees that she's given everything to someone she knows nothing about, with no possibility of getting it back.

But just as Eleonora lost it, she regains it – her faith. Her heart restores that faith to her, intact. She can't be so badly mistaken. Love is love, isn't it? It'll find a way. Aside from all the obstacles, above and beyond a few broken dreams and a few others that will have to be adjusted, life will triumph, and life is the two of them, after all.

Eleonora thinks of his father. She thinks of the man whom she has yet to meet. She thinks of the strictness that he described, the man's rigidity. She thinks that perhaps a man who loves his son so intensely will understand why she is now becoming so accustomed, so tenderly accustomed, to the fragment of life that she carries within her. There should be a certain degree of understanding, from one parent to another. Love is a universal language.

Eleonora looks around her. She chose to meet in the university park, the place they first met. It's a talisman, it'll bring her luck, of that she feels certain. She'll see him coming towards her, like he did the first time, with his easy, confident gait, his broad shoulders, slightly jug-eared – one more thing about him that she loves so much. She'll see him first and she'll smile in his direction. Then he'll see her and he'll break into a happy smile, as he does every time he sees her. And everything will be fine.

Everything will be fine.

Chapter 21

The old man walks by night down the street where the rich people live. He has read that prices go as high as a thousand euros per square foot around here. He's only interested in knowing whether there are security guards, and what their routines are.

The old man learns quickly. He takes note of schedules, situations, habits. If you cordon off a place, he thinks, then you turn it into a little world unto itself with only a few inhabitants, and people all move in roughly the same way. Of course, if it were one of those places where everyone knows everything about everyone else, like his hometown, then it would be impossible to pass unobserved; but here, he's become invisible. People's eyes slide over him and move on, as if he were made of air.

Which is a good thing, he thinks. A very good thing.

The other morning, in fact, he'd found himself face to face with the girl. He was following the route, he felt sure that she'd accept a ride from her girlfriend, the way she almost always did on Wednesdays when she had violin lessons in the evening. But, like everybody else, she failed to see him entirely. A city full of phantoms.

He walks past the park. He's decided that the right moment is in fact when she comes home from her violin lesson. The girl is right-handed, and she only uses her right hand: she'll shift her violin case over to her other hand, she'll pull out the keys to the street door, and she'll open it. She never buzzes upstairs. And her routine never varies by more than ten minutes or so. There's a night watchman in the park, but he doesn't start his rounds until ten, at times ten-thirty.

Next to the small entry door set in the larger carriage door is a stunted tree, a sort of dwarf cypress; the old man has a vague notion that this is called a thuja tree. A person could hide right behind that little tree, provided he weren't too tall. And that won't be a problem for him.

He pulls a tissue out of his counterfeit designer duffel bag to dab at his weepy eye, and his hand brushes against the cold metal. The old man finds the contact deeply reassuring.

The street where rich people live is deserted tonight. He's seen it at all hours, teeming with traffic or completely empty as it is right now.

A light rain starts to drizzle down, silently. The old man checked the weather report and knew that it would rain. It's not strictly necessary, but it's certainly helpful: there won't be a lot of residents out taking a stroll tonight. Lots of people here have dogs, but by nine o'clock they're all safe at home, eating dinner.

I bet it'll be someone taking their dog out who finds the body.

Not that it matters, the old man decides.

Chapter 22

Giuffrè rushed into the room, waving a newspaper in the air.

'Hey, Montalba', did you hear the latest?'

Lojacono looked up from his book.

'Listen, arsehole, stop calling me that. I told you already, I find it annoying.'

The diminutive sergeant shot him an offended look.

'Oh, nice manners! You know, I'm the only person in the whole city who even speaks to you. You could try to be a little more considerate, couldn't you? Anyway, if you're not interested, go fuck yourself.'

He turned to leave and Lojacono went back to his reading. Then Giuffrè stopped and spoke again.

'It's a pity, though. Because if you ask me, the news report I read in this newspaper really might interest you, Inspector Lojacono.'

Finally hearing himself addressed by his proper name, the inspector swung his feet down from his desktop and shut his book.

'All right, let's hear it. Anyway, I know that you won't

leave me in peace until you've told me, and this book is unbelievably boring.'

'I like you better when you play poker against the computer. Maybe you're frustrated because you always lose, but at least you're not angry. Anyway, it's big news. Yesterday, in the Via Manzoni, someone murdered a fourteen-year-old girl.'

There flashed into Lojacono's mind, crystal-clear, the final scene of the nightmare that had been persecuting him since the night of the boy's murder: his daughter hurtling into a car crash.

'That's a shame. But it's not exactly earth-shattering news, is it?'

'No, of course not. But if you put it together with the fact that since this morning Piras has called Di Vincenzo four times, and that right here,' he said, tapping the newspaper, 'they talk about a single bullet to the head, it changes things considerably, don't you think?'

Lojacono said nothing for a second, and then replied,

'First: how do you know that Piras has called so many times? And second: give me that newspaper.'

When Giuffrè was especially pleased about something, he swayed back and forth on the tips of his toes. Lojacono found this habit maddening.

'It's because Pontolillo, the guy who works in the admin department, has a mouth that's as loose as my mother-in-law's left slipper, the way he blabs. This morning, he buttonholed me over by the coffee machine and said she wouldn't stop calling. In fact, they had started to wonder if there wasn't a little flirtation developing, except that on the last phone call she was so pissed off that Pontolillo was actually scared. So I put two and two together because, what, you think you're the only cop in here?'

Lojacono considered the question.

'When I was small, I had an inflatable doll; I think I called it Ercolino, if memory serves. It swayed back and forth exactly the same way you're doing right now, and I used to rain punches down on its face, to see if I could make it sway even more.'

Giuffrè stopped short, wearing a baffled expression.

'Anyway, this thing is getting big. Read it. The newspaper even draws a link between the two murders. I wonder who their source is. And it mentions the notorious tissues. That's why Piras was so hopping mad, if you ask me.'

The article was pretty blistering. The journalist reported the murder of G. D. M., a fourteen-year-old high school student in the better part of town, adding that she'd been killed with a single shot to the head as she was returning home from her violin lesson, around nine o'clock the night before. Nothing had been stolen, apparently. On the ground near the corpse the police had found a number of used tissues, a detail that suggested a connection to the murder of M. L., a sixteen-year-old boy murdered in San Gaetano a few days earlier. The reporter wondered what links there might be between the two victims, and what the police were waiting for to arrest the guilty party and bring him to justice.

The tone of the article wasn't openly hostile, but it was clear that that was where it was tending. The article concluded with a striking image: a murderer waiting for his victims in the shadows, dropping tissues, wet with his tears, on the ground. A murderer's tears: the tears of the Crocodile.

In fact, the image had even inspired the headline: *Crocodile Killer Strikes Again.* Lojacono understood how angry Piras was, and why: her name was the only one mentioned in the piece.

The newspaper was one of the most widely read local publications, and the other papers were likely to adopt the moniker. That in turn would capture the popular imagination, inevitably sensitive to the deaths of young people. As long as it was young Lorusso, the murder could be dismissed as a result of gang warfare; but laying hands on a girl from the upper reaches of the social hierarchy was sacrilege, pure and simple.

Lojacono turned to look at Giuffrè, who had started swaying back and forth again.

'As far as you know, were there any reports on the shell casings found at the scene?'

The sergeant suddenly stopped.

'No, and how would I know anything about that? If you want, I'd be glad to look into it though. Not now – Pontolillo's already left for the day – but first thing tomorrow morning . . .'

Lojacono had glimpsed a useful scrap of information at the end of the article.

'Do me a favour: tomorrow, see if you can find out whether they found a shell casing and if it matched the one from Lorusso's courtyard. And one more thing: cover for me tomorrow. I have to attend a funeral.'

Chapter 23

His cheeks are burning. That's always been the symptom, ever since he was a small child, as far back as he could remember: burning cheeks.

And the sound of his pulse in his ears, as if his heart has climbed into his skull. Now, he's well aware of the effects of stress, because he's studied them, but that does nothing to diminish their scope and strangeness.

Donato walks out into the open air and heaves a deep sigh. He considers how in life you can do your best to plan things out, examine every angle, take into consideration all the pros and cons, but in any case it'll always turn out differently from how you expected; some unforeseen factor will always spin things on to another trajectory.

He knows that he didn't skip over anything; he studied the way he usually does. In fact, better than usual. He knows he even managed to find the time, in the last few days before the final exam, to go over the material one last time, making sure there were no gaps in his preparation, no chinks in his armour. He knows that he calmly reviewed his state of mind the night before, trying to ascertain whether he really was as well prepared as he felt.

In other words, he ran through every item on his usual checklist, and he even double- and triple-checked. So what went so horribly wrong?

As he runs his eyes over the gardens that surround the teaching hospital, teeming with the usual crowd of students, nurses, professors and assistants, some still in scrubs, others carrying their coats, straining to catch a few rays of pale sunlight after days on end of relentless, depressing drizzle, he starts to wonder whether his father might not have a point with that obsessive refrain of his. He always says that distraction, lack of commitment, are subtle, treacherous adversaries: that they worm their way in and then hijack your mind before you even realise what's happening.

He thinks about his father. About how he himself had hoped that this exam, his successful completion of it, would lay the foundations for the whole speech he was planning to deliver to him.

In his mind's eye, he sees again the professor shake his head in disappointment, toying with his exam booklet. He hears the silence in the lecture hall again, the silence that descended in the aftermath of his last answer. He remembers his own astonishment, confident as he was that he had given the exact answer required. He hears the professor's deep sigh again, then the words that followed: suggesting he come back for the next session, because it's such a shame that, with his grade point average and the family name he carries, this exam in particular, the most important exam of the whole semester, should be so far below his average.

And he sees himself too, stiff, cheeks flaming red, as he stands, nods, thanks the professor, and turns to go, with the burden of failure weighing on him.

He'll have to tell his father that the exam didn't go very well. He'll have to tell him because, no matter what, he's bound to find out from someone in his network of spies and informers, possibly the very same professor who conducted the examination. His father will sit there, without a word, he can just picture him, and then he'll finally nod his head sagely. If you did your very best, then you have nothing to be ashamed of. Which is to say: since failing the final exam is definitely not your very best, I feel sure you've done something you ought to be ashamed of.

And he'll have to break the news to her too. He'll tell her that there was an unexpected hitch in their plan, that the momentous dinner will have to be postponed. He'll see the disappointment in her eyes, the sadness that he'd never willingly meet with his own eyes.

It's only an exam, he tells himself. A goddamn university-level oral exam; just one of the hundred or so exams he's taken and the hundred more that still await him. After all, I have my whole life before me.

From a distance, sitting on a bench, someone he's never met watches him. And dabs away a tear from his left eye.

Chapter 24

Lojacono had decided to take a taxi. With his salary – eighteen hundred euros a month, less the money he had to send to that bloodsucking vampiress Sonia, who for that matter actually earned more than he did – and minus what he needed for basic survival, he certainly wasn't rolling in it; he could have taken public transport, no problem, and saved himself a little money.

But in that strange city, taking a bus could mean hours spent stuck in traffic, peering pointlessly out of the window, with the risk of missing the appointment entirely and leaving Giuffrè alone in the office too long. He'd taken the address from one of the numerous death notices that appeared in the paper. The disparity hadn't been lost on him: the boy from San Gaetano, zero notices; the girl from the Via Manzoni, at least thirty. The printed announcements had supplied him with the full name, so hypocritically concealed behind initials in the newspaper article: Giada De Matteis.

You could learn so much from a death notice. For

instance, it wasn't hard to guess that she was the daughter of parents who had separated or divorced long ago. Some of the notices – most of them – 'shared in the grief' of Marta, the mother; others 'extended shocked condolences to the grieving father', Luigi. It was clear that many were from friends of the girl, young people who must have been well off if you considered the sheer cost of all those announcements; a certain Debora had even published a lengthy poem that mourned a blossom cut short at the stem. Not many relatives, only an aunt and uncle, and the maternal grandparents. Lojacono had smiled dolefully as he read through the euphemisms and the circumlocutions: tragic passing, sudden loss, regrettable accident – as if one's head intersecting with the trajectory of a bullet were nothing more than a piece of bad timing.

As long as he was taking a taxi, he was determined to enjoy the ride. Ever since his transfer, struggling to deal with the tempest that raged inside him, he hadn't bothered to explore. He'd found a studio flat in one of the tumbledown buildings near the police station, and the only streets he saw were the ones connecting his office, his flat, and Letizia's trattoria. He'd pondered this fact, wondering why he felt no desire to see a little more of that city; after all, people came from all over the world to admire its beauty. But the answer was obvious: could you really ask a man to enjoy sightseeing in what was, in the end, nothing more than a prison cell?

Oncc, he walked down to the waterfront; he'd felt an urge to smell salt air, to feel a sea breeze. He hadn't found either at the city waterfront, with thousands of indifferent cars whizzing past the barnacle-encrusted rocks, under an endless spitting rain and a grey sky. The rancid stench, the white rocks piled up like a barricade, the casual litter, plastic bags bobbing in the stagnant water like so many jellyfish corpses.

He'd turned and fled, doing his best to reconstruct in his heart his beloved Scala dei Turchi, with the white limestone glittering in the sun, looking out over the friendly and unfailingly blue sea. And it became clear to him that this was no seaside city; here the city and the sea vied in their mutual indifference, ostentatiously ignoring one another like a couple of cousins in the aftermath of a terrible feud.

Now, as the cab climbed uphill and he looked out at the city that surrounded him, it struck him that this metaphor he'd glimpsed could be extended to the population at large. A scooter zipped recklessly between the two lines of traffic, and a woman at the wheel of a compact runabout jerked in alarm, startled by the engine's roar, glaring in hatred at the incautious rider. They loathe each other, Lojacono thought. They view each other as enemies; there is no shared identity.

He could sense the hostility like it was a scent in the air. Maybe that was why he hadn't yet felt any desire to take a stroll and sightsee, to gaze up close at the countless wonders he'd heard so much about. Better the daily indifference of his co-workers, or passers-by in the street, or cashiers in cafés. They had no need of him; he had no need of them.

He understood that he was now in the fancier part of town from the architecture, the flower planters and the quality of the shops; and he knew by the number of badly parked cars and the crowds of people walking towards a modern-looking church that he was approaching the place where the girl's funeral service would be held.

He decided to get out and walk the last few hundred feet, if it meant he would avoid sitting in traffic. He looked around him at the crowd: disconcerted faces, gazes lost in the middle distance. The death of a young person always hits people: it's unnatural, and it awakens a deep-seated, ancestral fear. He saw fathers and mothers weeping as they embraced their children, doing their best to shelter them from a fate that might prove to be contagious. He thought about Marinella, and he hoped that, wherever she might be right now, there was a smile on her lips.

It was a big church. The immense circular interior was drenched in the light that poured in through the high windows and the two stained-glass rose windows. It was also packed with people. In front of the altar, set on steel trestles, was a white coffin covered with flowers, photographs and teddy bears. A line of girls and boys streamed past, laying down objects or brushing the wooden casket with their fingers.

Lojacono pushed forward, taking up a position not far from the altar but off to one side: an ideal vantage point from which to observe the proceedings.

Set on top of the coffin was an enlarged photograph of Giada De Matteis, aged fourteen, cruelly torn from this life, as the mourning announcement at the church entrance stated.

For a few minutes, the cop and the young woman looked into each other's eyes, ignoring the line of her tearful classmates. What Lojacono saw in those eyes was embarrassment at being photographed, annoyance at the glare of the camera flash in her eyes, a burst of laughter poised on her lips. Normal emotions for a normal young girl, on a sunny day that would never return. The almond-shaped eyes never changed expression, the hands never left the overcoat pockets, but the inspector felt a genuine surge of hatred for the now notorious Crocodile.

Absurdly – though it was not that absurd after all – he was reminded of the day when he and Sonia had chosen their daughter's name, if the baby turned out to be a girl. It was raining hard, and the one-bedroom flat they lived in was the absolute centre of the universe. They'd agreed almost instantly on that song by Fabrizio De Andrè, and that sad but beautiful story by the Genoese poet, and that sweet name, redolent of the stars and the sea.

He tried to focus on what was happening in front of him. You could cut the grief with a knife; it was like some intolerable stench. What made an especially strong impression were the kids, sitting pressed close together on the floor in front of the first pew, crushed by a weight of emotion and sadness. Lojacono spotted a pretty fine-featured brunette and identified her as the epicentre of suffering: she must have been Giada's best friend. Everyone turned to look at her and took turns supporting her. She was clearly overwhelmed; she kept looking around her in despair, as if someone might wake her up from this terrible nightmare she'd wandered into. Her life, Lojacono knew far too well, would never be the same.

The inspector shifted his gaze, searching for someone in particular, and after a brief moment he spotted her. In the front row, standing rigidly, hair neatly groomed, impeccable dark outfit, a smile pasted on her face. Only her eyes gave her away: open a little too wide, staring fixedly. Lojacono hoped he wouldn't be there when Giada's mother's anaesthetised demeanour shattered under the impact of sudden realisation. Soon enough, that hope would be dashed.

The service began. The priest was fairly young, and might have been asked to officiate as an acquaintance of the girl, or perhaps as a teacher. His voice cracked more than once, heightening the general emotional pitch. Lojacono continued to watch the large congregation, mentally separating the curious onlookers wearing conventionally solemn expressions, from those who were merely uneasy, and those who displayed genuine signs of suffering.

The time came when classmates and friends took turns to speak at the microphone. The heartbreak of that young life snapped off in its bloom hung over one and all like a dark night that would never see its dawn.

The young girl with dark hair was the last to climb up to the pulpit, unsteady on her feet, guided by a couple of friends. She tried to speak but couldn't. In the end, she managed to murmur softly, 'Now what am I supposed to do, Gia'? Go to hell, how am I supposed to live without you?'

The curse hung suspended in mid-air, in horror and in grief. Then it evaporated. The priest leaned forward to speak into the microphone and resume the service when a clear, penetrating voice echoed from the front row.

'She didn't want to go. To her violin lesson. She told me she really didn't want to go. But I said, "No, Giada, you have to go. Because if you're not afraid to come home on Saturdays at midnight, then you shouldn't be afraid to come home on Wednesdays at nine. I have to raise you right, you know. That's my job in life." That's what I told her. I was right, wasn't I? You tell her I'm right, please, I beg you all. Mamma has to raise you, otherwise what kind of mamma would she be? You tell her, please. Tell her for me. Otherwise she won't understand; she'll go away for ever without understanding. Please. Please.'

Lojacono saw the people surrounding Giada's mother recoil in distaste, moving away from her as if she were a stranger, or some dangerous wild beast. The woman swivelled her artificial smile in all directions, eyes wide in panic. The policeman had never seen anything so horrible in his life. He thought back to the hiss escaping the lips of young Lorusso's mother, and his own nightmare: Marinella hurtling at insane speed towards her death.

And with shocking clarity, it immediately became clear to him what the Crocodile was doing.

Chapter 25

Sweetheart, my darling,

Scratch another one off the list. Let me tell you, I'm bone tired tonight. I'm really ready for a good night's sleep.

But not until I've told you all about my busy day. First things first: I've become famous! Not me, of course, but what I've done. As you know, I'm not bothering to hide what I'm doing. All I want is to complete my work as quickly as possible so I can finally see you again. And since they found the tissues I use because of this damned weepy eye of mine, a newspaper wrote that both things are the work of a single person, and they've dubbed me the Crocodile, on account of crocodile tears. Brilliant, aren't they? The crocodile cries as it eats its young. But, as you know very well, those aren't my children. It's pretty ironic, I'd have to say.

Crocodile or no crocodile, I had to go to church.

The last time, there was a small knot of onlookers and I was able to mingle with them to get a good look at her face. But this time it was too dangerous. In the gated park there were only local residents, and I would have been too conspicuous. Once I had finished, I had to get out of there fast.

Oh, I didn't tell you that I came very close to having to put it off entirely. That wouldn't have been a big problem; one day more or less was of no real importance. But it would certainly have been inconvenient. In any case, there was the usual tangle that's always waiting around the corner: the boy with the earphones, walking his beagle, took the dog out earlier than usual. You remember that that was one of the things I was afraid of? Well, for whatever reason, he went out a full hour earlier than his regular time, and just ten minutes before the girl was scheduled to return home from her violin lesson. And didn't the dog stop right next to the dwarf cypress I was hiding behind and raise his little hind leg? Funny, don't you think? Laugh, laugh, my darling, you're so pretty when you laugh.

But everything turned out fine; the boy walked away and I was able to finish the job. It was even easier than I expected: the girl rummaged around in her bag for a couple of minutes as she couldn't find her keys. I had all the time I needed to wipe my damned eye, so I could see clearly, exhale the way I used to do at the shooting range, and grip the pistol with both hands, even if the .22 practically has no recoil, which is why I picked it in the first place.

The one thing I was sorry about was not being able to stay and watch. But today I went to the church, as I was telling you, and, without boasting, I had my modest enjoyment. An interesting little show.

Then I took a look around, and who do you think I saw standing there? The cop with the Chinese eyes – you remember, I told you about him before. He was there, off to one side, standing next to a column. And he was staring straight where he needed to. He's smart, that one, like I told you before.

But not smart enough, in any case. Not smart enough to stop me.

Chapter 26

When Lojacono got back to the office, he encountered a highly excited Giuffrè.

'At last, at last, you're back. Mamma mia, what a morning! I have a lot of things to tell you. Come in, come in.'

The inspector shook his head wryly. His colleague's excitement amused him, and he sensed that the stout little sergeant cared every bit as much about what was happening as he did, if not more.

'Calm down, Giuffrè, you're working yourself up into cardiac arrest. Then I'd have to live the rest of my life with you on my conscience. So tell me: what happened?'

Lojacono used a distinctly Sicilian form of the past tense that seemed to catapult the question into a distant, ancient past. Giuffrè blinked.

'Listen, Loja', let's come to an understanding. There's a normal past tense in Italian, and there's your weird, remote past tense, but no one understands it outside of Sicily. If you want to know what happened this morning, ask me in plain Italian. Otherwise, I don't know what you're talking about.'

Lojacono shot the sergeant a disgusted glare.

'Listen, professor, if you want to tell me, go ahead; otherwise keep it to yourself. If I wanted to go back to school, that's what I would have done, and I would have gone one better: I would have studied up on how to deal with people like you.'

Giuffrè waved his hand.

'No skin off my nose. I'm smart enough to figure out what you're saying for myself. Anyway, while you were out, guess who came to the police station for a little visit? Piras, none other. As hot and furious as ever. She walked in and headed straight for Di Vincenzo's office, without even knocking – Pontolillo told me all about it. And then she started yelling: you could hear her downstairs. He kept coming up with explanations and excuses but she didn't even stop to listen.'

Lojacono received this information with interest.

'And just why did she throw this tantrum?'

'So the news does interest you, huh? Because you haven't seen today's papers. Well, here's the thing: this whole story of the Crocodile murders seems to tickle the fancy of the press. Every reporter in town is coming up with theories of his own – it's a new Camorra torpedo, a psychopathic killer, a sex maniac, a child molester. And every one of them claiming that the police, as usual, have no idea what's going on. Every article mentions Piras's name, and if you ask me, her career is hanging by a thread on this thing.'

Lojacono shrugged his shoulders.

'Well, what the hell do we care about Piras's career? If anything, I'd like to know what they suggest we do to catch the murderer, who might very well decide to go on killing.'

Giuffrè scratched his face meditatively.

'Well, it's not so much about Piras; it's the pressure this puts on Di Vincenzo, who turns around and squeezes all of us in here. I hear that ever since that little girl was murdered he's been out of his mind; he's afraid to go home for fear something'll happen when he's not here, and that poor Pontolillo is all over the place, running around like a headless chicken. Anyway, they've reached out to all their informants, they're going through the whole neighbourhood with a fine-tooth comb, trying to figure out what links there could have been between Lorusso and the girl from Posillipo. If you ask me, none at all. Those are two completely distinct and separate cities; at most someone like Lorusso might snatch a handbag from someone like De Matteis, and that's the closest they'll ever come.'

Lojacono was skimming the newspapers that lay spread out on Giuffrè's desk.

'Well, they're certainly tearing us a new one here. But these are strange murders. I'll say it again – if you ask me, this has nothing to do with the Camorra. In this city, you use the Camorra as an umbrella: anything that happens, you blame the Camorra, directly or indirectly. I know that habit – more or less the same thing happens where I come from. But I don't think people should let themselves be pushed off course. This time, I think these kids were killed for some other motive.'

Giuffrè started swaying back and forth on his toes again.

'But I know you have a theory. Why don't you tell the rest of us about it, Loja'? Maybe you're right – you catch this damned Crocodile, and you get us out of the loony bin. What a slap in the face that would be for that bastard Di Vincenzo.'

Lojacono shook his head.

'Giuffrè, you could make me seasick right here on dry land, even though I'm an island-dweller from birth. Do me a favour and stop bobbing around. And no, I don't have a theory. The only reason I went to the girl's funeral was so I could see if anyone there had also been present at the scene of the Lorusso murder, but there was no one I recognised. And the only reason I did *that* was to kill some time. You know I'm under direct orders to stay away from casework. As a distraction, in other words. To divert my thoughts.'

The sergeant stopped swaying but kept smiling.

'You can't fool me, Loja'. Someone who's trying to get his mind off something goes to the pictures or hires a whore; they don't go to the funeral of a murdered teenage girl. I know that the policeman sleeping inside you has been awakened. If you track down the murderer and they rehabilitate you, can I come with you? I'm sick and tired of being stuck here in the Crime Reporting Office, hearing people whisper behind my back that I must have received special treatment because I was a driver for a member of parliament. The truth is I'm a bloodhound, and I know everyone. I can be useful. Well, is it a promise?'

In spite of himself, Lojacono smiled back.

'You talk like we're a couple of prisoners exiled to the

island of Monte Cristo. OK, it's a promise. After all, what do I have to lose? The last people on earth who are likely to catch this Crocodile are you and me. Still, to kill time, we can keep an eye on the investigation. We need something to talk about all day, right?'

Giuffrè clapped his hands in delight.

'No, I have faith in you, Loja'. If you ask me, you're just like yours truly – much, much better than a few idiots upstairs think we are. The crucial thing is to find an opportunity, a situation, so we can show them what we can do. What do you think: is it a good idea to be going over the whole quarter with a fine-tooth comb in search of information, the way they're doing?'

Without even looking up from the newspapers, Lojacono shook his head.

'Information's always good to have, and they can't think of anything else to do. But you watch: it won't amount to anything. I'll say it again – there's only one thing I know for sure: the Camorra has nothing to do with these killings.'

Just then, Piras walked past the open door of the loony bin and came to an abrupt halt.

Chapter 27

The old man watches the young man.

It's stopped drizzling, and that has its upside and its downside, he thinks to himself. You stay dry, and there are more people on the street to mingle with. It's better for surveillance, for figuring out routines, for taking note of travel routes and schedules. But it's worse because there's more chaos, more people, and therefore a greater likelihood of unwelcome surprises.

Still, the old man thinks, the key to everything is time. If you have the time, and you're in no hurry, anything is possible.

As he sits there on the bench, next to an elderly woman feeding the pigeons, with the newspaper open in front of him as he watches the young man, the old man thinks about time.

He's had plenty of time on his hands. He's spent hours looking at a monitor, in the dark, hunting down names and addresses. He's spent hours in his garage, which he kitted out as a workshop, filing and threading a pipe and then filling it with fibreglass. He's spent hours at the shooting range, becoming comfortable with his pistol and smuggling out ammunition in order to avoid making a formal purchase and thus drawing attention to himself. He's spent hours thinking about what he was planning to do, reviewing each individual gesture, every movement. He's spent hours finding the right places, the right hotel, the right settings.

He dabs at his eye, under the lens turned dark in the pale sunlight. The last time he went in to see his doctor, she told him that it was a case of dacryocystitis, an inflammation that had become chronic, and its constant watering is called epiphora, and if pus develops then he'll have to use eye-drops.

He asked her, 'Could this cause me to go blind over the short term?'

She laughed and told him, 'No, don't worry. In fact, I don't know anyone your age who's in such excellent physical condition.'

I've taken care of myself, the old man muses. I've been prudent. To do what I had to it was important to be in good health. I certainly couldn't afford to have my body break down at the most crucial moment. I stayed in shape. I didn't do what she did: let herself be consumed by it until it killed her.

After all, the old man reflects while the young man, only about seventy-five feet away, takes a look at his watch, I'm here representing her too. She probably would have wanted the same thing. We never talked about it: that would have been too dangerous. The less you know about things, the less likely you are to let something slip.

I cased the locations a million times before actually coming to the city: flying over the streets with the satellite map, even studying the layout of the hotel rooms. It's incredible what you can do with a computer, and no one can see you.

I had time on my hands, the old man remembers. I found the right clothing, the most nondescript and comfortable clothing possible – things that don't change colour in the rain. The shoes, the glasses. Invisibility is a talent.

But I used the time to organise, not to gather my determination.

It only took a minute for that, ten years ago.

Over the edge of the newspaper, spread open to the page that is devoted to discussion of him, the old man sees the young woman arrive. He moves a little closer.

Chapter 28

Piras remained in the hallway outside the door of the Crime Reporting Office with a quizzical look on her face and her head tilted slightly to one side, as if making sure of what she thought she had heard. Her dark eyes slid over Giuffrè as if he were a piece of furniture and came to rest on Lojacono.

The inspector met and held her gaze, admitting inwardly that she was a good-looking woman. Now that she was fully lit, unlike the first time he met her, he could see the gentle lines of her body, lines that her business suit could not fully conceal. He noticed the perfect features of her face.

'Who are you? Do I know you?' she said.

'I couldn't say. But I know you: we met the night of Mirko Lorusso's murder. Evidently, I have a better memory than you do.'

Giuffrè let out a groan of terror. Piras was famous for her hair-trigger temper: now watch her pulverise Lojacono for his impertinent reply.

Instead, the woman slowly nodded her head as a derisive smile played over her lips.

'Now I remember. You're the one who noticed the tissues. And then got sent packing with a kick in the arse.'

Lojacono shrugged his shoulders without pulling his hands out of the pockets of his overcoat.

'True. The professionals had shown up, and in fact the first thing they did was solve the case.'

Piras weighed his reply. She nodded again, then she said,

'Come with me. I want an espresso. Point me to a decent café around here.'

Leaving an open-mouthed Giuffrè behind them, and trailing the curious gazes of a couple of colleagues who were coming in through the front entrance, Lojacono led Piras to a bar behind the police headquarters. The woman walked straight over to the only corner table in the place and sat down. She took a look around.

'Mamma mia, what a place. Cosy, isn't it? I'll take an espresso. Good and hot.'

Lojacono stood there, hands in pockets, his almond-shaped eyes focused on her face.

'Not for me, thanks. I'm afraid it might interfere with the afternoon nap I've got planned.'

Piras smiled.

'Do me a favour and stop playing the strong silent man who won't take orders. If you don't want an espresso, suit yourself. But sit down, please. I have something to ask you.'

Lojacono sat down.

'What can I do for you, dottoressa? I don't think I have any particularly useful information.'

The prosecutor shook her head.

'You never know where you'll find useful information. Please, remind me of your name.'

'Inspector Lojacono, Giuseppe.'

'Ah, now I remember – the Sicilian. I seem to recall reading something, a few months ago. I like to stay on top of things when it comes to the staff of the various police stations I might have to work with. What exactly happened? Some police witness, I think, must have mentioned your name . . .'

Lojacono stood up suddenly.

'So sorry, dottoressa, but I need to be getting back. I can't take time off my real work to sit here listening to fairy tales I already know by heart.'

Piras smiled again, openly satisfied.

'Whoa, calm down. No one's trying to insult you. I was refreshing my memory. I don't want to pry into your personal affairs, heaven forbid. Bad things happen to everyone, but there's a solution for everything. So what exactly do you do, here at the San Gaetano police station?'

Lojacono decided to give the woman another chance and sat back down.

'I'm in the Crime Reporting Office. But that's a front. I'm actually spending my days fighting a bloody poker duel with my computer. My weapon of choice is five-card stud.'

Piras smiled again.

'I see. Effective allocation of human resources, as they say.

Make the best possible use of all personnel to ensure that we give the criminals a generous head start.'

Lojacono shrugged.

'No problem. Mine not to reason why, mine but to do or die. It's sort of like being in purgatory; you take it and wait. And the truth is, I'm not dying to get back to where I was before, so it's really OK.'

The woman sipped her cup of coffee.

'I have to say, even in the least appetising dives, the coffee in this city is first rate. No argument. Now tell me, Lojacono, as one islander to another – what's your theory about these two murders?'

'Me? What evidence would I have, from my privileged vantage point in the Crime Reporting Office, that would even allow me to develop a theory? I'd have to be able to read the reports, go over the documents, see the transcripts of interviews. And consult with the station captains who have oversight, hear what forensics has to say . . .'

Piras snorted and lowered her voice.

'Stop pulling my leg, Lojacono. I know you have a theory; I heard you tell your colleague you did. Tell me more.'

'I really couldn't say. It's only a hunch, but we cops don't work on the basis of hunches; we base everything we do on facts. I wouldn't limit my investigation to the world of the Camorra, that's all. But as I say, it's nothing more than a hunch.'

Piras studied him at length. That man with his strange almond-shaped eyes provoked her curiosity. She sensed he was strong and also a little dangerous, but certainly intelligent. A rare quality, intelligence, she decided. Especially in this police station.

'In fact, there is some information you lack, Inspector Lojacono, Giuseppe. That's because you have no reason to know, since this is a high-priority investigation and it's off-limits to almost everyone. And so I'm not authorised to tell you – and I'll take care not to – that from a number of interviews it emerged that Lorusso, Mirko, the first victim, had only recently been recruited by a drug trafficker, a two-bit Camorrista from the outskirts of town called Ruggieri, Antonio; that this same Ruggieri had sent him to push wraps of cocaine outside a high school in the better part of town; and that it so happens that among the students attending this high school was De Matteis, Giada, the second victim. A set of facts that are intriguing at the very least, wouldn't you say?'

Lojacono turned his glass of mineral water between both hands.

'I don't know any of those things. But if I did, I wouldn't stop at appearances. Unless there's evidence of some deeper link between the two kids, then the murders might have nothing to do with that. Plus, bear with me: what's the point of killing both of them and bringing down all this attention on the case? The Mafia, as I know and you know, always takes care first and foremost to keep business front and centre. They could have arranged for the boy to vanish, leaving the girl safe and sound, and no one except his mother would have noticed a thing. Why unleash all this mayhem?'

Piras listened closely, then shook her head.

'Maybe the kids saw something they shouldn't have. Maybe they were planning to rip off the dealer. Who can say? Still, you have to admit that this contact is the only thing we have right now, isn't it?'

After a moment's consideration, Lojacono said,

'I guess it is. When you have a concrete piece of evidence, you have to follow it; you certainly can't chase after a vague impression. But I continue to believe that this case has nothing to do with the Camorra.'

Piras insisted,

'But all the hallmarks of a murder committed by a professional are there: the long-term stakeout, the painstaking selection of the time and place. No one saw a thing, no one heard a thing. He probably used a gun with a properly made silencer. A single shot, from close range, to make up for the lack of accuracy of the weapon itself, a .22 – easy to carry, easy to hide.'

Lojacono replied,

'Certainly. But you know as well as I do that this isn't the sort of hit we see from the organised crime families we have around here. They're much more arrogant and theatrical, especially when they're interested in teaching someone a lesson. Plus, this guy left tissues on the ground and didn't bother to pick up the shell casings. It's not exactly the work of a professional. I'm still baffled.'

Piras sighed.

'You're telling me. And these dickheads seem incapable of providing any help at all. What do you think of Di Vincenzo?'

Lojacono smiled.

'I don't know him at all. I've met him twice: the first time when I got here, the second the night of the Lorusso murder, and I think I might have run into him in the men's room another couple of times but he never even gave me a nod of the head. But he doesn't strike me as a yokel, I'll say that.'

'No, he's no yokel, but right now he doesn't know which way to turn. He's sticking to this theory of the Camorra connection, but only because he has nothing better. And the other station captain, the one from Posillipo, keeps passing the buck. This Ruggieri, the dealer who recruits children, is a lowlife. We grilled him but he's got nothing to tell us; he whines and denies everything. If you ask me, he really doesn't know anything. And I don't know which way to turn now. As you've probably seen, the press is ripping us to pieces.'

Lojacono nodded.

'Yes, I saw that. Unfortunately, I doubt they'll stop, at least until they know we have some real leads.'

'That's right. Which is why we're going to call a press conference and announce that we're following a lead on Camorra involvement, in connection with drug dealing at the girl's high school. There will be a collective closing of ranks in the city's highest social circles, a few indignant protests. But if nothing else, it'll drive the pushers out of the area for a while.'

Piras got to her feet. Lojacono understood that the conversation was over. He was sort of sorry: the woman knew her business, as well as being easy on the eye.

'That might even be the right solution, who can say? There's only one thing that can prove us wrong.'

'What's that?'

Lojacono was already on his way to the door. He paused.

'Another murder.'

Chapter 29

She lies motionless on the bed, staring up at the ceiling. Eleonora decides that she'd rather die. And so she prays for that.

The most absurd thing, the strangest thing of all, is that she feels guilty. As if she had been the one, all by herself, who had decided; as if she had laid the foundations herself, as if she'd conceived the child on her own, and she was trying to inflict it on him, as a penalty, as a condemnation.

She wonders whether she chose the wrong time. Maybe she should have talked to him in bed, after making love, when everything is tender and sweet and there is gratitude in the air for the pleasure shared. Perhaps she should have murmured it to him in the shadows, when the afternoon light poured in horizontal stripes through the half-closed wooden blinds, turning their bodies to gold and their thoughts to baby blue.

Maybe she shouldn't have arranged to see him at the university, in the very spot where they had first met. She should have avoided a place that could have completed the circle, imprisoning their emotions in crystal like the prince and princess in some fairy tale.

Fairy tales don't exist, and Eleonora knows it. Her mother had told her so, in no uncertain terms, during their last conversation before she left: Don't dream. Dreams will kill you if you're not careful.

But unfortunately I did dream, Eleonora thinks. I let myself be lured into another dream, where I was a penniless princess gathered up by the prince and carried straight into Paradise. But I was no princess. And he was no prince. And there is no Paradise.

She had told him as a gleaming shaft of sunlight suddenly broke through the clouds above them. She'd waited for it, that ray of light; she'd hoped for a good omen. And she'd even forgiven him for that first glance of terror and estrangement, aghast as he was. And the endless silence that had followed.

But not the words. Those were unequivocal, horrible. A chilly verdict.

'I can't,' he'd said. 'I can't.'

'What does that mean?' she had asked him. 'What can't you do?'

He sat there, shaking his head, without a word. Then he brusquely got to his feet, saying, 'I'm sorry, I've got to go now. I need to think.'

She'd talked to him that night, at the usual time. One ring, two, a third. Then his voice, so different from usual: frosty, distant.

'I need to think,' he'd said again. 'This changes everything; you understand that, don't you? It wasn't part of the plan. I need to think.'

'What about me?' Eleonora had asked. 'Don't you see that I'm part of this too? You think I don't have dreams, plans, opportunities? Weren't you there too, when this happened?'

Silence. Silence on the other end of the line, silence in his heart, silence in his soul. And then: 'Just think, what would my father say? Can you imagine? At the very least, I'd have to move, we'd have to move. And it would kill him. Plus, I'm a long way from getting my degree. I'd have to look for a job, give up studying. Scrape by, for the rest of our lives: me, you and . . . it.'

Eleonora decides that she could forgive him anything, except for referring to his child as a stumbling block on the path to happiness.

She'd sat there in silence for a long time. She'd listened to him breathing into the receiver, and he really had seemed like a stranger to her.

In the end, she had said to him, 'I don't want to lose you. I can't stand to lose you. Let me know what you decide to do.' And she'd hung up the phone.

A whole day had gone by. A night, a morning, an afternoon, an evening. And now it was night again. Eleonora hadn't eaten, she hadn't gone out, she hadn't got out of bed, she didn't remember sleeping, but she did dream.

She dreamed of death.

She saw herself in a bed, in the middle of the room. She saw, in succession: her mother, white-faced, dry-eyed; her father, distraught with grief, incredulous, despairing; her friends from the university, one by one, with the awkward expressions of people who have missed an opportunity, who are full of regret at not having had more time together.

Even his father was there: still a stranger, stiff, sanctimonious, a scrupulous shadow falling over his face, a hint of suspected guilt.

But not him. In the dream, he wasn't there. Eleonora wonders if she'll ever see him again.

Then the phone rings.

Chapter 30

She had been watching him all through the evening as he sat, lost in thought, his gaze wandering, one glass of wine chasing another. She couldn't wait for the dining room to empty out enough so that she could leave her young assistant to manage the tables and go to sit at his table.

It had been a while since Letizia had last seen him look the way he did when he first came to that city: bewildered, disoriented, unhappy. Slowly, one burst of conversation or smile at a time, he had opened up to dialogue and friendship, and a gentle and ironic nature had emerged, along with a flow of memories of another life.

With her heart rather than her head, Letizia sensed that Peppuccio – a nickname for Giuseppe that only she, in that city, used for Lojacono – was emerging from his solitude; albeit with effort, pain and regrets, he was starting to sit up and look around, the way someone might after suffering a terrible loss. After all, the man had left behind not only a marriage and a love story, but also his entire life. And his daughter – a bond that could not be forgotten.

She had known men devoid of all instinct for family, men who – once they were out of the house – thought of their children as financial burdens and nothing more. But that wasn't the way he was. The girl's silence, the barrier his wife had erected and his inability to alter his daughter's obvious intention to eliminate him from her life – all these things were wounds that refused to scar over.

She liked the man. She understood that it was time to level with herself. And the fact that Lojacono clung to his past the way he did, hindering any attempt to build a new life in the present, only prompted a sense of tenderness towards him in Letizia. In some odd way, in fact, it made him more attractive.

Over the last few months, night after night, she had seen that pain fade, become a mist hanging over his soul. The sudden moments of depression still came and went, but they became fainter with time. You get used to everything. Smiles had become more frequent, teasing jibes directed at her and the city, comments about the food. Peppuccio was starting to thaw, she had decided happily.

But tonight the pain and sadness were back, dense as a bank of winter fog. And they were looking for resolution at the bottom of a wineglass.

When she was finally able to take a break, Letizia wasted no time.

'So what's up? Are you trying to break the world record for the amount of red wine consumed in one evening? And look at that: you've hardly touched your pasta. Should I order a fresh bowl for you? Is there something wrong with it?'

The man raised his eyes to hers.

'I guess I'm not hungry tonight.'

Letizia sat down, drying her hands on her apron, and faked a laugh. She'd long since learned that it was pointless to question him; if he wanted to talk, he'd do so without prompting.

'That's a bad sign. Must mean you're in love.'

Lojacono said nothing, turning the wineglass between his palms. Then he spoke.

'You know, when that boy was killed and they called us, I was asleep, catching a nap on the foldout bed they have for the guys on the graveyard shift. I don't dream about Marinella often, though I think about her all the time, as you know. And that night, that very night, I dreamed about her.'

Letizia listened attentively.

'What did you dream?'

'She looked exactly like the last time I saw her, when I left and she refused to give me a parting hug. She was at a disco, or she had been, then ... Well, it didn't go well, I don't want to think about it. And as the car she was riding in ... That's when the phone rang, and I woke up. And as you can understand, I still have that weight on my chest.'

'I get it. But you shouldn't dwell on it. It was a bad dream, that's all. You know, in this city we say that dreaming someone has died makes them live longer.'

Lojacono smiled sadly.

'I know. I know that a dream is just a dream. But then, when I was there, I saw the face of the boy's mother. There was a woman, must have been a neighbour or a relative, I don't know who, comforting her. And she wasn't talking. But her face ... She was such a wreck.'

Letizia shivered.

'I can imagine. Poor Luisa. That son of hers was all she had in the world. Since then, I've heard she never leaves her flat, not even for food. Her neighbours bring her something to eat from time to time. I don't have the nerve to visit her, though maybe I'll try someday soon.'

'Sure, I can see why. That kind of grief is intolerable to be around, even at a distance. That night, it looked as if she was screaming but she didn't make a sound. Or she did, but it was a sort of sigh, a hiss. I can't seem to get it out of my mind. And I've seen dead people, in my time. And survivors, relatives of murder victims, plenty of them. But not like her.'

'Listen, Peppu', it strikes me that you're spending too much time on this thing. Those kids aren't your daughter. This is a nasty city and unfortunately this kind of thing happens.'

Lojacono's eyes were lost, empty.

'Then I attended the girl's funeral. I don't even know why I went; I just wanted to understand. And there were all her friends, her classmates – you can imagine, it was a terrible thing. And the mother, oh, the mother ... At a certain point, she started talking out loud, as if it were the most natural thing in the world. And the things she said ... She was raving, obviously. As if she'd lost her mind. I was right across from her, so I got a good look at her eyes. I felt as if I was looking straight into hell.'

Letizia decided to put an end to the torment. She took his hand.

'Now listen to me. I don't like this whole business. You're taking on a burden that doesn't belong to you, and in the shape you're in, you can't afford to. Otherwise you're going to lose your mind and then they really won't let you see your daughter ever again. These murders, these two dead kids – it's atrocious, chilling, unnatural. But we don't know who did it, and we don't know what it was about. Money, drugs, extortion; this city has a lot of different faces. But you have nothing to do with it, your daughter has nothing to do with it, none of us has anything to do with it. And you're not going to solve matters by hanging around eating your heart out over it.'

Lojacono stared at her. A light gleamed in his slanted eyes.

'You don't understand. The paper said he was a crocodile because of his tears, but that's bullshit. He's a crocodile, that's true, but it's his technique that makes him one. Do you know how crocodiles hunt? They can't swim fast, they have short legs and they can't chase their prey. And yet they're among the oldest animal species on the planet. Evolution left them as they were, and you know why? Because they're perfect. The crocodile is a perfect death machine.'

Letizia shook her head.

'I don't get it. What does a crocodile have to do with anything? That's a gimmick some reporter dreamed up.'

'True, but without knowing it that reporter hit the nail on

the head. Listen to me: a crocodile selects a location – in the swamps, in the muddy waters of the savannah – and it takes time making its choice. A lot of time. The place where it knows its prey will go, sooner or later, for water. And then it positions itself under the surface of the water, every so often breaking the surface with its nostrils so it can breathe. And it waits. It waits.'

Letizia was holding her breath. Lojacono's voice was little more than a murmur.

'Finally, the victim arrives. It sniffs, it looks around. Its instinct tells it that there's danger there, but it needs to drink. It sees nothing dangerous there, in that specific place. So it lowers its head to the surface of the water.'

Silence. At a nearby table someone laughed, and others joined in. Lojacono went on.

'That's how he hunts. And that's our Crocodile's technique. He knows their activities, their routines, their schedules. He knows where the kids will go, what they'll do when they get there. And when they approach his jaws, he fires. A single shot, with a small-bore pistol; not very accurate, but he can't miss. Because he's studied carefully. He's laid his plans, for who knows how long. And like real crocodiles, he's cold-blooded.'

For the first time, Letizia understood the hell that her friend carried with him in his soul. She also understood what a born cop he was.

'So have you told your colleagues about this? Have you talked about it to anyone else?'

'No. I told the young woman, the prosecutor, that as far as

I was concerned, the Camorra had nothing to do with it. But the things I've described are sensations, ideas, impressions. You can't work with your imagination; you have to work with the facts. What am I going to tell them: that I dreamed about my daughter and I saw the faces of two mothers and so I've decided that the killer isn't a Camorrista?'

Letizia thought that over. Outside, a motorcycle ripped through the quiet of the night.

'Well, I still think you ought to. Maybe you could talk to her, that prosecutor. From what you tell me, she's the only one willing to listen to you.'

Lojacono shook his head.

'No, not a chance. They already think I'm a bribe-taker, an incompetent who boosted his salary by taking money from a two-bit Mafioso in exchange for worthless information. They have all the reports, the information, the findings. And what do I have? A nightmare.'

'Then don't worry about it. Let them take care of it if they're so damn good. Maybe it's all about jealousy, some girl who was in love. Maybe they liked each other, who knows? Maybe you're right and the Camorra has nothing to do with it. Maybe it's all about love.'

Lojacono was silent, pensive, for a long while. Then he said,

'Maybe so. In cases of this kind, things bob to the surface sooner or later. In the middle of some other crime, or else by chance, the killer slips up. But that's not what I think will happen here. Someone who's capable of preparing two murders so meticulously, one right after another, isn't someone who's acting on impulse. It's someone who's given it thorough consideration. Someone who's gone to the location over and over again, staked it out, covered the ground, checked it out in every detail.'

Letizia's laughter had an edge to it.

'Really? Walking up and down past a place, like the courtyard where Luisa's son was murdered? Or letting himself be seen outside the girl's house, when I read that she was murdered near the front entrance of some flats a fair distance from the road? And you think that nobody noticed a murderer walking around with a handgun in out-of-the-way places like that?'

Lojacono ran a hand through his hair.

'You live in this city. You have friends here, you work here, you were born here and you know everyone in your neighbourhood. I've just got here. I've been here less than a year. But I can tell you that it's very easy to be invisible here. All of you are afraid of getting caught up in some mess that has nothing to do with you, so you mind your own business. You're probably right too. Still, the city's full of phantoms, people who come and go unnoticed in your midst.'

'Now you're trying to scare me. Just you wait – they'll find your phantom, and you can go back to getting a good night's sleep.'

'Let's hope so. But something inside me tells me that the Crocodile isn't finished hunting.'

Chapter 31

Donato worked up the nerve and called her. He spoke, he listened. He mirrored her dreams, her desires, and her fantasies in his own, and he found them intact in the aftermath of the storm.

Of course, it would have been better if none of it had happened. But there's a solution to everything, if you stay together, if you love one another. At the journey's end, no matter how gruelling it's been, there's a smile on your face – the right kind of smile.

First he talked to his father, and that was the hardest thing. He told him about the final exam, not about the two of them. Not because he was a coward, but because he believed that it was right for her to be present when he was talking about her, that any conversations about the future should take place in her presence. Because he is confident that his father, always so tightly controlled and cutting, will melt when he finds himself in the presence of those eyes, that smile. Donato decides that nothing in creation is so diamond-hard that it could withstand that smile.

Now he's smiling too, about her concern. She's tense, nervous, agitated. She's afraid of this meeting, but Donato knows that her fears are groundless. He himself had worried far too much about his unsuccessful exam. His father, with extreme clarity, made him understand that it was at his request that the professor, an old friend, had been willing to accept only an absolutely outstanding result. That the decision to advise him to retake the exam had been a way of allowing him to complete his preparation.

He had expected a scolding, an outburst of icy anger followed by a lengthy silence, the way it had been when he'd done something wrong as a child; instead he was greeted with tranquillity and understanding. His father truly was an exceptional man. At that point, he worked up the nerve and, taking advantage of the relaxed atmosphere, told his father about her. Not everything, because he didn't want to compromise his father's freedom to decide; a decision that could hardly be anything but positive. But the basics, yes, he had conveyed the essentials. And he had managed to secure a dinner date.

Now Donato knows that everything's fine, and that everything's going to turn out fine. He knows that he was unlucky to lose his mother as a small boy, but also that he was very lucky to have the father he has; and that luck has continued to favour him, allowing him to meet the most wonderful girl in the world.

Exams come and go, Donato tells himself, as he whistles

a cheerful tune and heads downstairs to the garage, to get the car out and drive over to her place. You can always retake an exam. Life always gives you a second chance. Starting tomorrow, he'll redouble his effort and resume his studies, and this time he'll give it his all.

Because I have my whole life ahead of me, Donato thinks, and one thing I know for certain is that it won't be a couple of hundred boring pages of text that will keep me from living it.

My whole life, Donato thinks. And he sticks his hand in his pocket, feeling around for the garage door remote control.

Chapter 32

It was clear that she couldn't stay awake any longer; her eyelids were growing heavy. So Laura Piras decided to turn off the light and see if she could get some sleep. Outside, the night was finally quiet. That meant it must be past 2 a.m.

It had been so long since she'd been able to get to sleep before the early hours that she couldn't even remember when that had been any more. Another lifetime.

Looking back on her own past, it was easy to split it into before and after.

She'd been a bright, happy girl. She loved to laugh, read, and study, play sports, dance. She loved everything. She loved life. She was curious and attracted by everything with the excitement and glee of a young girl. And that excitement had a name: Carlo.

She'd met him in junior school, back home in Cagliari. He was an extremely skinny, gangly boy, with perennially tousled hair that she tried unsuccessfully to brush into some semblance of order with her hands. Carlo, in his turtleneck jumper all winter long. Carlo, and his passion for political activism. Carlo, and his determination to play football, no matter how bad a player he might be. Carlo, who could make her laugh even at a funeral. Carlo, who had loved her from the moment he first saw her until the day he closed his eyes for the last time.

In the dark, as she sought sleep without finding it, Laura retraced her steps with Carlo. They spent every waking minute together, they studied together, they engaged in political activism together, they went to the cinema, and they made love. Everyone in town was used to seeing them together: the shapely, smiling girl and the gangly, bespectacled boy. Laura smiled at the memory of how they wanted to change the world by leaving their island. And at the way that coming from an island makes you different and determined for the rest of your life.

The thought of her island brought an oblique gaze and a half smile to mind, though they dissolved before bobbing to the surface of consciousness. And once again Carlo emerged, top grades like her after secondary school, and both of them opting for law – more concrete than philosophy and less abstruse than architecture.

And then, after the *summa cum laude* degree, the civil service exam. She was running a little behind schedule, what with her father's illness and subsequent death, in the atrocious grip of a cancerous tumour. So he was ridiculously embarrassed to tell her that he had become a public prosecutor at the age of twenty-four. She'd laughed, as usual, and told him, 'You know I'll not only catch up with you but I'll leave you in my dust.'

'I know,' he had replied, serious as ever. 'You always beat me, even at billiards.'

Together they had picked through a list of likely destinations for his posting, and together they had dismissed Lombardy, which, of course, was where he was assigned. In the early days it had seemed so strange telling him, in the foggy north, about the sunshine of home, studying by herself, turning around to make a wry comment and finding that he was no longer at her side. But there were always the weekends. She felt her mood lift at the airport when she saw him emerge from the crowd, a good head taller than her, with that bunch of bananas that constituted his hair.

'How on earth do they take you seriously up there, the northern polenta-grubbers, with that head of hair?' she'd say.

And he'd reply, 'Why, what's wrong with my hair?'

And they'd both burst into helpless peals of laughter.

There had been guys coming on to her even then. Laura was pretty, and she'd always exuded a feminine allure. But with someone like Carlo, she felt no need for anyone else. That's just how it was.

It happened, in fact, when he was on his way to the airport, to catch the flight down from Malpensa. Who knows why. Maybe he fell asleep at the wheel. Maybe he wasn't used to the fog yet. Maybe he was distracted, stupid, dopey bastard that he was. Whatever the reason, the fact remains, that Friday morning there he was, the usual hasty phone call confirming he'd be arriving, and that same Friday evening, a policeman on duty at Cagliari airport awkwardly broke the news to her that Carlo wouldn't be getting off the plane. Ever again.

In the silence of the night, broken only by the wail of a distant siren, she tried to remember that grief. Losing him was like an amputation – they say that you go on feeling the limb after you've lost it, that the body never cancels the memory of its missing part.

She changed. She studied even harder than before, came in at the top of the civil service exam rankings, and left the island of Sardinia. So eager to put a stretch of salt water between her and that odd couple that resembled the Italian *il*, she so short, he so tall; to put distance between her and a spirit whose hair was always rumpled and flyaway; between her and the person she had been, the one who always laughed too loud and too long. She no longer wanted to talk to anyone, neither family nor friends. She made a hasty, reluctant weekly phone call to her mother to see how she was, as if performing an objectionable task, and she'd hang up with a sense of relief, free until the following week.

She'd taken a posting to a dangerous, challenging place that none of her colleagues would have accepted. She could have turned it down; she could easily have opted for somewhere quieter, more attractive, that would have turbo-charged her already glittering career trajectory. But that was not what she wanted. She wanted to work hard, plunge body and soul into the dream that those two kids had once shared, and change the world from the ground up.

She knew that her attitude, the sharp edges that she did

nothing to conceal, the cutting harshness in her responses, were all viewed by others as signs of arrogant pride – the typical female prosecutor, young and attractive, who puts on a harsh, unyielding persona to establish her authority. But that wasn't the truth of it. Her harsh, brittle edge was nothing more than a manifestation of the permanent night that had fallen over her heart when the policeman at the airport, nervously turning his cap in his hands, had told her that she'd be alone from now on.

She had chosen not to let anyone get close to her. Not because she thought she should be faithful to a memory, but because she thought there was no point teaching the essence of herself to love someone who would never ever know her the way Carlo had. The call of the flesh was surprisingly infrequent, and anyway, it exhausted itself in brief, solitary moments that only left her feeling sadder than before. There were times when she thought she must be getting old without realising it. She saw herself as rigid, harsh and unlovely, and couldn't understand the allure that she continued to exert over the men that she met. In any case, she unfailingly rejected their advances, decisively and unilaterally.

The night dragged on and sleep gradually enveloped her in a murky fog. Those kids, those murders. The press and its damned Crocodile. She didn't mind the reporting of it per se; she just hated the way that the media attention created pressure and haste. Haste, as she knew all too well, made people do stupid things.

Maybe Lojacono, the Sicilian, had a point: the Camorra was a false trail.

Lojacono. Quite a guy. She'd felt his eyes running the length of her body but she'd picked up no attraction, not even when she'd impulsively invited him for a coffee. He'd struck her as different from the others. He was intelligent, that was obvious: he'd proved it at the crime scene, noticing the tissues before anybody else. And the observations he'd shared at the café hung together nicely too. She thought back to the file about him that she'd decided to read through once she got back to her office. A grim story: a police witness who'd decided to shoot his mouth off. Maybe the informant had simply been inclined to get rid of a talented cop.

Suddenly she shivered and pulled the blankets a little tighter. Somewhere out there was the Crocodile, probably alone, and possibly hungry. And there was a Sicilian policeman with almond-shaped eyes, whom she imagined was every bit as alone.

So many people are alone in this crazy, chaotic city, thought Laura Piras.

And she finally dropped off to sleep.

Chapter 33

Sweetheart, my darling,

I'm heading out soon.

As usual I've prepared it all in detail and I'm ready for any eventuality, including the possibility that I'll come back here without having achieved what I set out to do because something went wrong at the last second.

Because that's the key, my darling. To be in no hurry. To be sure you don't compromise your ultimate aim just because you must complete the job at all costs. You have to wait for conditions to suit the plan. However long it takes.

If you think about it, the ten years that have already passed are part of that philosophy. One day after another, building: in my head, on paper, on the computer, at the shooting range, in the garage. Readying everything, second by second. I never prepared a Plan A, Plan B and Plan C; I only ever had a single plan. And I have to wait for the parts – all the parts – to fit together before I make my move.

I creep around the city, doing what I need to. I watch from my hiding places, I never look anyone in the eye, crawling along, clinging to the wall. And I realise that all these people, running to and fro, cursing and swearing, listening to music on their headphones and chewing their gum, dead-eyed – all these people actually protect me. They're like a shifting wall that I can hide behind.

I think of you, my darling. I think of all the time you spent here, alone. Without me. I think of how you suffered. It won't be long now, you know. Not long at all.

This time it'll be even easier; this time there's no danger of anyone coming by with a dog. I still laugh. Did I tell you that I found some splashes of beagle pee on the cuffs of my trousers?

Writing to you keeps me company. I hope you like it. It warms my heart, makes me feel as if I'm talking to you, even if I can't hear you answer me. But soon we'll sit side by side, and we'll talk and talk – we'll tell each other stories until our throats are parched.

Sometimes I can hear your laughter. It's happened a lot in recent years. I took refuge in it, trying not to hear her gasp and wheeze.

I've often wondered about this thing I'm going through. I've thought about it, so much and for so long, about all this, every detail, every practical aspect, but I've never really wondered what I would feel. What emotions I would experience, in other words. And now I think I have the answer.

I don't feel a thing.

I love you, my sweet and only darling – that's the only thing I feel. I feel no joy, I feel no pain. I see them fall, I see them die. I see them pass away, give up the ghost. And I feel nothing when they do.

I stay and look, making sure that what I wanted to make happen really has happened. I watch as death moves from one corpse to another. I see a dawning expression on the faces of those left behind as the doors to hell on earth swing wide open. Which is what I wanted. But I don't feel any satisfaction, nor am I brushed by even the shadow of regret.

I feel nothing.

All I feel is the powerful, overwhelming love that I have for you.

Chapter 34

Dawn on a rainy day.

There's not a specific moment when you see the dawn, on a rainy day. Suddenly it's there, sliding into view while you had your mind on other things.

You feel it in the air. You watch as the night abandons the rain, step by step, and unexpectedly there's a pallid light, translucent as a wet silk sheet.

It descends gradually, like a disease. It settles on the smoke-grey trees, washes the walls with tears, turns the glittering cobblestones dull and opaque.

Dawn on a rainy day constricts the breathing and, to the sorrows of whoever is still awake at that hour, it adds pain.

A girl in love has checked the time over and over, dialling a mobile phone number over and over again, until she finally resigns herself to the fact that there's no answer, and she falls asleep, fully dressed, in an armchair. Dawn arrives in the rain and caresses her from the window, without waking her, regretfully.

A father awakes and, as he heads for the bathroom, notices an empty bedroom, an untouched bed. Suddenly he feels fearful and looks out of the window at the rainy dawn. Below, he sees the garage door open. He hurries down in pyjamas and slippers, steps outside, indifferent to the cold and damp. He walks into the garage.

A scream tears through the air.

The wet dawn folds back around that tear.

Like a chilly shroud.

Lojacono could hardly fail to notice that something had happened. In the alley, at the front entrance of the police station, there were two vans and a car emblazoned with the logos of the leading national television networks and surmounted by large dish antennae. The vehicles partly obstructed the already narrow passageway, and a uniformed policeman was arguing with the drivers in a spirited but unsuccessful attempt to get them to move.

Within the courtyard things were even worse. A platoon of journalists with microphones and digital recorders were pushing and shoving, trying to get inside the building, while two blank-faced cops barred the entrance. Lojacono was forced to signal to catch their attention before he could be allowed in. A young woman reporter wearing glasses realised that he was a cop and tried to grab his sleeve, but he wriggled out of her grasp.

Inside, it was relatively peaceful. Giuffrè was already swaying nervously.

'Do you mind telling me what the hell's going on? What is all this ruckus?'

The little man sniggered.

'Oh, right, I almost forgot: what with you living in a cave and all, you don't have a TV or a radio. But how do you manage to get any sleep with all that silence? I think I'd lose my mind.'

'Well, you're right. Who gets any sleep? Are you going to tell me what's happening or not?'

The sergeant puffed up his chest in pride.

'First item on the national news. The whole country is interested in us, as you can see. The Crocodile has struck again. A university student, in the better part of Vomero, same technique, this time in the garage at his villa. It probably happened last night. His father found him this morning at dawn – a prestigious doctor, well known in this city, apparently a gynaecologist.'

Lojacono flopped into his chair.

'So they're certain? There's no doubt about it? It was him?'

Giuffrè nodded gravely.

'Of course it was him. Unless there's already a copycat out there. You know how it is these days. The minute you're the subject of a front-page story, other people start trying to imitate you. But all the necessary elements were there: tissues on the pavement, a shell-casing from a .22 pistol, a shot to the head, fired point-blank. He waited for the boy to sit down at the wheel and then fired before he could close the door. So it was him.'

The inspector stared into the void.

'Another one. That makes three. What do we know about the kid?'

Giuffrè extended both arms.

'I can't help you there. All I know is what they said on the TV news. It happened last night, so the morning newspapers missed it. His name was Donato Rinaldi, he was almost twenty-three, studying medicine. He was on track for his degree, a good student. He lived alone with his father, a widower. He was an only child. His father's one of the most sought-after gynaecologists in town, plenty of money, they broadcast shots of the villa where they lived. They live there, instead of Posillipo like the other rich people in this city, to be closer to the hospital where the father is head physician. I don't know anything else.'

'I don't understand – if it happened on the other side of town, why are all these reporters here?'

The little man's expression suddenly turned crafty.

'Because we were the first to handle these murders, so we've had longer than anyone else to investigate, even if we haven't found out a thing. So we're especially to blame, don't you think? Now they're waiting for Di Vincenzo, to rip him limb from limb the second they get the chance.'

'Does he know?'

'Oh, you bet he knows. He's here, locked in his office, and he has been since seven-fifteen this morning. He's taking no calls. Pontolillo told me that Piras has already called three times. But he won't answer and he even has his mobile turned off.'

Lojacono shook his head.

'A single father. A widower. Lorusso was born to a single mother; no one ever knew who the father was. De Matteis's mother is divorced; the girl's father didn't even come to the funeral. I heard a couple of people talking about it – he wasn't able to get a flight back from America in time. And they're all just kids.'

Giuffrè listened, rapt, his eyes magnified by his bottle-bottom glasses.

'I can tell – the mind of the great detective is grinding into gear. Think, Loja', think. I know it – you're our one and only hope of ever getting out of here.'

'Get used to it, Giuffrè. I know less about all this than the others. All I'm doing is linking what facts I do possess, that's it.'

At that moment Di Vincenzo walked past their office door, heading for the courtyard. He was as white as a sheet. His gait was rigid and he stared straight ahead. An instant later, the platoon of reporters exploded with a shout.

Chapter 35

Now she knows she'll never see him again. Her fear has turned into certainty.

Eleonora gets out of bed, stiff-limbed. She feels completely drained of energy. She struggles against an immediate, violent surge of vertigo and the retching urge to vomit that follows. She leans back against the wall, inhaling deeply.

As she washes her face with ice-cold water she feels a distinctly odd sensation: she sees herself from outside. Right there, in the bathroom of the flat she lives in, as if it were a film and she were the only spectator, sitting and watching. She looks with detachment at this pallid, unkempt woman, with her rumpled clothing, her make-up smeared from sleep and tears. She could be any age, come from any walk of life. She is the very picture of loneliness and despair.

She's alone now. And she's scared.

She's terrified by the thought of having to make her way through a hostile world. Having to decide for herself, and defend her decision. Having no one to rely on, no one in it with her.

It's the first time in her life that anything like this has happened. There was always someone to take care of her, to point her in the right direction. Sometimes she followed her own instincts, but even then, she knew that she could count on help from others if needed.

Her family and her hometown surface in her mind. And she realises how long it's been since she bothered to think of them. What used to seem like a prison, an entangling net of pointless constraints, appearances and formalities, suddenly looks like a safe haven, but too far across stormy waters to be reached. Perhaps she was wrong to leave. But now it's too late, in any case.

She changes her clothes, every gesture slow and listless. She'd happily flop down on to the bed again, to sleep and sleep, to see if she could burrow into a place of peace amid her convulsive, agitated dreams.

But she can't do that. She has to solve her quandary, at least in part. The most important part, the most urgent part. How paradoxical, she thinks: being left without him has given her the strength to do what he wanted in order to stay with her.

She starts laughing, softly. Soon her laughter grows in strength, until she is left wrung out and collapses on to a chair, bursting into tears.

At last she recovers and gets to her feet. She picks up her handbag, rummages inside it and finds a crumpled scrap of paper. On it is a name and a phone number.

She remembers scrawling down that information with a pencil.

A sunlit morning at the university, her cheerful classmate catching up on missed studies. Wealthy, happy and glibly ironic – one of so many female students spending the winter at school. Daddy's happy to foot the bill, and in any case there's a line on Italian identity cards where you're supposed to state your occupation: you have to put something down.

Between classes, a group of girls would chat about life, professors and men. Not that Eleonora much enjoyed loitering there and engaging in that kind of conversation; her fellow students really did act like a flock of dumb birds. Still, that day the sun was warm and there were no dark clouds on the horizon. It was so agreeable to kill a little time like this, well aware that none of the tragedies the other girls were talking about would ever even graze her. To think about it now, sitting on the edge of her bed with that scrap of paper in her hand, prompted a stab of melancholy in Eleonora's heart and a surge of regret at her lost happiness.

Her classmate was the oldest girl in the group. She acted like the queen of the world, well versed in everything. She knew the city and all its most prominent citizens; she boasted that she could reach out to anyone at any time of the day or night. And she had told them, as a demonstration of her power, a story that now came rushing back to Eleonora – as arrogant and abrupt as a slap in the face.

She turns the scrap of paper over in her hands. She tries to recall what thought, or what premonition, had led her to jot down that girl's name and number. Once or twice she'd passed her in the corridors of the faculty, and they'd exchanged a fleeting smile. Nothing more.

And now, she muses, here I am. You're right. In the end everyone, sooner or later, needs something.

Eleonora gets to her feet and walks over to the phone.

Chapter 36

The old man gets up from the desk.

As long as he's been in that room, he's done nothing but write, sleep, change his clothes and use the bathroom. A few well-defined paths in the intervals between the long hours spent staking out places, monitoring and taking note.

Dabbing away at the perennial tear dripping from his left eye, the old man stands motionless. His thoughts run to what he has done. Slowly, methodically, he archives it all and focuses on his next move.

He's done the same thing every time: freed his mind of all the details that are no longer needed, all the things that have become superfluous, mere redundancy in light of what remains to be completed. Order, he thinks. First and foremost, order.

The boy, the student, was in a certain sense the easiest job of all to polish off. He had calmly catalogued his movements and activities, discovering to his relief that the boy was as methodical as he was, with strict routines from which he never wavered. And one in particular: Friday night.

Let the sky fall if it must, the boy went to his girlfriend's flat every Friday night and only returned home quite late. After returning from a day at university he spent time studying, then he'd shower, change, head downstairs to the garage to get out the car, drive to the far side of the city, and go up to his girlfriend's flat. The old man suspected that the boy's father knew nothing about the girl; from his usual safe distance he had observed the young couple argue frantically, as she insistently begged him to do something and he assumed a wait-and-see demeanour. Given the life he led as a student, a steady routine of home and university, and the fact that the old man had never seen the girl come to his house, she could only be demanding one thing: an official introduction. Times change, the old man thinks, but only to a certain extent.

Most likely the boy wasn't telling his father the truth. He was probably telling him he was going over to his study-partner's house to revise until late. It didn't much matter: the important thing was that on Friday night he could count on the father turning in at midnight as usual, unconcerned by his son's failure to return home.

The old man reviews how he came to the decision that the garage was the perfect place to settle the matter. The garage door closed automatically, a minute and forty seconds after the car exited the villa's front gate, which in turn remained open for one minute. In short, he had about fifty seconds to walk unhurriedly into the front yard, along the driveway on the side where the surveillance cameras were blinded by unpruned tree branches, check to make sure that no one was watching from the windows above, and slip into the garage.

He's already done it three times: dress rehearsals for a murder. A smile flits across his face at the expression. Funny.

The inside of the garage turned out to be ideal. Spacious, big enough for two cars, though only the boy used it because his father parked his in the space in front of the villa. Lots of clutter, a tool cabinet and a motorcycle covered with a tarpaulin. The old man had in fact opted for the space behind the motorcycle: a foot and a half from the driver's door, no more. He'd promised himself never to fire from more than a yard's distance. After all, his handgun – equipped with a silencer, to make the aim even more unpredictable – lacked the absolute precision he needed for the job.

This time he had had a little extra assistance from the garage door remote control. Maybe the batteries were low but, for whatever reason, it only worked if held outside the car, not from the interior with the door closed. So the perfect moment had been when the boy, already behind the wheel with his seatbelt fastened, used the remote control to open the garage door before swinging the car door shut.

Perhaps, the old man reflects, the hardest part was having to wait till dawn so he could watch the father come downstairs, still in his pyjamas and with those ridiculous clogs on his feet, to see him walk into the garage and come face to face with that grisly spectacle. But it was necessary, of course. Then he'd finally been able to head back to the hotel, leaving the property by the garden path, and remembering to put on his gloves. The last thing he needed was to screw things up by leaving a thumbprint on the release button of the gate, even though he knows perfectly well that his fingerprints, like his DNA, will be of no help to the cops if they have no prior records with which to compare them. But you never know, right? You never know.

Caution, in this phase, is of the utmost importance. Caution is the key to going the distance.

The old man has to admit that the outcome of all his work is entirely satisfactory. Everything has turned out perfectly, an impeccably clean job. But the most interesting part starts now.

He turns to the armoire, walks solemnly towards it, and pulls the door open. He lifts the wooden base and reaches into the false bottom, where a plastic tub is suspended from a hole cut into the floor of the armoire. He knows that the cleaning woman is sloppy and distracted but still, you never know, right? You never know. So it's always a good idea to assume the worst.

He pulls the pistol out of the plastic tub – a Beretta 71 with interchangeable barrels, specially modified to take the silencer he constructed himself, from instructions he found on an English-language Slovakian website. Another brief smile at how he struggled to translate the English instructions into Italian – a much more challenging task than constructing the silencer itself. He disassembles the weapon and lovingly cleans it, oiling each part on a cloth laid out on the desktop. He must be able to rely implicitly on the gun's flawless operation. He can't run the risk of it misfiring at the critical moment. He reassembles it with precision, checks it methodically. He loads it. As he does, he reflects that he'll only need to use it two more times. Not a lot of use, all things considered. He puts the gun back into the plastic tub and replaces the container where it was, hidden from the sloppy housekeeper who comes to clean the room every other day.

He pays his bill every four days, staying under the radar of the girl at the reception desk. He has calculated that four days is the right interval to convey an impression of transience and ward off the suspicions of the staff. The old man on the third floor, always about to check out, but lingering on, resting up for his health.

He takes a deep breath, standing in front of the armoire. Once he's cleaned and oiled his pistol, removing all traces of its last use, he similarly sweeps clean both mind and memory, eliminating every detail concerning the student's death. Every scrap of information is methodically removed – no longer needed. Then he catalogues everything he'll need to know for his next project, information that he'll flesh out in the next few days with surveillance and the investigation of even the smallest detail. If you've come up with a technique that seems to work, he thinks, there's no point in changing it.

For that matter, even the television used the moniker 'the Crocodile'. I'm a crocodile. Therefore, my chief characteristic must be that I'm cold-hearted.

With one last sigh, he turns towards the window. He walks the six feet separating him from the curtains and, for the first time since he moved in, pulls them apart, just the narrowest of openings.

And he starts watching the opposite side of the street.

Chapter 37

Di Vincenzo returned a few minutes later. The clamouring horde of reporters, their ear-splitting cries broken only by short intervals as they waited in vain for answers, had left the captain deafened. His face was ashen and expressionless. He had no idea which way to turn.

Giuffrè had learned from his friend in the admin department that Piras would be coming some time that morning, and that she'd called ahead to let the captain know that she expected to find him at his desk. The atmosphere was grim to say the least.

Lojacono had waited a reasonable amount of time before he ventured out into the courtyard, where he struck up a conversation with the bespectacled young woman who had grabbed his arm for an interview on the way in. She was now sadly putting her half-empty digital recorder away. Prefacing the conversation with a disclaimer that he knew nothing about the Crocodile that she didn't know already, he'd asked her what information she had about the latest murder.

The journalist, a freelancer named Ornella Cresci, accepted his invitation to swing round to the local café for an espresso.

'This story is fantastic,' she told him. 'It comes at a time when – leaving aside the occasional Camorra murder in the usual parts of town – nothing interesting is going on. And all of a sudden a serial killer pops up, preying on kids, and he practically leaves a signature on the crime scene, to say nothing of the fact that he weeps as he kills. Just think about it. I see a journalism award; I see a story that goes down in history. And the cops – no offence, but it's the blessed truth – the cops are digging into the Camorra, while the Camorra are caught completely unawares. The whole thing is a gift!'

Lojacono prodded further.

'And this last murder? What information do you have about the victim?'

Ornella was tiny and rail-thin. Her oversized glasses probably accounted for a full third of her body weight. But once she'd established that the inspector was paying, she'd grabbed a slice of pizza and was now devouring it ravenously.

'Oh, he's an ordinary kid. Outstanding student, top marks, but also the son of a famous doctor, and we all know how professors and chief physicians trade favours, right? He was keeping up with his coursework, no bad company that we know of. He spent his life at the university, at home and with his girlfriend – a nice girl from out of town he'd been dating for a couple of months. Only child of a widowed father, as the saying goes. Can I have another? I forgot to eat dinner last night.'

'Please, please, be my guest. Take your time, you'll choke if you bolt your food. What about the father?'

'Thanks. A glass of mineral water, sparkling, thanks. The father? A wealthy and respected gynaecologist, the first choice of footballers' wives and top-flight professionals, and a magnificent clinic in Via dei Mille, you can imagine. And you should have seen him this morning. He came out to ask us to ease the pressure a little bit, to let him grieve in peace. He was a wreck. He must be around fifty, but he looked at least a hundred. This was his only child; his wife died twenty years or so ago, and he never remarried. I don't think he'll ever recover from this blow. When you wind up in this sort of situation you have to wonder what the point was of devoting all that time to money, fame and a successful career.'

Lojacono nodded. A recurring motif.

'And the actual murder? How can you all be so sure that this was the work of the Crocodile?'

Ornella burst out laughing, scattering a mouthful of pizza in all directions. One elderly customer, receiving a direct hit on the lapel, glared over at her in disgust.

'Are you joking? It was all there: the tissues, the shell casing. And, as you cops like to put it, the MO: an isolated place, a lengthy stakeout, the late hour, the quick clean kill, plenty of time to get away undisturbed. Nothing was missing. It was him, as true as I'm sitting here about to order a caffè macchiato. No, wait, a macchiatissimo. Or better yet, a cappuccino. May I?'

Lojacono waved to the man at the cash register that he'd

be picking up the bill. The cashier nodded, his eyes widening at the woman's voracious appetite.

'And how did he gain access to the garage?'

'Ah, that's an interesting detail. He waited for the boy to use the remote control to open the garage door the last time he put the car away, at about two in the afternoon according to what the father said. And he must have slipped in after him. From what we learned from one of your colleagues on the forensics squad who worked on the crime scene, he sat behind a motorcycle, parked and covered with a tarpaulin. That's where they found the tissues. This cappuccino is delicious, but maybe another spoonful of sugar or two. It appears that he waited there until about nine o'clock, when the boy came downstairs and opened the garage to get his car and go out, and that's when he fired a shot right into the side of his head.'

'Just one shot?'

Ornella took a long slurp of her cappuccino.

'Just one, obviously, like all the other cases. In part because, whether it's intentional or pure luck, he always seems to be firing point blank, just inches from the victim's head. This time it appears that he was no more than a yard or so away. Excuse me, could you add a little more milk? Oh, you can leave that here, thanks. And the great thing is that he walks off, free and easy, on foot because they found no sign of tyre tracks on the driveway except for the doctor's car and his son's.'

'What do you know about the tissues?'

'Just ordinary tissues – the kind that the African guys sell at intersections. Nothing special about them. And as far as they're able to tell at this point, he doesn't seem to be crying after he fires the shot, the way a real crocodile might do, not that real crocodiles shoot guns, obviously. It's just that his eyes seem to be tearing up, which might be a case of conjunctivitis. I have allergies so I can sympathise. But what about your boss? From the little he told us, I get the feeling he's at his wits' end; he doesn't know which way to turn. I'm right, aren't I?'

Lojacono shrugged.

'I couldn't tell you; that's not my line of work. And anyway, it doesn't strike me as all that easy to get to the bottom of a case like this. You need to chase down the links between the kids, establish what relationships there might have been, any other connections. Assuming there is a link, of course. This could perfectly well be a psychopath, a maniac who leaves the house with a gun in his hand and conceals himself in dark corners, waiting for someone to walk by so he can put a pistol to her head. We live in exceedingly strange times, you know.'

Ornella had finished her cappuccino and was starting to pick absent-mindedly at the savoury bar snacks the barista had laid out on the counter for the fast-approaching aperitif hour. The cashier made a theatrical show of his exasperation by throwing both arms wide.

'I guess that's a possibility, all things considered,' Ornella said. 'Anything could happen. But the idea seems to be that this guy, the Crocodile, is carrying out a plan of some kind. He doesn't seem like someone operating on a whim. He appears to be highly organised. Don't you think?'

'Let me repeat: I don't know anything about it. I was asking purely out of curiosity. Excuse me, but I have to get back to the office now. Do you want anything else?'

'No, thanks. I try not to over-eat. If you ever want more information, you could take me out to lunch or dinner. Here's my card.'

When he got back to the police station, Lojacono found Giuffrè swaying so much he was on the verge of leaping into the air.

'Well, Loja', where the fuck have you been, if you don't mind my asking? Di Vincenzo has sent people looking for you three times now. He wants to see you in his office – immediately.'

Chapter 38

Orlando Masi thought about his father, dead now almost ten long years. He'd been a pillar of the community, a rigid man, difficult to get along with, a stranger to elation, indifferent to displays of affection. Someone who stirred fear in all those who had anything to do with him.

Old Masi, respected engineer, a man who had demanded outstanding performance from his son every day of his life, until he had almost driven him to the brink of outright hatred, who had taken strictness almost into the realm of cruelty. The day he lay on his deathbed, defeated by an illness that had eaten away at him from within until he was reduced to little more than a wraith, he had asked Orlando to come and sit with him, the two of them alone together. He'd raised his hand and placed it on his son's cheek, flat, motionless, as if to feel the texture of his skin more than to deliver a caress.

Then he had said,

'A son! You split my life into two parts, you know – before

and after. After you arrived, nothing was ever the same. Nothing, you understand me? Nothing.'

Orlando had waited. He'd expected those words to be the preamble; he expected his father would have something more to say. Instead, the old man had slowly let his hand slide away, and then he'd dropped off to sleep.

For a long time after that, he'd assumed that those words had been nothing more than the ravings of a man on the brink of death. But then, the day when he found himself unsteady on his feet, dressed in a hospital gown with sleeves too short for his arms, struggling with nausea after watching and hearing his wife give birth, it had suddenly dawned on him, clearly and unmistakably, what the elderly engineer had been trying to tell him.

A life split into two parts. Nothing ever the same again.

As he climbed the Via Orazio, pushing the pushchair in pale sunlight, and as he checked to make sure that the biting cold and seeping damp were unable to penetrate the plastic rain hood protecting his baby girl, he peered in, admiring the button nose of his tiny daughter Stella. And he decided that he'd never seen anything more beautiful, more miraculous in the whole wide world.

Just six months now. And every aspect of his life had changed completely. Perhaps, to an outside observer, Orlando's life might seem the same as it ever was. His job, as the chief engineer for a major construction company; his wife, the adorable Roberta, beloved of anyone who spent five minutes in her company; his wonderful house, with its perfect garden, an absolute rarity in that city, grounds that he tended personally, with scrupulous care. Everything perfect, everything untroubled.

But in fact, everything had changed, from the moment they had put that filthy, screaming little thing into his arms, wrapped in a towel. His daughter. Stella.

He had decided on the name at that instant. To ward off bad luck, he'd never talked it over with Roberta. In the long years of medical treatment, as they struggled to conceive a child who refused to come into the world, they had never once speculated about a name. His wife had always insisted that the name would pop into the mind of one of the two of them as soon as they laid eyes on her, and it had happened to him.

Stella – the name meant 'star'. Because a star shows you the way, guides your path, and he had understood at the very moment he'd first held her in his arms that every single step he took on earth from that moment forward would be directed towards that small screaming creature.

As he smiled and took a deep breath of the damp chilly air from which he was careful to protect his baby girl, Orlando considered how wonderful life managed to be sometimes. And he turned an affectionate thought to that gruff father of his, whose harshness had still been so crucial in keeping Orlando on track and out of trouble.

Certainly, there had been occasions when that harshness seemed like too heavy a burden to bear; certain impositions had struck him as high-handed and incomprehensible. Other times, the thought of his father's disapproval had steered him away from decisions that, left to himself, he would certainly have made.

When he wanted to become a professional football player. When he wanted to take off and travel the world. When he wanted to study philosophy at university. And of course when . . .

But this was no time to dwell on such things. It had taken him a little longer to get there, that much was true. And truth be told, his path could have been smoothed, with the help of certain friendships that his father had chosen not to use, convinced as he was that everything in life had to be won through determination and hard work. Life doesn't give you anything for free, Orlando mused, as he pushed his way up the last stretch of the street, passing by the front door of the hotel across the way.

Now, after the long climb, he had reached the safest place in the world: his home. And Roberta, with a hot cup of tea. And most important of all, his wonderful baby girl, Stella. He was about to lift her out of her pram and glimpse her smile.

Chapter 39

An ashen Di Vincenzo was sitting at his desk. He kept moving his files to one side and then back to where they'd been in the first place, as if his life depended on it. Lojacono, who stood in the doorway waiting for permission to enter the office, felt sorry for him: the weight that had suddenly been dropped on to his shoulders was clearly far more than he could handle.

'Dottore, may I come in? You sent for me?'

Di Vincenzo looked up at him with a chilly glare.

'Ah, Officer Lojacono, of course. Come in, have a seat. And close the door.

'Let me cut to the chase. For some reason that eludes my understanding, Dottoressa Piras would like you to be made a member of the team investigating this damned case, looking into the connections between the murders, even though the only killing that concerns us has to do with this kid – Lorusso, Mirko. I believe the reason for this development is that you – in direct violation of my recommendations, though I'm happy to let that slide for now – were the first officer on the scene of the crime. We are therefore summoned to police headquarters, in half an hour, to attend a meeting.'

There was no mistaking the captain's annoyance at having been forced to summon Lojacono. He did nothing to conceal his irritation: lips compressed, he avoided the inspector's gaze.

He went on,

'You therefore have a little more than ten minutes to have Savarese – who's been in charge of the case up till now – give you all the evidence we possess. I'm afraid it's not a lot of material; and I imagine that you already know most of it because it's been extensively covered in the press, on television and who knows where. Not that anybody else has made much more progress than we have, God bless them. But we seem to be singled out for the blame because the first killing took place in our jurisdiction. How absurd.'

Lojacono started to get to his feet.

'Well then, dottore, I'd better go and talk to Savarese . . .'

'Just a second, Lojacono. Tell me one thing: what did Piras tell you the other day when you went to the café together? And most important of all, why did you invite her to go?'

Lojacono considered the question. He'd had no doubt that Di Vincenzo would find out about what had happened immediately; what did surprise him was that the man had the nerve to ask him about it at all.

'Your informants seem to have their facts wrong: they should have told you that it was Piras who invited me to get a cup of coffee, not the other way round. She wanted further details about my first inspection of the crime scene, nothing more, nothing less. But I didn't have anything to add to my report. By the way, let me point out once again that the only reason I was on duty that night was the shift assignment that you countersigned. And I have no interest in taking part in any investigations, unless I'm ordered otherwise. Which is what you just did. Am I free to go?'

Di Vincenzo's neck had turned beetroot-red, but otherwise the man betrayed no emotion at all. He gestured vaguely towards the door.

'By all means, go. We'll see you at the car in twenty minutes.'

The short drive to police headquarters took place in silence. The documents that a disgruntled and openly hostile Savarese had handed over added very little to what Lojacono already knew.

Ballistics testing had been performed on both the shell casing and the bullet removed from Lorusso's head during the post-mortem, confirming the calibre of the weapon, a .22 pistol. Faxed copies of the police reports on the second murder further confirmed the correspondence between cartridge and projectile. An innovative computerised analysis had been used – the Integrated Ballistic Identification System (IBIS). It produced the same results: there was no doubt that it was the same weapon.

The tissues, on the other hand, offered little information. Apart from traces of a liquid that was probably human tears, there were also remnants of shredded epithelial tissue, plausibly the result of rubbing the eyelids. The DNA sequencing – completed in record time since this case involved a serial killer – provided confirmation that all the samples came from a single individual. Unfortunately, it matched none of the evidence on file in the database and so it was useless in terms of tracking down a suspect.

There was no trace of fingerprints. The kids' clothing and Lorusso's helmet only revealed the victims' own fingerprints. Either the Crocodile had touched nothing or else he was wearing gloves.

There were no reports on the third murder, which had taken place too recently, but Lojacono knew that certain elements must have been confirmed, otherwise he would never have been invited along.

Sitting in the back seat next to Savarese, a corpulent cop in his fifties with a perennially furrowed brow, Lojacono wondered why Piras had decided to summon him. He didn't think he'd shown any particular signs of acuity or demonstrated any special skills. The one explanation that struck him as plausible was the fact that from the very outset, more out of instinct than any strong line of reasoning, he had ruled out the theory that these were Camorra murders. Clearly, this third murder had persuaded the public prosecutor of the same thing.

When they reached police headquarters, both men followed Di Vincenzo, who knew the way, up to a third-floor meeting room. Sitting around a conference table piled high with documents were four men in plain clothes, a woman armed with a pen and notebook, and Piras, who raised a hand in greeting.

'Ah, there you are. Fine, you're all acquainted. Inspector Lojacono is here because I asked him to come, and I'll explain why later. Lojacono, these are the station captains within whose jurisdictions the murders took place, and their deputies in charge of the individual station investigations. To speed things up, I've asked them to introduce themselves whenever they happen to join in the discussion. This meeting became necessary because the latest murder, the one in upper Vomero, in my opinion casts a new light on the situation. It's crucial that we give this new development full consideration.'

A smartly dressed older man broke in with some annoyance.

'Scognamiglio, station captain of Via Manzoni. Dottoressa, I'm not really all that convinced, and I'd like to make it clear from the outset that the line of investigation we've pursued till now was the wrong one. We have ascertained, thanks to the interrogation of Ruggieri, Antonio, undertaken by our colleague here, Di Vincenzo, that the first victim, Lorusso, Mirko, was dealing outside the school attended by De Matteis, Giada, the second murder victim. That strikes me as a perfectly adequate basis on which to continue with this line of inquiry.'

Piras shot him a cold glance.

'Scognamiglio, that's not all Ruggieri said. He also declared that Lorusso was nothing more than a peripheral player, a petty apprentice dealer who was just getting started, who hadn't been out more than three times before. And there is not a shred of evidence, much less any solid proof, that the two victims even met, nor that De Matteis, a girl who has been described as absolutely irreproachable, both by her mother and by her classmates, ever used drugs. Last of all, the third murder, the Rinaldi case, looks to be entirely unrelated to the first two, though it was clearly carried out by the same perpetrator. Any objections, Palma?'

The man whose name she had called was the third station captain present, a guy in his forties with a rumpled look, his cuffs unbuttoned and the face of someone who hadn't had a wink of sleep in the past twenty-four hours or more.

'I'd have to agree. The forensics team, given the urgency of the case, has already delivered the ballistics report: bullet and cartridge line up. I spoke to the guy in charge and he told me, on an informal basis, that the tests on the exhibits recovered – the tissues in other words – show that it's the same individual. That's all we know for sure right now.'

Piras nodded.

'Just as we expected. Now, everything depends on how quickly we can shift our thinking and formulate new theories. And with that in mind, I'd say—'

Di Vincenzo cleared his throat. 'Forgive me, dottoressa, but I'm obliged to state that I find Scognamiglio's point of view persuasive. To discard so hastily the entire Camorra-related line of investigation in the aftermath of the Rinaldi murder, without first ascertaining the possible links between the medical student and the other victims, strikes me as premature at best. I'm of the opinion that first we ought to allow Palma and his men to investigate accordingly, and postpone this meeting until further notice. And when we reconvene, perhaps it might be with a shorter list of attendees, so that we can avoid distracting our colleagues from their work.'

Di Vincenzo's little speech fell into the silence with a boulder-like thud. Everyone in the room looked in other directions, studiously avoiding Piras's glance. Lojacono had no doubt that Di Vincenzo was referring to him when he mentioned the idea of pruning the guest list. Piras tapped her pen on the conference table, nodding in time with it. By now Lojacono knew her well enough to understand that this was her way of channelling her anger and averting an unseemly outburst.

'Di Vincenzo, you've had more time than anyone else to think about these murders, so we should pay special attention to what you have to say.'

The unmistakable allusion to the failure of his investigation landed like a resounding slap. The station captain sat impassive, but gulped visibly.

Piras continued.

'All the same, there are a number of factors that argue for a change in direction. First: the media are tearing us literally limb from limb. Every day, the television news and websites are having a field day, deriding us as incompetent. Plus the city is uneasy: murder is never a laughing matter, but when the victims are children, it's especially serious. Second: we've come to a complete standstill. No one is saying that we won't sift minutely through every aspect of what we learn about Rinaldi's life, but we need to start thinking about other leads, or else we run the risk of overlooking fundamental elements.

As we may very well have done already. Third, and most important of all: this damned Crocodile – and let me say parenthetically that there is no animal I find more despicable – may very well strike again. And correct me if I'm wrong here, Di Vincenzo, but we haven't shown any ability to predict his future moves.'

She fell silent, the pause heavy with meaning. She'd never once shifted her glance away from Di Vincenzo's face, and he had withstood her gaze.

'Finally, and I'd like to think that this is the first and the last time I'll be obliged to remind you all of the fact: I'm in charge of this investigation. My reputation rides on it. And when I wish for advice or opinions, I'll ask for them. Unless any of you consider yourselves better qualified, of course? If that is the case, then you are quite welcome to submit a written request and application to His Excellency the Director of Public Prosecutions of the Italian Republic. Anyone here planning to take that route? If so, I'd like to be made aware of it, if you please.'

You could have cut the silence with a knife.

'Now that we've got that out of the way, I owe you all an explanation for the presence of Inspector Lojacono. He was the first officer on the scene of the murder of Lorusso, Mirko, as he was on duty that night. On that occasion he noted the presence of the notorious paper tissues. In the aftermath of the murder of the young De Matteis girl, someone was kind enough to leak that detail to the press, giving rise to the legend of the now all-too-well-known Crocodile. I had occasion to meet with Inspector Lojacono subsequently, at the

San Gaetano police station where he works currently, and there I had the opportunity to learn that he does not subscribe to the theory of Camorra involvement in these murders. As long as we were working on that lead alone, it struck me as inadvisable to bring him into the investigation; but now that it's a cold hard fact that we have no idea which way to turn, it seems to me we might as well listen to anyone who has any ideas of any kind whatsoever.'

Scognamiglio, the station chief of Posillipo, stirred in his seat, clearly annoyed:

'Hold on now, dottoressa, you're undermining us here. We have ongoing investigations under way – my station inspector, Marotta, has questioned a good hundred young people to reconstruct the overall picture of drug dealing outside the local schools; he's worked hard, to the point of exhaustion, and now you see fit to sashay in and tell us we have no idea which way to turn.'

This time Piras made no effort to conceal her irritation. She slammed her palm down on the table, making pens and pencils leap into the air, and startling her secretary.

'Goddamn it, Scognamiglio! You've worked yourselves to the point of exhaustion, and what do you have to show for it? Nothing! Absolutely nothing! And the kids keep dying, different ages, different parts of town, with no evident links between them. Because of our incompetence we have three corpses on our hands, and there may very well be more on the way! You ought to be the first ones – you, Palma, Di Vincenzo – to display a little humility and be willing to accept a helping hand, whoever's offering it. If you don't like it, then you're free to leave and you'll be receiving detailed instructions on how to conduct investigations directly from me and the chief of police himself.'

Immediately after the hurricane subsided, a quick look around the room was enough to count the victims. Scognamiglio's ears were bright red and his eyes were fixed on the surface of the table in front of him. Di Vincenzo resembled a statue carved of granite. Marotta, who had interviewed all those kids and worked himself to the brink of exhaustion, was blinking his eyes at a rate roughly equivalent to the wing beats of a hummingbird. Lojacono cringed, afraid the man might be about to burst into tears. Palma hastily buttoned his collar, as if he'd just reviewed his personal appearance.

Piras coughed lightly and went on talking as if nothing at all had happened.

'Lojacono, as I was saying, seems to have a different view of what has emerged from the investigations. Could you tell us more, please?'

Lojacono was slightly sprawled in his chair, hands in the pockets of his overcoat, which he had not removed, unlike the others. It was as if he were emphasising the temporary nature of his presence in that room.

'Well, to my mind, dottoressa, these killings don't share any of the typical traits of Mafia murders. I'm referring to the technique. I'd posit that we could probably extend that to include the motive.'

Di Vincenzo snorted and muttered venomously,

'Sure, Lojacono. After all, you do know a thing or two about the Mafia.'

Lojacono gave no sign of having heard. But Piras snapped around and glared at the station captain.

'Another line like that, Di Vincenzo, and as God is my witness, I'll have you suspended from active duty. Don't test me, I urge you. You'd learn to your bitter regret how serious I am. Lojacono, you've already expressed these doubts to me before, and for that matter we've also had occasion to note the differences in style and method. It's also true that organised crime families have shown a willingness to turn to outside professionals, to outsource, so to speak, certain kinds of operations. That aside, do you have anything else to tell us?'

There was a moment of silence. Everyone was looking at Piras, and she in turn was looking at Lojacono, who was staring at the tabletop.

At last the inspector glanced up and said,

'Has it occurred to anyone here that the intended victims might be the parents, not the children?'

Chapter 40

She'd knitted the little pink cap herself, and she'd knitted the outfit too. She buttoned the outfit to the neck before sheathing the baby girl in her padded overalls and then strapping her into the pram.

In a way, Roberta misses the time she had spent waiting for the blessed event. Hours and hours spent poring over patterns, knitting, embroidering. And smiling, imagining. Understandable, she muses, after all those years. An endless series of days spent pursuing a single goal: to have a child. To hold a little piece of yourself in your arms, an independent life, possessed of its own breath and heartbeat. She enjoyed every second of her pregnancy, every tiny kick, every instant of nausea; she took it all as a blessing.

There are women who aren't cut out for motherhood. Roberta had known plenty of them: highly trained professionals devoted to their careers, athletic types, women in love with the nocturnal lifestyle, or adventuresome collectors of experiences – none of them willing to trade their personal freedom for a weak and needy creature demanding constant care.

But there are also women like her – women born to be mothers – though fewer and fewer in number in this world where selfishness and individualism triumph over all.

Not that Roberta ever gave up her profession or her career. She made her way in the world, working hard as an architect, at first in a larger firm and then as a freelance professional. She had her dalliances, a couple of relationships and one great passionate love affair, but the whole time she felt as if she were edging around a crater, an empty space at the centre of her life.

Roberta takes a look around outside. The temperature seems mild enough, and there's no sign of rain; in fact, a shaft of sunlight angles through the clouds and lights up the street outside her front door. Stella can go outside and get a breath of the fresh air wafting up from the waterfront.

Stella. So sweet and small. The destination and objective of an entire lifetime. Roberta remembers when the doctor told her she was sterile, ten years ago. She hadn't believed him at first. She hadn't wept, she hadn't slid into a slough of depression; she'd put on a smile and girded for battle.

The old man emerges from the shadows and starts walking, on the far side of the street. He's careful because there aren't a lot of people out and about so he's more visible than usual today.

A woman doesn't spend her entire youth waiting for Mr Right, the great love of her life, the man with whom she can finally start a family of her own, only to give up passively when faced with a sentence printed on a sheet of paper. Not on your life.

And Roberta hadn't given up, not in the slightest. She had recruited Orlando to fight the battle alongside her; her husband had followed her willingly, but more than once she had been forced to rekindle his determination. Everybody knows it's different for men. For men, a child becomes important once it's there, but not before; women, in contrast, are born with the maternal instinct. That's nature's way.

The old man stops suddenly, because the woman is tucking a blanket in the pram. Twenty-five feet from the other side of the street: not an inch less. Invisible. He must remain invisible.

Orlando. She'd met him at work. A smile, a lingering gaze, and the magic spell had been cast.

He was older than her, by a good fifteen years: reassuring, strong, sensitive. The right man, the right husband – the right father. When it comes to the idea of a family, the concrete reality of the thing, it's a matter of degrees, a gradual thing, Roberta thinks. You might yearn for it as an abstraction, but when the time comes to build it, actually create a family, that's quite another matter. Orlando clearly had a long history of relationships. He didn't talk much about them, but the scars were unmistakable. And a man still alone at his age suggested a troubled past. His father's long drawn-out illness – a father to whom Orlando had always been very close, a father whom she'd never met – had left its mark on him too.

Still, they were a perfect couple, bound together by a powerful force from the very beginning. Maybe they'd been looking for each other all their lives. Maybe that whole time they'd been waiting for each other.

There was no way they'd stop at the first diagnosis. Roberta had always known that she'd be a mother some day – a mother of her own biological child, not an adopted child. She wouldn't turn to those horrifying baby markets. She would have a child of her own.

The old man starts moving again, his feet dragging, his gaze low, clinging to the sides of the buildings. No one knows him. No one sees him. Twenty-five feet, not a foot more, not a foot less.

Roberta had always loved to sketch; that's why she became an architect in the first place. And she'd always sketched the face of her future daughter. She hadn't stopped even when a second and then a third doctor confirmed the first doctor's diagnosis.

She listened, smiled politely, and then went out to find another doctor. And meanwhile, she went on sketching. The loveliest portraits – the ones that vaguely resembled the wonderful features of her daughter as if they were intimations of some future beauty, some foreshadowing of grace – Orlando had had framed and now they hung on the walls of the little pink nursery where they safeguarded the most loved of all Roberta's and Orlando's treasures.

The old man stops when he sees her step into a shop. He backs away a short distance until he finds a bench, pulls his newspaper out of his pocket, and pretends to read. But all the time he's watching and waiting.

In the end, they found the right doctor. Not that they'd have ever stopped looking, of course. But this one had smiled and explained exactly how to go about it. With a minor operation and a course of pharmaceuticals it might be possible to achieve their goal – those had been his exact words. And Roberta remembered the sound of his voice as if it were a chorus of angels.

The old man breaks his self-imposed rule and draws closer. The woman stands in the shelter of a doorway to protect the baby girl from the wind and so she won't see him. Twenty-five feet, fifteen feet, ten feet. He leans against the wall, as if catching his breath after a long walk. He pulls out his tissue, dries a tear from his cheek and then rubs his eye. He looks closer.

The baby girl opens her eyes and smiles at her mamma. Stella. The most magnificent spectacle in the universe.

Roberta immediately accepted Orlando's suggestion; she knew she could never have come up with anything better than that. Stella. Star: beautiful, luminous. A light in the darkness, the strongest light of all. Her North Star, her *Stella Polare*, the star that would guide her footsteps for the rest of her life. The daughter she'd hoped for, wanted, searched for. Her dream come true.

The woman can't resist. She gives in, planting a kiss on the baby's face before laying her down on her back in the pram again. The girl cheeps like a chick and smiles once again.

The old man looks at the baby girl. This is the first time that he's had a chance to see her up close like this. The risk was worth it. She's lovely: a button nose, chubby cheeks. The old man searches for a feeling, any tinge of emotion, and comes up with nothing. His eyes remain expressionless, the hand holding the tissue steady. He looks at Roberta's smile and decides that this woman must truly be a fine person. Someone who wishes the whole world well. And therefore trusts the world to feel the same way towards her.

The old man retraces his steps. Thirty feet back, at least, he decides.

Chapter 41

Lojacono's words had landed in the middle of the conference table like a hand grenade.

Everyone stared at him as if he'd cut loose with a stream of profanity.

The first to regain his composure was Scognamiglio.

'What the devil did you just say, Mr What's-your-name-again?' he barked. 'What do the parents have to do with it?'

Di Vincenzo snorted again, rolling his eyes skyward. Palma, the Vomero station captain, lunged forward:

'But why would he do that? Sorry, but wouldn't the Crocodile have gone after them directly?'

Scognamiglio turned to glower at him, practically foaming at the mouth.

'Palma, don't tell me you've decided to start calling him the Crocodile too? What, are we going to let the press influence the way we think now?'

Piras hadn't taken her eyes off Lojacono's face for a

second; in turn, he'd gone back to staring at the tabletop, like a student in the principal's office.

'What do you mean, Lojacono? In what sense could the parents be the victims?'

Lojacono looked up and met the prosecutor's gaze.

'I think that there could only be one thing worse than dying, and that's losing a child. It's a blow, a crushing grief from which you can never recover.'

Di Vincenzo muttered through clenched teeth,

'What are we doing now, philosophising?'

Piras shot him an eloquent glare and the station captain lowered his eyes. Unexpectedly, Lojacono started talking again.

'Three kids, each of them an only child. Three single parents. Lorusso, a young unmarried mother. De Matteis, a divorced woman with her ex-husband on another continent. The father of this boy murdered yesterday: I hear he's a widower.'

Piras turned to Palma.

'Can you confirm that? Is this true about Rinaldi's father?'

Palma nodded, rapt in thought.

'Yes, I think that's right. The two of them definitely lived alone. To tell the truth, we were focusing on the technique of the killing. Excuse me, Lojacono, but how did you find that out?'

Lojacono shrugged.

'A journalist, a young woman who was in the crowd outside the police station this morning. I bought her an espresso.'

Piras's jaw muscle twitched.

'That's a nice way to get information, taking people to a café and buying them coffee. I'll keep that in mind for future reference. What else did you learn from this woman journalist?'

The edge in Piras's tone was not lost on those present, and they exchanged disconcerted glances.

Lojacono replied nonchalantly,

'That this Dr Rinaldi was distraught, at his wits' end, devoid of any interest in life, and practically on the verge of insanity. Just like the two mothers, Lorusso and De Matteis.'

Scognamiglio blurted out,

'Dottoressa, seriously, do we have to sit here and listen to this utter nonsense? We've had three young people murdered here, probably selected at random, or maybe because they were easy targets, or else because they were somehow involved in the same drug deal. We need to take the time to investigate this thing, go into it in depth; maybe this Rinaldi had some contact that could be traced back to the other two. But we're wasting our time here.'

Lojacono spoke to him directly.

'True enough, this might not be the right lead. But nothing says we can't consider a theory, explore a hypothesis, does it? I'm not saying we should stop investigating, that's the furthest thing from my mind. Still, if I wanted to inflict a fate worse than death on someone, I'd murder their child.'

Palma scraped his chin. A five o'clock shadow was beginning to show on his face.

'True, this latest murder seems to have no connection to the first two. It wouldn't be easy or fast, but we could start digging into the parents' past. It wouldn't cost us a thing, really.'

Di Vincenzo shot back with a cold retort.

'Speak for yourself, if you have extra men to assign to your case. In my department we have the whole staff working full-time on the first boy's case. The boy's mother? She's nothing but a home-care nurse, just a poor woman. She can't have ever done anything to make anyone want to take revenge.'

Piras felt obliged to break in.

'There's something that still baffles me. The way these murders have been carried out is strange, there are odd details. I've studied the modus operandi, the process, the routine, and the third case only reinforces my impression. On the one hand, they all point to careful study, patient preparation, an attention to detail that would have to be the product of a lengthy and painstaking organisational effort. It can't be pure chance that no one has ever seen him; it can't be dumb luck that he's struck repeatedly without encountering resistance, getting away with it three times. But on the other hand, there are aspects that cry out that this is the work of an amateur: like the tissues, or the weapon he used. The two sides of the equation don't add up.'

Lojacono sat up straight in his chair.

'That's exactly right. The overall picture points to someone who's had a long time to prepare, but who's still no professional killer. A blackmailer, perhaps. Or someone out for revenge. But not a professional criminal.'

They all thought over what Lojacono and Piras had just said, trying to modify their points of view after spending days on the theory that there was a Camorra connection between the first two murders. At this point Savarese broke in, with the scowling expression of someone who'd been insulted.

'All right then, let's say that the Camorra has nothing to do with it. How on earth can one person move undisturbed through three isolated locations, two of which are low-traffic areas where the inhabitants all know each other? How can he kill three kids and then fold his tent and silently steal away without being seen? Riddle me that.'

Lojacono gave him a melancholy smile.

'Trust me, Savare', it's much easier than you think to move around in this city without anyone noticing you. If anything, that's helpful. We're looking for someone nondescript, an ordinary man in every sense of the word.'

Piras nodded.

'And what should we do now, Lojacono, in your opinion? What's our next move?'

Lojacono seemed completely unaware of the irritation of Scognamiglio and Di Vincenzo. He looked Piras in the face.

'In my opinion, the first thing we should do is bring the three parents together and arrange a face-to-face confrontation. Let's try to find out what they have in common, or what they might have had in common in the past.'

Scognamiglio spread his arms out wide.

'Absurd. It's completely absurd. You're suggesting we take three people who have suffered a calamity of this magnitude and subject them to questioning as if they were three criminals. Moreover, you're suggesting a confrontation, all three of them face-to-face! If we're going to question them, let's talk to them one at a time, at least. Let's not bandy names around; let's move cautiously. The De Matteis woman has friends in high places, and so does Doctor Rinaldi. We could be asking for serious fallout, take it from me.'

Palma agreed.

'He's right. I've already received a number of phone calls to my police station, and one of them even came from here, from police headquarters. I can't imagine it would be a straightforward matter to question the doctor about his past even on his own; it would become impossible if we put him in the same room as other people. There's also the question of whether he's in any kind of shape to put up with questioning at all. This morning the man looked like he was dead himself: staring eyes, a face I couldn't really describe.'

Scognamiglio couldn't believe that someone was actually throwing him a lifeline in his quandary.

'I won't even try to describe the De Matteis woman. If you ask me, her testimony would be unreliable; in fact, I'm not sure she hasn't lost her mind.'

Lojacono nodded in agreement.

'I can well imagine. And I understand perfectly, you both have a point. But it's absolutely necessary, and we'll need to move fast too.'

'Why on earth should we move fast?' asked Di Vincenzo. 'They're certainly not going to run away. We can give them a little time to recover. Try to show a little consideration.'

'Simple. Because the Crocodile, or whatever we choose to call him, might not be finished yet.'

This time the silence around the table was tinged with fear. Finally, Piras spoke softly.

'Here's what we'll do: you go on investigating, but on a broad basis. Don't neglect any clues, even if it takes you off the Camorra trail. It's what we would have done in any case after this third murder. None of you will be involved in questioning the three parents: I'll take care of that myself. I'll summon them all in here, and there will be no pressure on any of you. Lojacono and I will handle the confrontation ourselves, and from this point on he's assigned full-time to this investigation.'

Di Vincenzo started to object, but Piras shut him up with a wave of her hand.

'That's all for today. You're free to go.'

Chapter 42

It's not enough. Knowing what needs to be done, having made the decision. It's still not enough.

Eleonora learned this at her own personal expense.

She waited, right up to the very last minute. A phone call, a word would have been sufficient. She waited to be picked up and carried off, to be given some crumb of comfort. If nothing else, to be told that she's not alone, in this steep uphill climb, on this sheer mountain face that she's trying to scale.

Instead, only silence was forthcoming. She fought against her temptation to break that silence herself; to pick up the telephone receiver, or even to present herself at his front door, on the threshold of that house she'd never even seen. And to say: Here I am. Here we are. Now tell me what it is you want me to do. And tell me clearly; don't expect me to guess what you want from your absence.

It wasn't pride that kept her from doing it. Her pride had died days ago, the instant that she saw the bewilderment and fear that filled his eyes. And the mistrust. At that exact instant, just as a part of her had decided days ago, she should have turned her back on him and on her dreams and run away.

But then what would she do?

If only she had the courage she lacks, she would have kept the baby. She would have gone back to her hometown, defying the disapproving eyes and the secret exultant triumph of all those who had envied her independence, her talent, and her determination to make something of herself.

If only she had the courage she lacks, she would have searched her mother's and father's gazes to find a new awareness of herself. The tenderness that had always been there, and a new sentiment: an acceptance that their dreams would have to be adjusted.

If only she had the courage she lacks, she would have been able to forget about love, a little at a time. She'd have cleansed her heart and soul of all sentiment and steeled herself against the fear of loneliness – a fear that right now clings to the walls of her heart like an irremovable encrustation.

If only.

But she doesn't possess that courage in her heart. She has only grief, sorrow and silence.

As she searches for an address in the rain, she thinks that – however paradoxical it might seem, when all is said and done – if she'd kept the baby she would have had the strength to face up to her family's disapproval, the vicious gossip of the place where she was born, and even the abandonment, the shameful way that the man she loved took to his heels when confronted with adult responsibilities. But by letting the baby go, she's condemned herself to endless silence; to the lack of any human caress.

Her classmate, the one who knows everything, also knew exactly where to send her, whom to put her in touch with. She called her back, not ten minutes later, with an address and phone number. At that point, the only thing still lacking was the money.

There was only one source available to her, the only one she could ask for help. Not him, of course, not the man who was old enough to father a child but lacked the maturity and the willingness to bring that child into the world. The other one. The man to whom she was accustomed to turn, to confess her sorrows and her innermost thoughts. Even though she knew that by doing so she was wounding him deeply. Even though she knew that she was condemning him to know what no one else would ever find out, ever.

She'd had to tell him. Him and no one else. And the money had arrived promptly.

Now, faced with a locked street door and a nameless intercom buzzer, standing in a fine misting drizzle that penetrates her heart like a probing needle, in the silence of her soul, in the desert of her heart. Now. Now, she'll have to find the strength to say farewell to her dreams, to the smiling little girl she once was.

Now she's going to have to find the strength to say farewell to her child.

Chapter 43

In the end, Lojacono fell asleep.

He'd spent the rest of the day reading reports, transcripts and test results concerning the other murders. Di Vincenzo had brusquely enquired whether he'd need an office to himself, but Lojacono had told him that he preferred to remain at his usual desk. He had good concentration and, in any case, there really wasn't much traffic through that office. Giuffrè was beside himself with excitement, and from time to time he'd pepper him with questions about the Crocodile, but Lojacono mostly ignored him.

He didn't have any answers. The documents only reiterated what he already knew. And the more he thought it over, the more deeply Lojacono became convinced that there was no link at all between the three murdered kids.

Tomorrow was going to be an important day: for the first time, the parents would be brought together in one place. Lojacono hoped they would recognise each other, that they would reveal a relationship that could set the police on the right track.

The best thing now was to get some rest; but that was no simple matter. After a year, he could finally go back to doing his real work, the work he felt cut out for, the work he'd wanted to do ever since he was a boy. He had to admit there was a rising tide of excitement inside him, a euphoria that he hadn't expected. The thrill of the chase.

He stretched out on his bed and toyed with his mobile phone. He scrolled through the few numbers in his contacts list and, as always, lingered over one. The display read: Marinella. He imagined her in her bedroom, the room he'd never seen, in their new flat in Palermo, intently reading one of those strange romance books she liked so much, or chatting on her computer with some girlfriend or other. He smiled in the dark, and fell asleep.

He dreamed he was flying, dragged by his mobile phone as if it were a jet engine, or a flying carpet. In silence, he was whisked high over the bay, immersed in the darkness of night, crossing the Calabrian coast. He hurtled over the strait of Messina, floating thirty feet above the face of the water that separates the island from the mainland. He dreamed he was flying over the sleeping city of Messina, and it took him only seconds to travel the road that leads to Palermo. He reached the town from the sea, from the waterfront down by the port. He crossed Via Crispi and climbed Via Notarbartolo, remembering in his dream the elegance of the palazzi, the grand shops with their metal shutters rolled down. He travelled the length of Via

Leonardo da Vinci, where, to the best of his knowledge, Sonia had chosen to live now. In his dream, he knew the house number, and he gently alighted on the balcony of his daughter's bedroom.

He went in. Marinella was hunched over her desk, her back turned to him, and so she didn't see him. He didn't want to startle her so he just stood there, looking at the curve of her spine. His heart throbbed with tenderness. He noticed how she tilted her head to one side as she wrote, like a little girl: his little girl. He let his gaze wander and a wardrobe door, standing ajar, caught his eye: a dark closet.

From within the wardrobe were a pair of yellow eyes, staring fixedly at the girl.

They were reptilian eyes, the pupils a pair of vertical slits, unblinking, lidless. Lojacono watched, hypnotised, rooted to the spot. He couldn't seem to wrench his gaze away, and he couldn't intervene: he was paralysed, the way it often is in nightmares. His daughter went on writing, focused, oblivious to the lurking danger. The wardrobe door began to inch open.

In his sleep, Lojacono was moaning, but in his dream no sound issued from his lips. He desperately struggled as he realised that the monster was about to emerge from the darkness and devour his daughter.

Suddenly, behind him, he heard two pistol shots ring out, and he saw the two yellow eyes in the darkness waver and then sink shut. As if freed from an enchantment, he turned and saw Piras, in perfect firing stance – legs braced, body angled forward, aiming her duty revolver in a two-handed grip. She looked at him and smiled. She struck him as beautiful.

He woke with a start, drenched in sweat. He got out of bed, went to the window and opened it.

Four storeys below, the street glistened with rain. A light flashed on a waste disposal lorry as two binmen hooked bins to the hydraulic hoist that emptied them into the back of the lorry.

He looked up over the roofs, towards the lights glittering in the night. You're somewhere out there. I can sense it. I know it. Maybe you're still not finished with your horrible task. But I have to find a way to stop you.

From out on the water came the sound of a departing ship. Lojacono thought of Sicily and Marinella.

Both of us are alone in this city. Otherwise someone would have seen you, someone would have recognised you. But you're invisible, like me. This city is nothing but a damned wall, and you're hiding behind it. And I don't know how to batter down that wall and get to you.

But I'll find you.

You can bet on that.

Chapter 44

The parents had been summoned for a ten o'clock meeting. Piras, who had made the phone calls personally, would have preferred to give Doctor Rinaldi the time he needed to come to terms, at least to some minimal extent, with the terrible trauma of his loss. His son's funeral could not possibly be held until the day after tomorrow at the earliest as the autopsy was still under way. But they couldn't spare that much time.

To her surprise, and in direct opposition to what Scognamiglio had expected and feared, she'd encountered a spirit of willingness and accommodation on the part of all three of the victims' parents. She'd told them that this meeting was considered to be crucial to the investigation; she hadn't needed to say anything more.

Lojacono headed straight over to police headquarters from home, getting there early. He looked as if he'd slept badly. He was ushered into Piras's office immediately.

'All right then, Lojacono: how do you think we should

proceed? Should we have them all come in together?'

'The thing we need to know first and foremost is whether they know each other, if there's a relationship. Whatever contacts there might have been between the three of them could very well be at the root of everything. I'm not saying they're even aware of it, I'm not saying they'll remember then and there. It could be something that seems trivial to them, something that happened a long time ago. What we need to determine during this meeting is whether there is any acquaintance. That's all. If there is, we can start digging deeper.'

Piras ran a hand over her eyes.

'I'm tired, Lojacono. I'm tired and I'm worried. Did you see the papers this morning? One newspaper actually interviewed an American profiler who's concluded that the tissues are a diversion, and that the murderer is a psychopath who's bound to kill again. The tone of the articles and the news broadcasts is growing steadily more menacing.'

Lojacono shrugged.

'But isn't that something we only care about to a certain extent, dottoressa? What matters is that we figure out whether this murderer means to kill again, and try to stop him in time. And if we hope to do that, then we have to figure out why he killed in the first place.'

Piras shook her head.

'No, that's not the point. The media hoopla provides cover for the murderer. It hinders us, keeps us from acting freely, conditions the things that we are able to do – and it means that he's free to work in blessed peace. We have to move quickly, before the rot sets in. What I'm most afraid of is that they take the case out of our hands by sending a consultant down from Rome. They pay a lot of attention to public image these days.'

Lojacono smiled sarcastically.

'I don't doubt it. That's why we need to take action. This is what I suggest we do: let them come in one at a time, and we'll study their expressions closely. We'll speak openly to them, tell them what we think might be the motive linking all the murders together. And we'll see what they tell us.'

Piras looked baffled.

'Listen, Lojacono. Make no mistake, I have every intention of supporting and pursuing this idea of yours to the bitter end, but it's not necessarily the only option available. You heard your colleagues yesterday, didn't you? There's still a possibility that the Camorra is involved in this case, in some way, shape or form, or else it could simply be a psychopath who's killing at random but choosing different parts of the city to keep from spreading the alarm too quickly. The kids' parents have full access to the press and to the television coverage; two of them certainly have connections in high places. I wouldn't let them in on your theory, and I wouldn't give even the faintest impression, for their own good, that we're feeling our way in the dark.'

Lojacono considered the matter.

'That's fine, whatever you say. We'll watch them carefully, and ask a few neutral questions. But unless we track down the connection, we'll never be able to stop this Crocodile. That's one thing I know, and you know it too.'

Before Piras could come up with a retort, the secretary stuck her head round the door and announced the arrival of Doctor Sebastiano Rinaldi, the father of the third victim.

The gynaecologist was a distinguished, well-dressed man, somewhere in his mid-fifties. He was wearing a sharp grey suit, a dark-blue tie and a still-damp raincoat. His hair, grey, flowing, swept back, gave him an authoritative air. His face was smooth, shaven with care. Image counts, Piras had told Lojacono. He decided that he was looking at living proof of that axiom.

Perfect in every detail: except the eyes. They were a window on to misery and despair. The emotion that he could glimpse in the man's eyes made a mockery of the painstaking care he'd devoted to the presentation of his appearance: this was a man on the verge of collapse.

Piras, doing her best to avoid his gaze, invited him to take a seat in any of four armchairs surrounding her desk.

'Doctor, first of all let me extend my condolences for your loss. And I apologise for having invited you down here so soon after, but we absolutely must move quickly if we wish to bring this murderer to justice as soon as possible . . .'

The man sat down stiffly. His voice was harsh, scratchy.

'Signora, let me tell you something, and I insist on telling you this immediately. My life ended yesterday. My son, Donato, is . . . was the only reason I had, after my wife's death, for getting up in the morning and going to work. I was laying the foundations for his future, minute by minute. I knew his life, the things he did, the thoughts he had, and I can assure you that nothing, nothing that he was or that he did or that he thought, could possibly have led to . . . to this thing. I haven't thought about anything else for the past twenty-six hours. I've reviewed his life, step by step, and nothing, no one, could have had the slightest motive for taking that life away from him.'

The words poisoned the air like a bad odour. Piras looked at her hands, spread open on the tabletop, as if she were deep in other thoughts. Then she looked up, and Lojacono heard a gentleness in her voice that he never would have expected.

'Believe me, I understand. Even though I don't have children myself, I understand. You know that the murder of your son is the third, from what we're able to determine, in a series committed by the same killer. We don't know whether or not the murderer is finished with this . . . this series. We have to assume the worst, so we're asking for your help. This is Inspector Lojacono, one of the investigators assigned to the case, and if you have no objections, he'd like to ask you some questions.'

Rinaldi turned to look at Lojacono, as if he had only just noticed his presence. Beneath the grief and sorrow in his eyes, Lojacono could also read an uncomprehending rage.

'I won't be able to rest until whoever did this thing has been punished. Whatever the cost. Ask away, Inspector.'

Lojacono wasted no time on preliminaries.

'Doctor, I need to ask you a very specific question, and I hope that you won't take it the wrong way, as there is no offence intended. My purpose is to attain an objective I believe we both hope to achieve. You said that you've thought thoroughly about your son's life, and that you could find no conceivable motivation for what, sadly, has actually happened. Is that right?'

The doctor nodded slowly.

'Absolutely. For the past few months he'd been seeing a girl; he'd made passing reference to it, and I imagine he planned to bring it up again once things had become a little more serious. I'd asked around, discreetly, and I knew she was a good girl. She came to the house this morning. She's crushed. I had to comfort and console her. Me. Can you imagine?'

'I'm sorry, I do understand. But I have another question, Doctor, and it has to do with you yourself. I'm going to ask you to think carefully before you answer: was there anyone who hated you so much, for whatever reason, that they might have been tempted to do something like this?'

The question fell into a chilly pool of silence. The man's expression remained unchanged as he sat there, rigid and proud in the chair, his overcoat draped over his legs.

Then he said,

'I get it. The time has come to dig into the lives of others, since nothing has emerged from the lives of the victims themselves.'

Piras decided it was time to come to Lojacono's assistance.

'No, Doctor, that's not right. But we can't leave any stone unturned. You are a prominent, well known professional, and you work in the field of people's health; if there was someone who had any reason to be angry with you, they might very well have chosen to take revenge in this manner.'

'As well as killing two other children who have nothing to do with it, to cover his real purpose? Doesn't that strike you as a bit much, signora?'

Piras maintained a neutral expression, but her tone of voice grew harsher.

'Do you have any better theories, Doctor? Can you point us in some other direction?'

The doctor sat in silence for a moment. Then he turned to look at Lojacono.

'No, Inspector, I can't think of anyone who hated me enough to . . . excuse me . . . to put an end to my son's life. The prosecutor is right when she points out that I work in the field of medicine, and inevitably there are cases that turn out less successfully than others. But I've been lucky, it's never happened to me – the way it has to certain colleagues of mine, perfectly capable physicians, by the way – that anyone has accused me of malpractice, of making a fatal mistake. Over time, I've managed to consolidate my patients into a single, let us say, restricted speciality. I've had the advantage of being able to work with patients who were, for the most part, not in a serious condition, and that has meant a particularly low risk of error. I work with hospitals, which further eliminates the margin of error present in my line of work.'

Lojacono nodded.

'How about other areas? Your finances, for example, and investments. Or personal relationships.'

Piras shook her head. Rinaldi took a deep breath, then answered.

'You're sorely trying my patience, Inspector. I'm going to answer your question because I've undertaken to do so, but I'll do it this once, and that's it. After my wife's death, many years ago, I devoted myself to my son and my practice. I entrusted the handling of my money to my accountant, an old family friend, who has a mandate to invest, at moderate risk, in public stocks and bonds. You can check; it's all there in my tax returns. I've done my best to stay away from that side of my life. I look at the final end-of-year statement and, to tell you the truth, I only check to see that the number is bigger than it was last year. From now on, most likely, I'll stop checking entirely. As for personal relationships, as you put it – nothing at all. I never felt I could bring a woman other than his mother into our house; there was no one who could ever have compared to her in any way. And in any case, at my age, I feel no need for companionship.'

Lojacono thought about the Crocodile and found renewed strength.

'I'm very sorry, Doctor. But what I want – more than anything else, and you must take me at my word on this – is to catch this bastard. And if I have to make a fool of myself in the attempt, believe me, I will, without thinking twice. So I can't really bring myself to ask forgiveness for my indiscretion.'

Unexpectedly, Rinaldi flashed a grimace that might have distantly resembled a smile.

'No, I owe you an apology, Inspector. The habit of pride is a nasty disease, and there's no cure for it. Believe me, I'll give your questions some thought. And if I happen to discover, in my past, some element that might point to this … this thing, I'll call you immediately.'

Piras broke in.

'I'm going to have to presume even further upon your patience, Doctor. We've asked the mothers of the two other children to come in, and I'd like to ask you to meet with them, if only for a brief moment. I have something I'd like to say to you, all together. Would you be so good as to wait?'

Rinaldi nodded.

'I don't think I have anything more important in my schedule right now, signora. I'm at your complete disposal.'

Just then, the secretary stuck her head in and announced, 'The two ladies are here.'

Chapter 45

Sweetheart, my darling,

We're almost there. The last spin of the merry-go-round. Not a bad metaphor, you have to admit; it suits the situation, doesn't it? Or maybe not, now that I think about it. It's still a little early for the merry-go-round.

I've finally opened the window. Not too much. Let's say that I've drawn the curtain a bit.

The panorama of this city seems so strange to me. It's like a pasteboard backdrop. You know what I mean – the kind of props you see on low-budget TV shows. But really, there's nothing there.

Everyone walks with their head down, rushing around, and if anyone looks anyone else in the eye, it's with hatred or with fear. Of course that's fine by me, you know what we have to do. But for them? I remember what you said, when you told me about the people here, and as usual I couldn't agree with you more. You're so right.

But I don't have time to waste pondering these matters. I have a lot of things to do. I really can't spare a second for anything else.

Yesterday, I drew up an initial action plan, and I think I'm going to have to forget about the idea of doing it with him still in the house. It's too risky; there are too many variables. This isn't like the other times. I'll have only one chance and I can't afford to make any mistakes. So like a good boy, I sat down and wrote out the whole timeline, all the arrivals and departures. It's no simple matter: his work varies, he goes to construction sites, he drives around, he has no fixed schedule. Sometimes he even spends the whole afternoon at home. I can see him from here.

He plays with the baby girl.

It's odd, don't you think? An older father, so in love with his daughter. If you have such a powerful instinct, if it's something that's so important to you, you'd think about it earlier, wouldn't you? Well, it doesn't matter to us, does it, my darling?

The important thing for us is that I'm almost finished, and soon I'll be able to wrap my arms around you again.

She, on the other hand, strikes me as a woman from bygone times. She reminds me a little bit of my own mother. She's Mamma to a tee, inside and out. You should see her when she looks at the baby: she's transfigured, as if there were a light glowing from within her.

I've decided that I'm going to have to equip myself in a slightly different way than I expected. But I'm not going to tell you quite how. I want to leave an element of surprise for you. Otherwise, how boring, don't you think?

In any case, there's really very little time left. It's a matter of days. Maybe only a day or two.

Sweetheart, my darling.

Chapter 46

Lojacono concentrated to the best of his ability, aware that the first time the three of them came into contact would be absolutely decisive. He had arranged for the two women, upon arrival at police headquarters, to be taken to separate waiting rooms: he would have to observe instantly whether or not they recognised each other, or whether there was at least a hint of uncertainty.

He and Piras had evaluated the real possibility that Rinaldi and De Matteis already knew each other. They were members of the city's high society, a fairly restricted milieu, so it was virtually impossible to think that they'd never met before.

De Matteis walked in, accompanied by a policeman. She was well dressed, the same as she had been at her daughter's funeral, her hair neatly groomed, lightly but neatly made up, an elegant dark dress suit, a silk scarf around her neck. Her eyes were shielded by a pair of dark glasses. Lojacono recalled the delirious expression she'd had the last time he'd seen her. As she came in she nodded to Piras, who'd already questioned her, and then she recognised Rinaldi and extended her hand.

'Ah, Doctor. I heard. My condolences.'

Rinaldi smiled with his mouth, if not his eyes, and gave the woman's hand a faint squeeze.

'Signora. I'm so sorry to hear about your loss.'

Passing acquaintances, nothing more, Lojacono concluded. Those two have nothing more in common than a small circle of friends.

All the same, he ventured, 'Do you two know each other?'

Rinaldi turned to look at him.

'We've met at a few benefit dinners, and perhaps at a party or two. I don't actually get out much. But Signora De Matteis is not a patient of mine.'

The woman confirmed with a nod.

'Yes, I think the last time was more than a year ago, at the Piromallis' place, if I'm not mistaken.'

So there was nothing between the two of them.

The woman took a seat in an armchair, and Rinaldi also sat down, as stiff as before. Both of them were embarrassed by the other's grief. They didn't know each other well enough to give full rein to their grief as they might have wanted; a long, well-consolidated habit of formality prevented them from doing so. It was a difficult situation to manage.

Piras took a stab.

'As I was explaining to the doctor, signora, we're here to try to see if we can find another way to fathom the tragedy that has struck you both. You must surely understand that any connection between the victims – that is, if there is one, and we know of none at this point – would narrow the field considerably, helping us to identify any potential suspect. Of course, this means we'll be asking questions that may appear, how to put this – indiscreet. We would ask you to have a little patience.'

The woman grimaced.

'A little patience, you say? We're so far beyond patience, dottoressa. We're at the bottom of a pit, and we'll never get out of here. Nothing's going to change for us, please believe me, even if you do find out who did this and you draw and quarter him in front of our eyes. There's no remedy for this . . . this tragedy. That's all I have to say.'

De Matteis's words came out as little more than a whisper, but it still caused a chill to run down Lojacono's spine. Piras, however, was not someone who could easily be silenced.

She replied sweetly,

'Well, that's one more reason to lend us a hand, then. I'm going to ask you the same question we asked Dr Rinaldi: is there anything in your life, recent or past, that might be cause for revenge or extortion? Any reason for ill will, anyone who might harbour a grudge towards you? Thus far, we've only looked into your daughter's circle of acquaintances, and as you know, nothing has emerged. Now I'm referring to you, yourself.'

De Matteis sat for a long time without saying a thing, lost in thought.

Then she said,

'Dottoressa, I have a complicated, stubborn personality.

My Giada and I often argued, to say nothing of our arguments with others. We argued a lot recently, but not when she was little; things were different then. But there's nothing that could make me even remotely imagine such a thing. A couple of years ago I fired a housekeeper for stealing, but she went back to her home country and we never heard from her again. Of course, there is a person I hate, and he hates me, but he's Giada's father, so I'd rule him out, in part because he came back from America purely to upbraid me and accuse me of every crime under the sun. And then left.'

Piras nodded.

'Fine. And there are no relations with Dr Rinaldi sufficient to make us think of a connection between the two families. So we're back to square one. Let's bring in Signora Lorusso, whom neither of you have ever met before, I imagine.'

The two exchanged a glance. Rinaldi shook his head no, and De Matteis shifted uncomfortably in her seat. Lojacono decided that De Matteis wouldn't be able to hold out much longer and was liable to get up and leave any minute.

At a signal from Piras, the secretary left the room and returned immediately with Mirko's mother, Luisa Lorusso.

The woman was unassuming, dressed in black, her face creased with strain. A tragic mask of unremitting sorrow and grief. Her hair hung grey, lank and lifeless, her hands were reddened, and there was no sign of make-up. At her neck she wore a pendant with a picture of her son as a child. Her eyes, empty and expressionless, lazily ranged around the room with indifference.

Lojacono, who remembered the terrible voiceless scream that had disfigured the woman's face the night of her son's murder, felt a stab of pain for a person who clearly had no intention of submitting to considerations of form or style, unlike the other two, distraught though they clearly were. This really was a dead woman walking. The fact that she was still breathing was a chance detail, and in any case it seemed unlikely to persist.

Immersed in these thoughts, Lojacono came dangerously close to missing the one flash of consciousness that glittered through Lorusso's glazed eyes. It only lasted an instant, so brief that he almost doubted he'd seen it, but Mirko's mother had recognised someone – Dr Rinaldi. Lojacono immediately swivelled his gaze over to the man, and he glimpsed a faint blush on his cheeks. But the doctor had turned his eyes away and now he was staring intently at his coat that lay neatly folded over his legs.

Bingo, Lojacono thought to himself.

He turned to glance at Piras and immediately understood that she had noticed the same thing. Her large dark eyes were wide open and alert.

'Signora, thanks for coming in. We're on the case, as you well know, and from what we've found so far, your son was killed by someone who employed the same technique to kill the children of the other lady and gentleman we've invited here this morning. Do you happen to know each other?'

Lojacono appreciated her style: an offhand question, as if merely a round of introductions for the benefit of her guests. Lorusso had regained her composure and was now staring fixedly at Piras. She was still standing, though she'd been invited to take a seat.

'No. I've never met the lady and the gentleman. And I don't understand why you've asked me to come in. I've already told you everything I know, and your officers have also questioned everyone in the building and all of Mirko's friends. It seems to me that you already have everything you need.'

The woman's hostility was unmistakable. She came from an environment where the police were the enemy – certainly not a source of help or assistance. It was equally obvious to Lojacono that when she said that she didn't know anyone there, she was lying. He decided to go along with it.

'Signora, we've seen each other before; I was there that night. You're right, we talked to you, and to everyone we could track down. We're trying to understand what happened, and who killed your son. To do that, we need all the help that this lady and this gentleman – and you – can give us. It's a possibility – and I repeat, just a possibility – that the murderer actually had nothing against these children; that all this is directed against . . . someone else. And that organised crime, for once, might have nothing to do with this murder. If we can only establish some relationship linking the three of you, then we might be able to pinpoint a motive. And once we have a motive, we can catch the killer.'

Lorusso said nothing. She stared at the inspector wild-eyed, as if she were looking right through him.

'What do you think, dotto', that if you catch the guy who murdered my son, I'll come back to life? Do you think that if you put him in jail or whatever, I've suddenly got a reason to get out of bed in the morning, get dressed and leave the house?'

The same line he'd heard from De Matteis, thought Lojacono. In his mind's eye he glimpsed again the vision of his dream: the curve of Marinella's back, her head bent to one side in the effort of writing.

Lorusso went on, in a conclusive tone of voice.

'And in any case, let me say it one more time: I've never met this lady and this gentleman. And there's nothing in my life – like there was nothing in my son's life – so terrible that he deserved to be murdered. I'm a nurse, dotto'. Every day all I do is tend to people who suffer, people who despair, people who want nothing better than to die. My son wanted to live, and he was my one reason for living. There was no one out there who had it in for him, and even if he was doing some bad, stupid things towards the end, he was doing them to improve our lives. Before long, though, I know he'd have told me all about it, and I'd have put a stop to it. So can I leave now, please?'

Rinaldi and De Matteis got to their feet too. Piras wearily waved them to the door and they filed out.

Chapter 47

Stella breathes. She smells the odours and remembers the flavours.

She recognises her mother, that warmth. Her shape is indistinct, but that skin against her skin, that hand on her face, is something she recognises, for sure. Unmistakable.

As soon as she feels the pressure, that special smell, Stella starts suckling. She knows that any second now, along with that smell, she'll sense the taste of that warm gooey substance that gives her nourishment. Her mouth waters, but if food is not immediately forthcoming, she doesn't cry. Stella is a happy baby.

Stella recognises the smell of Papa too. The strong grip of his fingers, his long arms. The sensation is different with him. She feels safe, protected. She feels sleepy, and she falls into a contented, smiling slumber, safe in her papa's arms.

Stella plays.

She feels like laughing when she senses the arrival of the part of the nursery rhyme that she knows. And when they bounce her on their knees, up and down, up and down. She can recognise the colours of the little balls; she especially likes the red one when it rolls to a stop and they hand it to her. She wants to bite it, but they take it right away from her again. Still, even then Stella doesn't cry; she takes it in good grace.

Stella recognises her name.

They pronounce that name with infinite tenderness; they whisper it in her ear with a sigh. Every time they say her name, someone caresses her, and so she's happy and smiles again.

Stella recognises love.

Her button nose senses love like a scent. She hears love like the beat of the heart that accompanied her for nine months, she feels love pour over her like a warm wave from those who sang her lullabies long before she was born, when she was nothing but a wonderful idea in the mind of the woman who wished for her so ardently.

Stella loves back.

She's enchanted by the sound of her father talking, by the warm, deep vibration of his voice that echoes in her chest.

And she presses her face against her mother's cheek when her mother pulls her up out of her bath and into the warm vapour that surrounds the two of them.

Stella sleeps happily, preparing to live her life.

Chapter 48

When they were alone again, Piras turned to Lojacono.

'You saw it too, right? Lorusso's met Rinaldi before. She saw him, there was a flash in her eyes, and she immediately regained her composure.'

She had begun addressing him more informally, using 'tu' rather than 'lei'. Lojacono noticed and followed suit.

'Yeah, I saw it. He recognised her too, and he looked at the floor. I told you, there's a relationship of some sort. Now it's up to us to figure out what kind of relationship.'

'And we have no time to waste either. What worries me most are the time lapses in this thing: one week between the first murder and the second one, then only three days between the second murder and the third. If the Crocodile has something else in store, he won't wait long. It all seems so strange to me: murders that are apparently so difficult to carry out, kids murdered practically right in the safety of their homes, one after the other, and he gets away with it every time. He must be on a winning streak not to have had anyone see him.'

Lojacono stood up and started pacing the room. His eyes had narrowed to slits, further accentuating the Asian appearance of his features.

'Luck has nothing to do with it. It's a matter of technique. It's very simple: it's preparation. He prepares every step, minute by minute. The Crocodile's technique: he stakes it out, he stands watch, he waits patiently. And when the prey is within reach, he strikes. He can't afford to make a mistake, so he only moves when he's absolutely certain.'

Piras followed his reasoning, but something still didn't add up.

'Then isn't he moving a little too fast? Isn't the interval between one murder and the next too short to allow him to prepare so thoroughly?'

Lojacono stopped and turned to look at her.

'Not if he started preparing a long time ago. Not if he planned all of the murders at the same time.'

Piras thought that over for a while. Then she said,

'We need to figure out how and why Lorusso and Rinaldi know each other. Because if there's one chance of tracing back to the Crocodile, it's by finding that out. What do you suggest?'

Lojacono grabbed his coat.

'I'll go and see Lorusso. If that doesn't work, we'll try with the doctor. If we try talking to him first, he could reach out to someone and then we'd be hamstrung.'

Piras nodded.

'Then get moving. And let me know as soon as you learn anything. It's about time we had a stroke of luck.'

*

Before returning home, Luisa Lorusso had gone to the cemetery. She went every couple of days; she felt she had to. That was the only time she felt even partially alive, that she had a purpose, when she could neaten up the flowers, make sure the little lamp was still glowing.

She'd felt she was alive for Mirko and for him alone, when she used to iron his shirts, used to tidy that bedroom of his when it looked like a bomb had gone off in there. She'd felt alive when she sat up waiting for him to come home, so that he'd at least have some idea of how dangerous the night really was – he considered himself a crown prince of the night. She'd felt she was alive when she dreamed of that happy, invincible boy's future, day after day. The future he'd never really had – something the two of them couldn't have predicted.

On her way home, Luisa wondered how she'd find the strength to go on living for even a single day. What reason would she have? Seeing the doctor had caught her by surprise, but beneath all her grief and pain, she'd felt nothing more than the distant echo of a remorse long since buried. A chance occurrence, a coincidence, nothing more than that. The lunatic, the murderer, had taken other people's children too, what of that? What did it change for her? She had died along with Mirko, and that was all she knew. The whole world could die now and it wouldn't change a thing as far as she was concerned.

At the top of the staircase, in the arch of the doorway, stood the policeman from that night, the one she'd seen at police headquarters.

'Now what do you want? What do I have to do to get you to leave me alone?'

Lojacono looked at her, expressionless.

'I need to speak to you, signora. May I?'

Luisa walked through the door without a word, but she left it open behind her. The inspector entered and gently shut the door behind him.

'Signora, I can't believe that you don't give a damn about your son's murderer being at large, on the street, free to kill again. I have a daughter myself and if I thought that someone wanted to harm her, I'd want that person dead. How can it be any different for you?'

The woman stood motionless, her eyes resting on the policeman's face, her hands hidden beneath her black shawl. She looked like a statue. Then she slowly pulled a chair out from the table and gestured for the man to take a seat.

'I've only had one man in my life. He was already married, and he had children of his own. A *malamente*, we say – a bad egg. Someone who did dangerous things. But we loved each other. And just when I got pregnant, he was killed. I couldn't even go to his funeral. The family was there. They'd have beaten me to death; everyone knew about the two of us. I had a nursing certificate. I'd always liked studying, unlike my brothers and sisters who were out on the street from morning to night. So I found a job.'

Lojacono waited. He hoped that at the end of this story he'd find the nugget of information he needed. He knew that the story she was telling him was a slender thread, the only one that could keep his hope alive.

'A neighbour used to look after Mirko for me – the same woman you saw crying with me, downstairs, that night. You know the way it is here: it takes a whole building to raise a child. Gang war rages in the streets, but it came all the way into the building to get my son.'

The woman spoke under her breath, and Lojacono had to make a special effort to understand what she was saying. A radio in a nearby flat was playing folk songs at high volume.

'The lady, back in police headquarters, said that *maybe* the Camorra has nothing to do with it. But I'm sure the Camorra had nothing to do with this. That's not the way they do these things. They make noise, they want everyone to know what's happened and why no one should ever make the same mistake. Whoever this was, he was hiding in the shadows. Like a rat.'

Lojacono nodded in agreement.

'Yes. I'm convinced that these murders, all three of them, are about something else. And if I am able – if we are able – to understand what and why, then we can catch him. We can stop him.'

Luisa suddenly burst out laughing. It was the laughter of a madwoman; she was laughing with her mouth, not with her eyes. With a shiver, Lojacono watched her and suddenly realised how young she really was, and how irredeemably old she had become.

'You want to stop him? Now that he's already done everything he wanted to do?'

Lojacono waited for the hysterical laughter to subside, then he spoke.

'Signora, I think I told you that I have a daughter of my own. Last night I had a dream: someone was watching her from the shadows, threatening her. And there was nothing I could do about it. That's the way it works in this city: there are many who watch from the shadows but no one seems to see them. Your son was the first, and no one could foresee what would happen next, no one could do anything to prevent it. Then the girl from Posillipo was murdered, and once again no one could imagine or understand why. But now this killer has murdered Doctor Rinaldi's son. I understand that you already knew Rinaldi. Don't deny it, please. I remarked upon it, and Dottoressa Piras saw it too. That's why we brought you together, to see if any of you knew each other. And you two do know each other.'

Luisa stared into the middle distance. Tears ran down her cheeks from her convulsive laughter, or perhaps she was crying again.

Lojacono went on.

'Until today, Signora Lorusso, none of what's happened has been your fault. You couldn't know, you couldn't help us to prevent it from happening again. But from now on, now that you know that these innocent victims might be a result of something you know which you're keeping to yourself, blame attaches to you. If another kid is killed, it will be as if your son, my daughter and all the children were dead because of you. Do you think you can bear that burden?'

The silence that followed weighed heavy like the silence of death itself. Outside, the folk singer sang about a good friend's infamous betrayal. And a strong odour of cooking onions blighted the air.

Luisa looked up into Lojacono's face.

'Sure, I know him. I know him very well. Doctor Sebastiano Rinaldi. I knew him before he was a famous doctor, when he needed money, lots of money. When he performed clandestine abortions in a block of flats on the Via Foria. When I was his nurse.'

Chapter 49

Luisa Lorusso's words came out broken, fragmented, pierced by the present pain of time now past.

The words came out and mingled with the notes of the Neapolitan neo-melodic songs wailing out of the neighbours' radios.

The words came out amid the stink of garlic and onions for the lunches that were being prepared, amid the sound of sirens cutting through the air, the car horns and roaring engines of the traffic that suffocated the city.

Out came the words, in the leaden light of another early afternoon of drizzle, beneath the tears of a sky that incessantly mourned its dead.

Out came the four years of working together – the nurse from the poverty-stricken quarter of the city, earning a living so she could carry on her affair with the Camorrista who was an outcast to both warring families; the nurse who needed money to buy the flat where she still lived, the flat where some day she'd give birth to her son. And the up-and-coming, ambitious gynaecologist – a young man who wanted it all and wanted it now, who needed money to set up his most important and high-profile clinic in the aristocratic centre of the city.

They had met by chance at the home of an elderly woman, an invalid; she was there to change the old lady's IV. The doctor decided she would be perfect: they had no shared acquaintances, she was entirely outside his social circle, she was competent, efficient and determined. Moreover, she was unhindered by any troublesome concept of legality. She was also capable of finding customers outside the regular circuits.

The logistics were simple: a rented flat in a transient neighbourhood, anonymous, easy access. The lease was made out to a non-existent company; there was to be no name on the buzzer downstairs. The phone number and the name circulated only discreetly. It had become a silent and efficient factory of tiny angels, with the mutual understanding that they'd both stop once they'd achieved their objectives: the flat on the top floor of the run-down old building in the working-class neighbourhood for her, and the clinic in the Via dei Mille for him.

And that's exactly how it went.

From 1992 until 1996 – the year Mirko was born. That's when Luisa got out. Now that she had a child of her own, that kind of thing was hard for her to take. She'd started to spend her time running up and down the steps of the flats, visiting sick people, providing home-care nursing, administering injections and IV drips. She earned less that way, much less. But at night, she took Mirko in her arms and smiled down at him, and he smiled up at her. That was enough – more than enough.

'The reason I've told you all this is that I didn't want to kill any more children, once Mirko was born. And I don't want to start again, now that he's gone.'

Lojacono thought it over: four years.

'And do you remember anything, anyone, an operation that had serious complications or anything of the sort?'

Luisa shook her head.

'There was no reason for complications. The operations lasted half an hour, we wrote the names of the antibiotics that the patients were supposed to take on a sheet of paper, and then it was *arrivederci*. They never came back, so we had no way of knowing what had become of them. They laid down the money, in cash, and left. Some of them were crying, others were smiling in relief, happy to get it over with. When I found out that I was expecting Mirko, I never thought of it for a second, the idea of doing such a thing.'

Lojacono stood up. Suddenly he felt all the urgency in the world bearing down on him.

'Signora, you've done the right thing, believe me. And I promise you that you won't get into any trouble over what you've told me.'

Luisa, who had been standing the whole time, suddenly collapsed into a chair as if all the energy had been sucked out of her.

She looked up into Lojacono's face and smiled sweetly. It

was the first time that he had seen that expression on her face.

'Trouble? Then you really don't understand. No one can cause me any trouble, dotto'. I'm a dead woman walking, and nothing matters to me now. Nothing.'

Chapter 50

Laura Piras remained impervious to Lojacono's frenzied excitement.

'Of course I get it. Rinaldi and Lorusso were doing illegal, clandestine abortions together twenty years ago. That explains the relationship between the two of them, but we still can't figure out how De Matteis fits in – that is, if she does. Plus, we need to get Rinaldi to admit it, which I doubt he's going to be especially eager to do, considering what it will do to his reputation and standing. So we're back to square one.'

Lojacono shook his head.

'Laura, listen to me. I understand and I agree, we'll never get Rinaldi to confirm any of this; but in my view we don't need him to. All we need is to understand how De Matteis fits in – she's the missing piece of the puzzle. We're not trying to solve a cold case; all we care about is understanding what the Crocodile is up to. We'll have plenty of time afterwards to take care of matters with Rinaldi, if we can. But right now, this is the only thing that matters. The more we find out, the more obvious it seems to me that the killer still has work to do.'

At the sound of his uttering her first name, Piras felt a clutch at her stomach. It was the first time in many – far too many – years that she'd felt any such feeling. She put off her examination of that feeling to a time when she wasn't so busy, and focused on the topic currently under discussion.

'OK, I agree. Right now, squeezing a confession out of Rinaldi would only take up precious time and might trigger some disagreeable intervention from on high. It turns out that even the public prosecutor's wife is one of his patients, or so I'm told. But tell me this: what gives you the feeling that the Crocodile might kill again?'

Lojacono sketched a vague gesture with one hand.

'More than anything else, it's a matter of timing. You said it yourself that much less time passed between the second and third murders than between the first and the second. Given his technique, which is clearly based on constant surveillance, shortening his lead-time means an enormous increase in the level of risk. Why should he increase his risk, unless he has something else in mind? If I understand anything about the way this suspect thinks, we should expect another murder. And, unless it's the last in the series, I expect the interval to be even shorter.'

They sat there for a long time, looking at each other. Piras ran a hand through her hair and started toying with the ends of one lock of it. Hard as he tried not to, Lojacono found this irresistible.

'I have to admit, it kind of scares me how clearly you can see into the Crocodile's head; it almost seems as if you're in touch with him, somehow. But you're right: we need to figure out De Matteis's role. That is if it turns out that she's the murderer's target and not, say, the girl's father, or her grandfather, or her best friend. We're groping in the dark here, and we have been since the very beginning of this case.'

Lojacono smiled.

'Well then, we're due a little luck, aren't we? I'm going to go and question the signora.'

Piras stood up.

'No, I'd better go and see De Matteis; she might refuse to speak to a policeman. She might stir up some trouble in high places, which is something you can't afford. And for once, I want to smell the smoke of battle. After all, we are pursuing this line of inquiry together, aren't we? Or are you trying to hog all the glory for yourself?'

Letizia went to the Crime Reporting Office at San Gaetano. It had been no easy matter to make the decision to go there, but in the end she'd managed to work up the courage.

Night after night she'd waited for Lojacono to show up at the trattoria. The corner table had sat empty, even when there was a queue of customers on the waiting list outside, getting drenched in the rain. She'd waited for him, at first curious, then annoyed, with a slight stab of jealousy and, in the end, with a shade of genuine concern. She went on serving tables, accepting compliments for her spectacular ragù and graciously batting away the misplaced gallantry of her male clientele, but deep down there was a growing sense of apprehension for her new friend's welfare.

He lives alone, she mused. If he had a heart attack, who would even notice? Certainly not his co-workers who, from what he told me, barely speak to him at all. Nor his wife, in a faraway city – his contact with her is only sporadic and thorny. And much less his daughter, whom he hasn't spoken to in almost a year. He has no one. Except for me.

Little by little, the thought grew more pressing. In the end, she decided to go and find out.

She didn't know where he lived. Lojacono had always been very vague on that topic and she would never have dared to ask such a bold question outright. Over there, he would say, waving his hand airily towards the trattoria's front door. One of the thousands of lights burning in the night. Too little information to think of trying to hunt it down. And she could hardly ask around the neighbourhood without fanning the flames of gossip, something for which she felt no need or desire. That left only the police station.

She'd made a tray of pastries, purely to avoid showing up empty-handed: small *pastiera* ricotta cakes. It was the right season for them, and she remembered the night she'd offered him a slice of *pastiera*. At first he was sceptical, saying that no pastries could rival the ones from Sicily, but once he took a bite, a look of surprise had come over his face, gradually fading into a reverie of enchantment. In the end, he'd asked for a second slice.

She crossed the courtyard, feeling the eyes of the policeman on duty at the front entrance on her back the whole way. She climbed the steps and followed the signs to the office where she knew Lojacono had been assigned. In the office there were two desks, one of them unoccupied. At the other desk sat a small man with thick-lensed glasses. The minute he saw her, his face lit up.

'*Prego*, signora, *prego*. Come right in. Was there something you needed?'

She walked into the office hesitantly.

'I was looking for Inspector Lojacono. Isn't he here?'

The man's disappointment was obvious.

'No, he's not. I'm Sergeant Giuffrè, his colleague. If I can be helpful in any way . . .'

Letizia stepped closer. The man was courteous, and perhaps he could provide her with some information.

'My name is Letizia and I own the trattoria in the Via San Giuseppe, not far from here. Pepp— er, Inspector Lojacono always dines with us in the evening. Since he hasn't been around in a few days, well, we, that is the staff and I, we were a little worried. The young people wondered if he was sick, or if . . . er, that is . . . whether he might have had to leave town because of something that happened back home, where his family lives?'

Giuffrè knew the way the world worked, and to some extent he knew women as well. It didn't take him much more than a fraction of a second to figure out that the concerns of the restaurant staff were all concentrated in the person now standing before him.

'No, signora, you can all rest easy at the restaurant. Lojacono is fine, he hasn't gone anywhere. He's working on a case right now, and it's taking all his time. He's working hard, that's all, and most of the day he's not in the office at all.'

Letizia nodded, both reassured and puzzled. Finally she screwed up her courage and asked.

'A case? Are you sure? It's just that, you see, he told me … he told us that he wasn't supposed to work … that is, he wasn't assigned to investigative work. In fact, he said that he was strictly relegated to office work.'

The sergeant's curiosity was piqued. Such a good-looking woman, not only attractive but also the owner of a restaurant that everyone was talking about, one of the few fashionable establishments in that part of town. And she was so unmistakably smitten with Lojacono, a man who was always threadbare and rumpled and had a personality that was as prickly as a cactus. There's no explaining it: women are an unfathomable mystery and that's a fact, he decided.

'Well, he told you the truth, signo'. But then what happened is that, in this particular case, he turned out to be the only one with any idea of how to proceed. Of course, he and I did talk it over, and I have to say, all modesty aside, the most important insights probably came from yours truly. However it happened, the prosecutor in charge decided to bring him in on the investigation directly and she summoned him to police headquarters. And that's where he's been ever since, practically full-time.'

Letizia took in this new information, once again with mixed feelings: Peppuccio was finally back doing the kind of work he felt he'd been born to do, and she knew that he had missed it much more than he'd ever been willing to admit. But now he was in close contact with that female prosecutor, the one about whom he had said: 'she's not just pretty, she also knows what she's doing'.

She felt an urgent need to leave and hurry back to the safety and tranquillity of her trattoria.

'I understand. Well, if you'd be so kind, please tell him that I dropped by when you talk to him.'

She turned on her heel, took a few steps, then stopped and came back.

'Actually, just forget about it. Don't tell him anything about me coming by. Ah, these are for you, thanks again and *arrivederci*.'

She fled, leaving Giuffrè behind her, open-mouthed at the unexpected and two-fold gift of a tray of pastries and the sight of a marvellous derrière disappearing into the distance at a trot.

Chapter 51

The mansion block where De Matteis lived was part of an elegant complex in the most exclusive quarter of the city. As Piras rode along the tree-lined streets, designed to ensure that the flats were shaded by leafy foliage, she reflected on the fact that isolation and privacy might sometimes be to the detriment of security, as the facts had made so sadly clear.

It was an observation she'd already had occasion to make when she'd participated in the forensic investigation of the scene of Giada's murder. Lots of greenery, lights that illuminated only the pavements, a large dark area where a recently built swimming pool awaited its summertime inauguration: dozens of places where a wrongdoer could lurk in hiding.

As her driver approached the front door where the girl had been murdered, she thought about the sound of De Matteis's voice on the phone when Piras had called her to ask for a meeting: metallic and distant. She felt as if she were talking to an answering machine. She was almost tempted to think that the woman didn't care a damn about what was going on around her, including the investigation into her daughter's murder.

She spoke her name into the buzzer and went upstairs to the second floor. A black woman in a checked dress and white apron opened the door and ushered her into a large living room. One of the walls was glass from floor to ceiling, offering a spectacular panoramic view.

Even on a grey day like this one, tormented by a relentless rain of varying intensity, the sea, the mountain, the peninsula and the island, whose silhouette was reminiscent of the profile of a woman's face with her hair cascading down, were a canvas whose beauty clutched at the heart and took your breath away. Piras thought to herself, as she had many times before, that the city looked out at that landscape with a certain impatience: the way an old and unsightly woman might open an armoire and gaze at the dress, now yellowed with age, that she'd worn to her debutante ball.

De Matteis walked in, saying goodbye to someone on the phone and making no secret of her annoyance as she ended the conversation.

'Excuse me, dottoressa. One of my so-called girlfriends, who keep persecuting me with their fake comforting phone calls. All they really want is a little gossip to trade during their hour-long chat fests. I know, I've done it myself: car crashes, divorces, bankruptcies, cheating husbands and wives. Always the same merry dance, as long as there's some nugget worth sharing. Please, make yourself comfortable.'

Piras took a seat on the sofa, facing De Matteis, who had sat down in an armchair. She was no longer wearing dark glasses and Piras could finally scrutinise her gaze, but it didn't do a lot of good: the woman's eyes were completely devoid of expression.

'Signora, you may well be wondering what else we have to say to each other after our initial meeting in police headquarters, and why I asked to see you at your home. The reason is simple, and I'll come right to the point: I am here to ask for your help. We have a new development that might possibly bring us close to a solution, and you may be able to provide us with some crucial information.'

De Matteis heaved a sigh.

'Dottoressa, I'm so tired. No, it's not only that I'm tired. It's that I don't care any more. My heart is dead. I wake up, I get dressed, I keep everything in order, as you can see, the apartment, my help. I fill my days, I talk to my accountant, I supervise the charitable activities of the foundation named after my father. I use every minute of my day, to try to fill up the space . . . the space that's been left empty. I always try to have something to do. But if I look inside myself, I find nothing. If I look up, peer beyond the next urgent thing, the practical nature of whatever I'm doing, there's nothing left. I have to watch out because if I stop and ask myself the reason, the motive for doing all this, then my only option is to put an end to it all, there and then.'

Piras understood perfectly. She remembered the days and weeks that followed Carlo's death as if in a dream, a life lived through a mist of fog; she could clearly recall how unreal it felt to do a thousand trivial daily things while constantly bearing that immense burden in her heart.

'Believe me, I have some idea of what you're going through. I went through a loss of this kind many years ago, and I can remember the feeling very well. But we've got a murderer to catch. And we need your help to catch him.'

De Matteis grimaced.

'I really don't see what help I can provide. You see, in the past several days I've thought deeply, and I've discovered a terrible truth about myself: I've lived my life based on two emotions, which, when all is said and done, were two faces of a single emotion. Love for my daughter, and hatred for her father. The two things that sustained me; my only two topics of conversation. Giada's education and upbringing, my responsibility alone for seeing to that; and my constant resentment towards this man who humiliated me as a woman and as a mother, abandoning us to flee to another country in the company of a cheap prostitute. Now, suddenly, I've lost everything. My daughter, and my pride in watching her grow up to be beautiful, caring, sensitive and intelligent; and paradoxically, at the same time, her father, whom I no longer have any reason to loathe. I not only lost my daughter, dottoressa, I also lost myself, the person I've been until now. So let me tell you, I am deeply indifferent to anything you might be about to tell me, believe me.'

Piras smiled sadly.

'I asked to see you here, in your home, for a specific reason, aside from the fact that this is an informal meeting. Let's call it my womanly wiles. A hostess in her own home cannot simply turn and walk out of the door the way you did at police headquarters; here, in your own living room, you're obliged to hear me out. And I do have something to tell you.'

As raindrops carried by a listless wind streaked the plate glass, distorting and defacing the view of the bay, Piras recounted the story of a nurse who had an affair with a married man; of a doctor, still young and ambitious, who wanted an office in the fashionable centre of town. She told her about an address on a nondescript street in a transient neighbourhood, about young women eager to rid themselves of what they'd come to think of as nothing more than a burden. She told her about the duo's four years working together, about how that period came to an end with an awkward, unplanned pregnancy that resulted, however, in a baby boy who was wanted and loved, in spite of all the challenges.

De Matteis sat bolt upright, listening, without any change in expression. When Piras had finished speaking, De Matteis sat for a moment in silence.

Then she said:

'How ironic. Just think, Rinaldi's now famous all over the city for his fertility treatments. It's entirely possible that among his clients are some of the girls who went to see him back then for the opposite problem.'

'In any case, if Inspector Lojacono's theory is correct – that the Crocodile's intended victims are you three and not your children – then you're the missing piece of the puzzle. I'm here to ask you to make an extra effort, signora: I'd like you to try to remember whether, in the years between 1992 and 1996, you had any contact with this business of Lorusso's and Rinaldi's. Any interaction, direct or indirect. Please.'

The silence dragged on. Piras couldn't tell, as she looked at De Matteis's rigid expression, whether she was making an effort to remember, or if she was thinking about something else, or whether she was simply searching for the right words to put an end to the conversation. At last, she spoke.

'I never got my degree, and I had absolutely no interest in education. But my father did set one condition on the money he gave me: I had to study. So I was still enrolled, technically, and I'd make sure to sit my course exams every so often until, in the end, I got married in 1998 when I was pregnant with Giada. At that point, my father resigned himself to the situation too.'

Piras waited, relieved that De Matteis was finally reconstructing her memories.

'Back then, we had a lot less fun. We tried things out a little at a time. It wasn't the way it is these days; today, a fourteen-year-old girl could teach us things. Why, I've read text messages that girlfriends of Giada's sent her that would ... But let's forget about that. We got started at an older age, and we were far more naïve, and as a result some of us got ourselves into trouble. And among the girls of what we used to call good families, it was a much more common occurrence. Of course, we couldn't go to a hospital or a private clinic; our parents were sure to find out, and they'd have heart attacks at the very least. They belonged to a generation that was much less open than we are to dialogue and forgiveness.'

She paused to take a sip of the tea that the housekeeper had brought in. The two women looked as if they might be talking about the weather, or their holidays.

'It had never happened to me, until Giada. And at that point I wanted a home of my own, and he was handsome as could be and rich to boot, so why not? But it did happen to plenty of my girlfriends, many of them now anti-abortion crusaders. There was an address and a phone number circulating among us, though none of us knew exactly who the doctor was. I'd heard that he was good, fast and, most important, very discreet.'

Piras took in every word, her attention focused closely. She was afraid that if she asked questions, the woman might shut down again. But still, she needed to narrow the field.

'And thinking back to that period, do you remember having contact with any woman who might have known him in any way?'

'I never went there, not even to accompany any of my girlfriends. I vaguely remember that it must have been on the street you mentioned, and I remember that fact because it wasn't far from the university, but at the same time it wasn't so close that you might happen to pass by, and I decided that the choice of location must have been intentional. But it could have been a different street number, and we might be talking about two different things, I couldn't say.'

Piras made one last desperate effort.

'And can you remember if you recommended him to anyone, possibly a girl from outside your social circle? I don't know, some girl you'd only met once or twice, at the university or at the beach, anywhere else ... '

De Matteis, who was finishing her tea, furrowed her brow. She carefully set down the cup and dabbed at her lips with an embroidered napkin. Then she turned to look at Piras as if she were seeing her for the first time.

'You know, now that you make me think about it . . . I couldn't say exactly when, but not too long before I quit university entirely, so it must have been in 1996 when I sat my last exams . . . There was a girl there, cute, from out of town. She was young, much younger than me, I'd say early twenties, maybe twenty-two. We used to hang out, chatting, with a bunch of other girls, and we hit it off. We never saw each other off campus. One day she called me at home. I didn't even remember who she was – she had to remind me. And she told me that . . . yes, in short, that she needed that address and number.'

Piras held her breath. A gust of rain splashed against the plate glass.

'I remember her: a little wisp of a voice, a delicate face. She wasn't from here. You could hear the accent, but ever so slightly.'

'And what did you tell her?'

De Matteis shrugged her shoulders.

'I decided to give her a hand. I felt sorry for her. Who knows what son of a bitch had wormed his way into her heart. I got the information and gave it to her.'

Piras gave a long sigh and then asked,

'Do you remember this girl's last name? Or the town she came from, or anything else that could help us to find her?'

De Matteis shook her head decisively.

'I don't think I ever even knew her last name. We were taking different courses and anyway, like I told you, I didn't spend much time at the university. It's been so many years, I can't even imagine how I came up with the memory just now.'

Piras couldn't conceal an expression of bitter disappointment. She had felt she was so close to the solution and now she saw it slipping through her fingers again. How could she track down that girl and complete the circle without more information?

Then suddenly De Matteis said,

'But I do remember her first name. She had the same name as the main character of my favourite novel, *Il resto di niente*. Her name was Eleonora.'

Chapter 52

Eleonora finishes writing and gets wearily to her feet.

Her fever has been rising relentlessly over the past few days. The boundary between sleep and wakefulness has grown flimsy; she can no longer distinguish between thoughts and dreams.

Earlier, she'd been stretched out on the bed, flat on her back. The pain has faded from stabbing to dull, as if her weakness and listlessness had struck some sort of pity into it. She should have taken her medicine but the scrap of paper with the name of the antibiotic that the doctor dictated over the phone is still at the bottom of her bag, forgotten.

She looks around: her bedroom looks like a dump. Remnants of food she tried to eat, half-finished drinks, dirty clothing. It's obvious from every detail that she no longer has any desire to live, Eleonora thinks.

It's odd, what happened to her. Until she made her way to the address that her classmate at the university gave her and she climbed the stairs of that building, deep down she'd never really thought about the baby. She'd only thought about the man she'd loved, about what he'd given her and what he'd taken away. She'd thought about her father and her mother, about how they'd react, about what they'd say to her. She'd thought about herself, about what would become of her, about what she ought and ought not to do. She'd even thought about the people from her hometown, about the gossip that would undermine her parents' respectability.

But she'd never thought about the baby.

A clump of cells deep in her belly, like a piece of undigested food, something to be expelled as soon as possible, and then forgotten.

A piece of lost love, or a piece of love that never really existed except for in her imagination, the fantasy of a small-town girl living in a big city for the first time.

A mistaken dream, an idea of happiness posited at exactly the wrong moment.

An impediment, an insurmountable obstacle lying between her and the attainment of her dreams.

It had been everything to her, from the moment she first glimpsed it in the form of a line of type on an impersonal lab test result, except what it really was.

A baby. Her child. Flesh and blood, a gaze, a voice, thoughts in a mind. A hand on her face, the smell of its breath, the intensity of love. Her child.

In a feverish dream, in the pain of her own empty womb, Eleonora glimpsed him. She imagined seeing him at school, serious and responsible, his little black smock and a book bag. Playing football with grit and commitment, not especially good but fiery and stubborn. Running straight towards his grandparents, hugging them tight. And in her arms, fast asleep with a smile on his face.

In the fever and the pain of her own empty womb, Eleonora met the son whose death she had decreed. She watched him being born a thousand times; she felt the searing pain of losing him. She felt him sail away from her on the wings of her own lost love, becoming a ghost of the past like the man who, together with her, had conceived him on that very same bed, on an afternoon of dreams and caresses.

Eleonora waited for her fever to subside and then she dragged herself to the table. She picked up her pen and wrote a note to the one person who had always understood her even before she opened her mouth to speak, and she enclosed the story of the seed that had been planted in her belly. She told that person of her dreams and her illusions, describing how they had vanished into the air so that she no longer wanted to go on breathing. She described places, faces and feelings. She included first and last names, because she wanted to be sure that none of this would be forgotten.

Most importantly, she described her baby, the baby that would have been: the facial features that now no one would ever see, the imaginary resemblances and the hypothetical character traits. And as she re-read it, she decided that there had never been a baby as real as this one.

As she wrote, in order to ensure that all of this would be remembered, Eleonora realised that without her little angel she had no desire to go on living. Without her child's love, without the honour and affection of her family, she knew she lacked the strength to go on. She could have overcome every obstacle, but not the absence of her baby.

As she wrote, Eleonora realised that she had striven, paid for and pleaded for her own unappealable guilty verdict.

Eleonora has sealed the envelope. She's written a name on the front. Someone will deliver it.

She gets up and struggles to open the window. The air – damp, muggy and foul with smog – rushes into the room. Eleonora climbs on to the windowsill. It takes quite an effort, what with her fever, what with her empty womb.

And like the rain, like her tears, she falls.

De Matteis looks thoughtfully up at the ceiling. Then she turns to Piras.

'And there's one more thing that I remember, now that I think about it. A few months later I went back to the university, to pay my enrolment fees, and I bumped into a classmate who told me that the girl had killed herself. Sad story, eh?'

Chapter 53

The old man keeps the lights off. He's accustomed his eyes to the shadows; he can make out the silhouettes of the furniture and other objects. That's all he requires. He has what he needs in his hands, the only object of any importance.

A pair of binoculars.

He took his time picking them out – almost twenty days of internet research. The street is twenty-five feet and five inches across: the satellite map is accurate to a twentieth of an inch. The thickness of the two walls amounts to one yard eleven inches, and it's twenty feet from the outer wall of the property to the wall of the villa. His choice had fallen on a pair of roof-prism binoculars – an older technology but much more reliable over short and middle distances.

The old man moves cautiously over to the curtain and, without opening it, focuses his binoculars on the villa through the central opening.

There are two windows lit up, plus one that emits the pale blue brilliance of a television set. On the upper floor is the baby girl's bedroom. He can just glimpse the bars of the cot, with the colourful butterflies turning overhead. Every so often, the baby's hand spins the butterflies as she extends her fingertips to touch the lowest-hanging one. The little one learns quickly.

In the kitchen on the ground floor, the woman moves around, busy with countertops and utensils. Near the microwave is the baby monitor, picking up the sounds in the child's bedroom. He'll need to keep that in mind.

In the little living room he can glimpse, in the half-light, the silhouette of the man's feet propped up on the coffee table in front of the sofa. Still at home, the old man thinks.

He looks at his watch – the glowing phosphorescent spheres show 9.05 p.m. He sees the small red car slow down and pull up in front of the gate. The young woman says goodbye to her boyfriend, their heads merge in the shadow for a long, lingering moment: a sweet kiss, see you later. She gets out and blows another kiss, then wiggles her fingers. *Ciao, caro*.

She walks up to the single-button intercom and rings. Through the kitchen window, the old man sees the woman move briskly and buzz the front gate open. She presses the lower button. So that means: top button, answer; bottom button, open gate.

The girl enters, turning one last time to look at the red car, which pulls away and vanishes down the street. Good boy, the old man thinks. Never leave a girl alone waiting to be admitted. These are dangerous times we live in.

The hall light comes on; the woman opens the door and

welcomes the girl inside. *Prego*, come right in. Come with me to the kitchen; let me show you what I've prepared for the evening. You can eat some of this, and here I've got milk for the little one – all you have to do is heat it up.

The old man follows each movement and reconstructs snippets of the conversation. He almost has the impression that the binoculars are transmitting the audio as well as the video.

The father has risen from the sofa and climbed the stairs, perhaps to put on his jacket and overcoat. From his observation point the master bedroom is out of sight. Then the woman goes upstairs, while the girl lingers in the kitchen.

Now the girl heads upstairs too. She enters the nursery, at the top of the stairs, first door on the right. Seven seconds at a normal pace. The girl leans over the side of the cot and starts to coo at the baby; the old man can see the little hands in the air. The girl picks her up. She smiles at the little one.

The parents come in: now everyone is in the nursery. They say goodbye to their daughter. They're all dressed up, going out for the evening. They disappear from view and fifteen seconds later they emerge from the front door and head for the garage. The old man counts, murmuring under his breath: one, two and so on, to twenty-five. Then the garage door opens and the black Mercedes glides out silently. The automatic gate swings open, then the car pulls out and turns up the street, heading for the corner. The old man manages to glimpse the brake lights as they glow red at the junction, before pulling out into the traffic on the main road.

He turns on the desk lamp and jots down a series of numbers on a sheet of paper. Intervals, he thinks. The timing of the intervals: that's fundamental.

Once he's finished making notes, he switches the light off again and picks up the binoculars. In the kitchen, the girl is talking animatedly on her mobile phone. In the baby's room, the little nightlight glows sky-blue.

The old man moves his chair over to the window and settles in for the night.

Chapter 54

Piras went to see Lojacono at the San Gaetano police station so she could give him the news immediately.

The driver hadn't even brought the car to a halt before she'd already thrown the door open and was out, racing up the stairway leading to the offices. The inspector was at his desk in the Crime Reporting Office, killing time by re-reading for what seemed like the thousandth time the ballistics report, and formulating theories on what make of gun had been used in the murders.

Giuffrè had told him about Letizia's visit to the loony bin. Lojacono was sorry to hear that his only real friend in this city should have felt so neglected that she had begun to worry about his health, but he was also a little flattered. Maybe this evening, if he had time, he'd drop by the trattoria.

Piras burst into the room like a cyclone.

'Giuseppe, big news: De Matteis remembered something that strikes me as important.'

Giuffrè, blasted awake by Piras as he was dropping off for a nap, leapt to his feet and executed a comical rendition of a salute while at the same time trying to put on his glasses. Piras didn't even seem to be aware that he was there.

'Really? That's great, Laura. And what did she tell you?'

'She remembered that, when she was at the university, she gave the address of the place where Lorusso and . . . '

Just then she noticed the existence of Giuffrè, and said,

'Giuseppe, maybe we should talk this over outside, don't you think?'

'Sure,' Lojacono replied, grabbing his coat.

As he followed her out of the office, Giuffrè murmured,

'What now, you're on a first-name basis? With Piras? By any chance . . . ' The open-ended question was accompanied by a graphically obscene gesture.

Lojacono responded silently with another equally offensive gesture and caught up with Piras in the courtyard.

'So, you were saying?'

Piras told him briefly what De Matteis had remembered about her old classmate: how she had decided to have an abortion and then committed suicide.

Lojacono scratched his chin thoughtfully.

'Then we need to get to work immediately. We need to go through the records for 1996, find out whether a girl named Eleonora, residing in this city but born elsewhere, actually killed herself. If we find her, then once we've determined her last name and hometown, we find out whether she has relatives, and if so, talk to them to learn whether this event can in any way be linked to these murders.'

Piras nodded.

'I've thought of all that already. On my way over here I called my assistant and asked her to get on it right away. She's searching through the archives as we speak. What do you think will happen now? Do you think the Crocodile might stop, now that he's killed Rinaldi's son?'

Lojacono squinted in thought.

'It depends. We still lack the evidence to determine whether this is revenge or something else. To my mind, murdering children is too big a statement to make extortion the likely motive; and if this is vengeance, then we have no way of knowing how many people are involved.'

Piras agreed.

'Well, how do you think we should proceed?'

'First of all, we need to identify the suicide as quickly as possible; only then can we try to figure out whether a family member of someone connected to her is involved.'

Piras was perplexed.

'But if this is about revenge, why would he wait all this time? It's been, what, sixteen years?'

Lojacono shrugged.

'I don't know. We don't have enough information yet. We need to keep digging. And hope for a little more luck.'

Just then Di Vincenzo hurried over, all out of breath. He didn't give Lojacono so much as a glance and instead spoke eagerly to Piras.

'Dottoressa, they told me you were here. What's going on? Is there any way I can be helpful?'

Piras gave him a frosty reply.

'No, Captain. No more helpful than you've been so far, at any rate. But tell me: have there been any developments in your investigation?'

Di Vincenzo flushed bright red.

'We're in the process of checking out Ruggieri's alibi and the alibis of his entourage. They claim that they were dining in a restaurant in Piedigrotta, and so far the waiters have all confirmed his story. Of course we won't stop there, and—'

Piras interrupted him with a wave of her hand.

'That's fine. Draw up a nice report, in triplicate, and let me have it. Not until you've checked it all out, of course. Let's go, Lojacono. We've got a lot to do.'

They vanished with a squeal of tyres, leaving Di Vincenzo fumbling for something more to say.

Chapter 55

'Hello?'

'Doctor Rinaldi?'

'Yes? Who is this?'

'*Buon giorno*, Doctor. This is Marta De Matteis. We saw each other a few days ago at ... We ran into each other a few days ago, if you remember.'

'Ah, signora. Of course. Tell me, what can I do for you?'

'First of all, let me apologise for the intrusion. I asked a mutual acquaintance for your number – perhaps the only person we both know who has a modicum of discretion – Rosy Stammati.'

'I'm at your disposal. Please tell me how I can help. Would you like to make an appointment?'

'No, Doctor, no. That's not the reason for this phone call. Actually, I'm calling to tell you a story.'

'Signora, excuse me, I'm rather busy just now. I'm organising ... Well, you can imagine what I'm referring to. And I have a number of decisions to make, I have so many things to … Perhaps a little later in the month, in a couple of weeks, we could speak again and—'

'Doctor, please listen to what I have to say: this is the first and the last time you're going to hear from me. But you're going to have to show me the courtesy of hearing me out. It will only take a minute.'

'Then go ahead, have your say.'

'Yesterday, Laura Piras came to see me. You know, the prosecutor who's working on … on this case. It was an informal visit. She told me that what they're thinking, their theory, is that you and I are linked in some way. That the kids … that this whole thing happened because this person, the one who did these things, has a motive, and the motive is us.'

'Signora, I know, but it's clearly completely absurd. I can't for the life of me imagine—'

'Doctor, please. She told me that the only way, our only hope of working back to an explanation, is to establish what the connection might be between the three of us: me, you and the Lorusso woman.'

'Signora, now I really must put a stop to this, it's nothing but a waste of both our time. As you know perfectly well, there is no connection between us. Unfortunately they're simply stumbling around in the dark and this theory is proof if any were needed. As soon as I have the … as soon as I've organised this … thing, I'm going to make my voice heard at the highest levels, I promise you that.'

'They're right, and you know it.'

'What are you talking about? I don't know anything of the sort! This is utter nonsense and—'

‘All right then, listen closely to what I have to say. I’m going to tell you a story, and we can pretend that I’m talking about other people, in a long-ago time and a faraway place. A young girl from a small town – let’s say in Irpinia, or even from the Foggia area – comes to the big city to study. She meets a boy, she falls in love, they have sex, she gets pregnant. We don’t know the details – maybe because she’s afraid to tell her parents, or else the boy doesn’t want to become a father, or maybe she doesn’t want the child herself. In any case, she decides to have an abortion. She doesn’t know how to go about it and—’

‘Signora, this whole conversation is absurd. And in any case, as you know full well, it’s perfectly legal in Italy to contact a hospital and request a voluntary termination of pregnancy—’

‘I know that, Doctor. And it was legal even in the years when this story takes place. Just let me finish, please, and I won’t take up any more of your time. The girl, for reasons of her own that we don’t happen to know, decides not to go to the hospital. So she asks someone she knows. This person asks around and gives her a number and an address. The girl goes to that address and there she meets with a nurse and a physician.’

‘Signora, that’s quite enough! I’m not going to sit here and be—’

‘Afterwards, I don’t know exactly how much time later, the girl kills herself. That’s the end of my story.’

‘I’m going to hang up the phone now, signora. At the risk of seeming discourteous, I’ll ask you never to call me again. I don’t know what it is you’re trying to insinuate—’

'You see, Doctor, I'm the someone who asked around and got this girl – whose name was Eleonora and who was a classmate I met at university – the number and the address. It was back in 1996.'

'What is this, an attempt to blackmail me? Listen, I don't accept your insinuation. I'm terribly sorry about what happened to you but—'

'Doctor, it's a completely different matter. The Lorusso woman recognised you, and she told Piras how and why. I was able to reconstruct the role I played in this story, and that role is the only link between us.'

'Signora, once and for all – what do you want from me?'

'At police headquarters, when Piras and that Sicilian cop whose name I can't remember mentioned this to us, I told them that I didn't care whether or not they caught the murderer. Because my life ended with Giada's death. And that's certainly true; nothing will change. I still won't have any reason to get up in the morning, get dressed and leave the house. I won't have any reason to eat, read or sleep. Ever again. Any more than you will, or the Lorusso woman. But if I have some way of understanding why this thing happened, if I think that I might have prevented it from happening again, to some poor innocent child that, even as we speak, that ... man is watching, the way he did my daughter, before killing her, or him ... I believe, Doctor, that if something we did resulted in our children being killed, then we need to know what it is.'

'Signora, grief can drive a person crazy. I know, I'm experiencing it myself right now. I beg you, get some professional help: you're seeing ghosts that simply don't exist. None of what you say is true, you've only been influenced by the incompetence of a prosecutor who's in over her head and a policeman who's out of his mind.'

'I did my part, Doctor. I remembered the face of that poor girl; I remembered her first name. I remembered how stupid and frivolous I was, how recklessly I obtained an address for her without stopping to think or care what might happen later, or whether that poor young girl needed help, money, or even just someone to talk to. I remembered the nonchalance with which, perhaps, I put an end to my daughter's life so many years before she was even born. I did my part. And now that I've told you about it, I can go back to dying in peace for all the years that it finally takes.'

'I really don't know what I can say . . . '

'Indeed. Don't say a thing. *Buon giorno*, Doctor. And thanks for taking the time to hear me out.'

Chapter 56

He came in a little after eleven, when she had already resigned herself to another night without seeing him. It was as if he'd never been gone, the way his long, narrow eyes were lost in who knows what thoughts, an indecipherable expression on his face, hair unkempt, overcoat permanently rumpled and creased.

She happened to be looking towards the door at that instant, and so she saw him scanning the room for her before turning towards his usual little table in the corner, beneath the television set.

Letizia immediately turned to focus on the customer she was serving, feigning a cheerfulness and a friendly solicitude that she was very far from genuinely experiencing. She didn't want to give Lojacono the idea that she was angry, nor did she want to rush to his side, as if she hadn't been waiting for anything else all these days. More than anything else, she wanted to put him at his ease while he was there. If there was one thing she had figured out in the past few days, it was that under no circumstances did she want to become a burden to him.

She pretended that she hadn't even noticed him come in until he was comfortably ensconced at his table.

'Well, look who's here. How are you? Everything all right?'

He gave a weary smile.

'Sure, everything's fine. I've been working overtime, so I haven't been around much. But I swear to you that I never cheated on you once: grilled panini and beer, and a lot of the time, not even that.'

Letizia laughed.

'Of course I'm sure of it: in this whole city the only place you can get a really outstanding meal is right here, don't kid yourself. Hold on, I'll bring you something.'

She let him have plenty of time to eat, lending a distracted ear to the television news reports that included, as it did every night, references to the elusive Crocodile, the child-murderer who wept before he killed. And of course the inability of the forces of law and order to bring this Crocodile to book.

As usual, once the dining room was partially empty, she came over and sat with him.

'You feel like telling me about it?'

Lojacono was draining his last gulp of wine.

'We don't have a lot of evidence in hand. Something is brewing, but it's still not enough. I'm more and more convinced of what I told you before – that he's doing this to get even with the parents. They're the ones he's interested in punishing. And I don't even think any more that he's interested in extracting ransom, the way I did at the beginning. Unless all these dead children are a tool to threaten someone else, like: "You see the way I kill other people's children? I could do the same to you, or to your son or daughter, so pay up."'

Letizia listened attentively.

'I don't think so either. In that case all he needed to do was send a letter, right? If you ask me, he's taking revenge. And nothing more.'

Lojacono sat with his glass suspended halfway between the table and his mouth.

'You think? How can you be so sure?'

'According to what I've heard on television, this man doesn't care whether or not he's caught. He drops tissues at the crime scene, he always uses the same gun, and always the same technique, as you described it to me – the crocodile's technique. He's following a path, that's all: nothing more, nothing less. He's taking the steps he needs to. Someone who's doing that has no interest in a future for himself, right? He's not being tactical. Like someone who, I don't know, goes to a friend's office to see if he's all right, if there's some reason why she hasn't seen him for a while. Completely untactical.'

Lojacono nodded, smiling.

'Giuffrè told me all about that. And he told me about the little pastries too, which he took home and ate himself, every last one. Didn't save even one for me. I owe you an apology, I dropped out of circulation without a word, but it's just that this case has been eating me up.'

She smiled back.

‘Don’t worry about it. I wanted to be sure you were doing all right, that’s all. I’m really happy to know that you’re involved in your work; I know how much you missed that this last year. And then that Giuffrè, once you get to know him, is very likeable. So I’m glad I had the chance.’

‘You think so? Having him around all day long tends to change a person’s opinion. He never shuts up for a second. Still, he is what he seems, and that counts for something, in this city.’

‘Don’t forget that shutting the door and leaving the rest of the world outside, the way you do, might not be the best way to lead a life. But I’m happier to see you with a purpose, the way you are now; you’re tired and you’re worried, but you’re thinking about something. Much better than the way it was before.’

Lojacono looked her in the eye.

‘You’re right. As you seem to be so often. And maybe you’re right about the Crocodile too. Let me ask you something though, as maybe you can see the situation with the right degree of detachment, while we’re in it too deep to see things clearly. Let’s say you had a person who was dear to you, like a fiancée, a girlfriend, someone who had been forced to have an abortion and in the wake of that abortion, as a result of it, she had killed herself. And now let’s say you wanted to take revenge, like you said before: who would you focus on first?’

Letizia was paying close attention.

‘So this is it, this is what happened? An abortion, then she killed herself? And who was she?’

Lojacono shook his head.

'We don't know yet. For that matter, we don't have any confirmation that we're pursuing the right lead. For all we know this might be a damn lunatic, or it could be the Camorra after all, as everyone else working on this case seems to think.'

'In other words, the only people pursuing this lead are you and her, right? You and that prosecutor, the one who's not just pretty but also knows what she's doing.'

She put a fake cheerfulness into her voice.

'That's right. She's the only one willing to support me on this crazy manhunt. But there's no reason for you to make fun of me: it's work, work, nothing but work. I couldn't imagine, given the tragedies we're dealing with here, having anything else in mind. But why don't you try answering my question: if something like that had happened to you, who is it you'd want to take revenge on?'

Letizia tried to put herself into the situation. Then she said,

'Everyone. Everyone who had a hand in pushing her to that decision. But especially whoever got her pregnant and then abandoned her to that solitude and loneliness. If she decided to kill herself, it was because she had been abandoned and was utterly alone. There's no doubt about that. If she'd still had the man she loved, she would have found a reason to go on living.'

Lojacono sat for a long time without speaking, reflecting on the simplicity of this drive, the extreme purity of the most human emotion there is: the thirst for revenge.

'You're right. You're dead right. I could tell that he wasn't finished yet. That he hasn't stopped. The last target is himself: it has to be himself.'

He stood up, as if a sudden sense of urgency had come over him. He reached out and caressed her face. Letizia felt the warmth, rough texture and scent of his skin. The first physical contact with him.

She half-closed her eyes, and by the time she had opened them again, the door was slowly swinging shut behind him.

Chapter 57

Sweetheart, my darling,

I think back to the ten years it took me to prepare everything I've done. And I have to say that I'm very proud: proud that I was able to predict every imaginable outcome, and its opposite.

Many things, obviously and luckily, weren't necessary after all. With all the eventualities and unpredictable twists of fate that I'd imagined, at a certain point I began to feel a little ridiculous. All that was missing was a military invasion and an alien landing, and then I could say that I really had foreseen everything. But you know, my darling, when someone has nothing else to do for so many years, nothing else to think about, with no company other than a death rattle coming from the next room, planning becomes a comparatively agreeable pastime.

You might ask me: why did it take you so long? You know, the actual decision to take concrete steps, to put it into effect, only came after a number of years. I've wondered about that more than once.

Maybe I wasn't sure if I was up to it, wasn't sure I could pull it off. It was something too alien to the way I was, to the principles I used to hold dear, to my way of thinking. Maybe I was too physically beaten down, out of shape, inadequate. Maybe I was just waiting for her to show me the way; after all, she'd always been the decision-maker for the two of us.

Instead she got sick, and as time went on, sicker still. She'd stopped talking, you know. She'd spend hours at the window, looking out. As if she was expecting something; or someone.

It's a strange thing, my darling, the way the human mind operates. Or maybe it's the heart I'm thinking of. For years and years I folded in on myself, clutching at memories and at what could no longer be. Then you became my one reason for living: to see you again, to be able to hold you once more in my arms.

Perhaps the spark, or should I say the detonator, was the handgun. Do you remember my Uncle Nicola? No, *maybe you don't. He was my mother's brother, a glorious head on his shoulders, a legend to the rest of the family: he'd never resigned himself to the sleepy atmosphere of the town, he said that he was the only one left in the whole valley with any life in him, while everyone else was happy to sit in one place and breathe. Well, there wasn't a single undertaking or initiative that didn't have his fingerprints on it: film clubs, dance halls, cultural associations. If there was something to be started up, he was ready and willing. Then one unfortunate day, a stroke carried him off, and he died in his sleep.*

A couple of days after the funeral his wife called me and asked me to hurry over because she had a problem. Who knows how and who knows why, but in the back of a desk drawer, buried under a messy heap of papers, she'd found a box with a handgun inside. Perfectly cleaned and oiled, a working pistol in good operating order.

My aunt asked me: What should I do with it? I'm afraid to throw it away, and I'm even afraid to take it outside and bury it somewhere. Could you take care of it for me?

Of course I can, I tell her. And I leave, with the box under my arm.

Back at home, she was already quite sick and sleeping through much of the day. I put the box on the table and I sat down in front of it. I sat there for a long time, more than an hour. By the time I stood up, I'd had the idea.

Of course, it was still in embryonic form, and I lacked a plan. It would be a long, long time before I worked that out. But that was the idea, or this was the idea, I guess I should say. And if you want to know the truth, I believe that this, along with the desire to see you again, of course, is what has sustained me for all these years.

Then I bought the computer and got on the internet. And I started searching and researching.

It took time, a lot of determination and a lot of hard work. I built my workshop so I could make the silencer. I researched everything I needed to know about the lives I was interested in. I studied locations, conditions, even factors such as the weather. I put together a wardrobe, selecting the most nondescript clothing I could find, and whatever I lacked I procured, one item at a time.

When I went out shopping, there were those who asked me what I was doing with myself. It was a polite question, a form of courtesy. I would tell them that I was taking care of her, and it was true: I kept her clean, I kept her fed, I gave her her medicines and injections. When she started to get bedsores, I'd turn her over to keep her from suffering too much.

Every once in a while she'd look at me, with those despairing eyes, the way a prisoner looks out from behind the bars of his cell. She said nothing. She asked nothing.

I think she knew what I was doing, and she couldn't ask me to stop. Perhaps she wouldn't have asked it, even if she'd been able to speak.

Well, this is it, right? Now we'll see how it all turns out.

Now we'll all see.

Chapter 58

This time Piras sent a car to pick up Lojacono. When the driver looked into the Crime Reporting Office, Lojacono was in the bathroom, which gave Giuffrè the opportunity to mock him upon his return, even as he was still zipping up.

'Your lordship, as your butler I'm honoured to inform you that your carriage is ready and awaits you in the courtyard. Which suit will you be wearing this morning, sir: dinner jacket or full dress tailcoat?'

Lojacono shook his head and gathered up the papers on his desk.

'If I had the time for it, I'd tell you to go fuck yourself. But since I'm in a hurry, you'll have to take my word for it.'

'At your service, your lordship, I'll take care of it immediately. Consider it done.'

During the brief journey, Lojacono thought the summons over. There must be major new developments, otherwise Laura Piras would have called him on the phone; and she must need to speak to him in a hurry, otherwise she wouldn't have sent a car. After all, it was only a ten-minute walk, maybe a little more. What could have happened?

With a mixture of excitement and trepidation, he walked into the conference room that she'd practically taken over as her office. Piras's eyes were glittering but impenetrable.

'Well? What's going on?' Lojacono asked.

'I've got bad news and good news. The bad news is that according to the city's police archives, there were no suicides named Eleonora in 1996. At least, nobody was called out to investigate one.'

He felt something collapse inside him, but he immediately started thinking over possible alternatives. 'That doesn't mean it didn't happen. There may have been no call-out if, say, the girl slit her wrists, or took an overdose of barbiturates. That happens sometimes, you know, especially if the family is trying to hush it up, and—'

Piras raised her hand to halt the rush of words.

'Stop right there. Don't you want to know the good news?'

Lojacono looked at her quizzically.

'The good news, Inspector Lojacono, is that while it may be true that there were no such reports during the year 1996, we do have one for 1997. Specifically, for Sunday, January twelfth: the day that De Falco, Eleonora, aged twenty-three, put an end to her life by throwing herself out of the fifth-floor window of her flat in Via dei Cristallini, number sixteen.'

As she said it, she tapped her index finger on a file in front of her on the table.

Lojacono shook his head.

'Dottoressa, you pull another stunt like that on me and I'll leave you to fend for yourself, helpless without my indispensable assistance. Sunday, eh? The worst day of the week for suicides. The world over, Sunday afternoon is when people kill themselves. It's a given.'

Piras grimaced.

'True, very true. In any case, don't underrate yourself: your assistance really is crucial to me. In fact, when we're done with this case, we'll need to have a serious talk about the best use we can make of you.'

'The best use you can make of me? Like a horse, in other words. Here, let me take a look at these papers.'

The contents of the file were actually fairly meagre. Just three documents: the report from the police car that responded to the emergency call from the doorman of the mansion block, a certain Martone, Giovanni; the medical examiner's report, based on his on-site inspection of the body; and the autopsy report, filed subsequently.

In the first report, the author ascertained that De Falco, Eleonora, born in San Gerardo Valle Caudina in the province of Benevento on 24 September 1974 and residing etc., etc., had been identified by the informant etc., who stated that he had heard a loud thump at about 10 a.m., while he was sweeping the atrium of the mansion block, whereupon he promptly dialled the emergency number from the telephone in his flat.

The coroner's report, with its impersonal bureaucratic language, took Lojacono back to that pavement on a cold January morning.

Initial Post-Mortem Examination Report:

Upon removal of the sheet covering the deceased, it was determined that the subject was clothed in a pair of sky-blue pyjama bottoms, a long-sleeved blouse and white woollen ankle socks.

The deceased lies on the ground in a prone position, with head closest to the pavement, twisted to the left, immersed in a puddle of blood. The upper left limb is flexed, with the forearm lying on the edge of the pavement; the upper right limb is extended alongside the torso; the lower limbs are both slightly flexed and spread.

The cadaver in question is that of a person of the female gender, apparent age corresponding to the chronological age of 23. Skin and muscle mass is normally developed; subcutaneous adiposity present and distributed as one would normally expect; regular skeletal structure in conformity with age and gender standards. Scattered light-red hypostatic marks were in the process of formation, present on the anterior regions of the body, as to be expected from prone extension, responsive to finger pressure. Signs of incipient rigor mortis. Corneas clear. Rectal T of 35.5°C at 11.05 a.m.; ambient T at the same time in the vicinity of the corpse: 10°C, with light breezes.

The following traumatic alterations were detected:

- Diffuse ecchymotic excoriation affecting the right hemifacial area, with further soiling of dust and grit;

- Upon palpation, evident bony fragmentation is detected, compatible with multiple cranial fractures in the right parietal and temporal region.
- Upon palpation of the thorax, bony fragmentation of the frontal costal arch and of the sternum can be detected, compatible with thoracic collapse.

Taking into account the technical evidence that emerged from the inspection of the cadaver and the external circumstances surrounding the event in question, we can safely state that the decease occurred as a direct consequence of a very grave traumatic shock (cranial and encephalic trauma and thoracic trauma) with virtually immediate arrest of all vital functions in the aftermath of a *fall from great height* (more than 10 metres). The absence of any further traumatic lesion to the dermal organ, save for that caused by the fall, suggests a conclusion envisioning behaviour of a self-destructive nature.

The period of decease, taking into account the thanatological phenomena set forth here, can be established at roughly 2–3 hours prior to this inspection of the cadaver.

Lojacono looked up from the document and his eyes met Piras's: she was watching him attentively. All his years as a cop hadn't worn away his ability to feel pity at the picture, in his mind's eye, of that poor bloody bundle on the pavement of an unfamiliar city, on a cold morning many years ago. Behaviour of a self-destructive nature, the report said.

Piras pointed to the other flimsy sheet of paper: the autopsy findings. He picked it up and started reading.

Autopsy Report:

Head: Following removal of the pericranial tissues, there was detected an intense subgaleal and subperiosteal haemorrhagic infiltration. Once the extraction of the periosteum was complete, numerous fracture rimae were identified, of various width, diversely parallel and curvilinean, in the right occipital and temporal region.

Thorax: Following the extraction of the perithoracic tissues, there was identified a vast haemorrhagic infiltration into the muscular tissue as well as a flattening of the thoracic cage, especially marked on the right anterior arch. Upon the removal of the sternal plate, which showed extensive fracturing to the manubrium and sternal body, abundant hemothorax in the pleural cavity were detected.

Abdomen: Following opening of the abdomen, the omental apron appeared to be covered with haematic material. Upon inspection of the abdomen there was detected serum stratification in the area of the spleen and wall, with lacerations of the splenic capsule. Careful inspection of the pelvic cavity allowed determination of the presence of a yellowish corpusculated serosal fluid, with opaque peritoneal serosa. Following the removal of the intestine, which showed no macroscopic alteration, the Fallopian tubes appeared ectatic, congested and greyish in hue. Upon section, purulent material issued. The uterus, displaying augmented volume, with conserved shape, when cut displays an endometrium slightly accentuated on an irregular basis, with areas of mucosa regeneration. The uterine neck with a slightly dilated external uterine orifice and with areas of erosion of the mucosa.

Diagnosis of death: Polytrauma resulting from a fall from great height (cranial and thoracic fractures, haemothorax and haemoperitoneum with extremely grave traumatic shock), in the subject in question, with a context of pelviperitonitis and bilateral sactosalpinx of recent date, with uterine mucosa in a phase of re-epithelisation. This anatomo-pathological context, observed in relation to the pelvic organs, is extraneous to the traumatic context and can be ascribed with a criterion of elevated likelihood to infectious complications, which can be correlated to surgical procedures involving revision of the uterine cavity, in all probability in relation to a voluntary interruption of pregnancy.

He read it twice. Aside from the difficult-to-decipher technical terminology, he'd understood the basics: the girl had killed herself, and when she died she was suffering from an infection, the result of the abortion to which she'd subjected herself.

He looked at Piras.

'We should contact the Carabinieri in—' he checked the incident report, 'San Gerardo Valle Caudina.'

Piras smiled.

'I was waiting for you to arrive to do it. That's why I sent for you.'

Chapter 59

My baby girl. My beautiful baby girl.

For Orlando, coming home, climbing the stairs and picking her up out of her cot has become a wonderful little ritual on those days when he's able to get away at lunchtime.

Who'd have ever thought it?

He thinks back to the way he was until a few years ago as he buries his nose in Stella's tummy and blows raspberries there, making her chortle in delight. He was the kind of guy who lived his life for his own pleasure – or at least he thought it was pleasure. He hadn't met Roberta yet; he didn't feel any need for a wife or a home of his own, much less a child.

He liked women, fast cars and sailing boats. His friends were just like him, some of them worse – divorced men with children out of sight and out of mind, appointments on their calendars to spend a weekend with them every five weeks or so, a cost to write down on their personal spreadsheet and nothing more. Their sole concerns were to organise their holidays and to focus on their work and the steady climb to the top. Who gives a damn about the rest of it? he thought at the time. There's still plenty of time for that.

Now, as he carries his wonderful baby girl around the room, perched on his shoulders as he gallops in circles and trumpets like an elephant, it's impossible to understand why he was willing to waste all those years. Or perhaps, he thinks, perhaps it was precisely that very chase after the emptiest of vanities that kept him from understanding how important it might be to have some part of him that could live on. To become immortal, in a certain sense.

Stella emits her customary little shriek, an uncertain mix of fright and amusement. Her tiny hands grasp at his ears as he holds her wrists; he can feel her little fingernails scratching away. God, how he adores her. Every smallest detail of her, whether it reminds him of her mother or of himself. She's his ticket to the future, the bridge built by his love into the years that are yet to come.

A glare of light from the window strikes his eye and instinctively he looks outside, at the wall of the hotel across the street and the line of windows, some with the wooden shutters rolled down, one with the curtains drawn. Through another window, on the top floor, he glimpses a woman languidly cleaning a room.

Obviously, he thinks with some small portion of his brain, the woman swung the window open and the sunlight was reflected off the glass for an instant.

He picks up his baby girl and tells her, 'Mamma mia, what

a smell on you. We made a little poop, didn't we? Now Papa will change your nappy, my wonderful little star, my Stellina.'

Less than fifty feet away, the old man carefully puts away his binoculars. He knows how risky the slightest mishandling can be, because at that time of day the sunlight can reflect off the lenses and attract attention. He pulled away from the opening in the curtain in the nick of time: the man came that close to getting a glimpse of him.

For the first time, he betrays an emotion, biting his lip and slamming his fist down on the table. He made a stupid mistake. He'd never have made it this far if he'd started out doing things like that. What a fool. Just an instant, a single instant in the whole day when the sun beats down directly on to the window, and that's the instant when he picks up the binoculars to watch.

Ever so cautiously, after dabbing a tissue at his eye behind the lens of his glasses, he moves over to the curtain. He knows that the instant has passed and that the sun is no longer directly overhead, but still, the risk he ran has made him especially cautious. With two fingers, he gingerly parts the curtains and peers across the way.

In the nursery the father is leaning over the changing table, at the opposite corner of the room from her cot. The old man finished his floor plan of the room a couple of days ago. Thanks to an armoire with mirrored doors that the babysitter opened once or twice, he even knows that on the wall with the window there are only framed pictures or photographs, no furniture.

Now the father, his back to him, picks the baby up from the changing table. Two skinny little legs extend from the nappy, kicking away happily. The father turns, showing his profile and revealing an expression of enchantment.

Unmistakably, the baby is laughing. She's always laughing, the old man thinks. A happy, untroubled baby. Surrounded by love.

The father joins in his daughter's laughter, then he acts out a dance, cheek to cheek with his baby girl. The old man imagines that the father is crooning aloud.

They dance together for a while, father and daughter, lost in an imaginary waltz, swaying to a tune that exists only in their intertwined imaginations.

The old man draws the curtains together, closing the narrow gap, and tosses the damp tissue into the wastepaper basket.

Chapter 60

The Carabinieri station at San Gerardo Valle Caudina was small but efficient. Piras announced her credentials and was immediately put through to Warrant Officer Giaquinto, the station commander.

Piras quickly apprised him of the urgency of obtaining as much information as possible about the De Falco family, informing him that she was unfortunately unable to provide either the addresses or names of the family members and how many there were. The only detail she possessed was the fact that the daughter, Eleonora, had committed suicide at the beginning of 1997, here in the city she was calling from.

The warrant officer explained that he hadn't been stationed there long, and that he'd call back shortly. In fact, he returned the call five minutes later, asking Piras if he could put her through to Brigadier Mariani, who had been stationed there for over twenty years and practically knew everyone in town.

The brigadier had a deep rolling voice.

'Dottoressa, *buon giorno*. The warrant officer tells me that you need information about the De Falcos, the family of the girl Eleonora. A very unfortunate family.'

Piras took notes as she listened, then she put the call on speakerphone so that Lojacono could hear the information too.

'Yes, we know about the girl's death. Who else is there in the immediate family?'

'Let me tell you that at first, no one in the town knew about the ... the way the girl died. We knew that she was attending university in the city, and that she'd been involved in a serious accident. The father and the mother – she was an only child – went to get the body and held the funeral here. It was only later, with the transfer of the documents, which of necessity included the police reports, that we learned that the girl had killed herself, but since her parents were decent people who kept to themselves, no one ever mentioned it.'

'What do you mean they "were" decent people? Are the parents dead?'

'The mother came down with a nasty disease, something to do with her lungs, a few years after the death of her daughter. Poor woman, she never recovered; she was little more than a ghost.'

Lojacono and Piras exchanged a glance. The man was a bit verbose, but his comments might prove useful, so Piras decided to encourage him.

'Did you know them personally, Brigadier?'

'Yes, of course I did. This isn't a big town, though in the summer the emigrants come back and the population swells.

The De Falcos are good people. He was an accountant for a company in Benevento but, after the daughter's death, he took early retirement so he could look after his wife. In any case, they were well-off: a few properties here in town, a couple of commercial premises they rented out. They had plenty of money.'

Lojacono broke into the conversation.

'*Buon giorno*, Brigadier, this is Inspector Lojacono. What were Eleonora's parents' names?'

'*Buon giorno*, Inspector. Felice is the father, and the mother, God rest her soul, was named Gemma.'

'When did the mother die?'

Mariani's booming voice turned sad.

'I think a month and a half ago. She was in bad shape, poor thing. He stayed with her till the very end.'

Lojacono leaned towards the speakerphone.

'And the father, Felice, is he still in town?'

Mariani replied hesitantly,

'Well, sure, I think he is. He's not someone you see much of in town, to tell the truth, as he tends to mind his own business. He's the kind of person that tends to keep to himself, so to speak.'

Piras interjected.

'In any case, we need to speak to him. I wonder if you'd be good enough to bring him in to the station. And let us know when you have him.'

Lojacono broke in again.

'One more thing, Brigadier. Are there any other relatives?'

'Um, you know, Inspector, in these small towns, more or

less everybody's related. My wife, who is from here, has a ridiculous number of uncles and aunts and cousins, for instance. I know for sure that the De Falcos have at least two groups of relatives, but I don't think they see a lot of each other.'

'Is there anyone who was especially close to the girl? An old boyfriend, for instance, or some dear friend?'

Mariani said nothing for a moment, obviously trying to gather his thoughts.

'I seem to remember that there was a young man, maybe a distant relation of some sort, who used to see her; but then he left too, went up north for work. Though I could certainly be mistaken, it's been so many years.'

Piras cut the conversation short.

'Maybe the girl's father will remember that boy's name. Brigadier, please call me the minute you get back to the station with De Falco. We'll have a chance to talk and then, if necessary, we'll come out to see you. All right?'

'Certainly, dottoressa, right away. I'll call you later.'

Chapter 61

Roberta finishes dressing Stella and gets herself ready to go out. Luckily, it looks like the rain is subsiding for today. The baby's only been out for some fresh air a couple of times in the past week, and the paediatrician insists on her getting outdoors as much as possible.

Perhaps this is the new frontier of medicine, thinks Roberta: the return to nature. She believes in it up to a point. Nature is fine if you're in the foothills of the Alps or in Polynesia, but not in this city, where the air you breathe is made up of black exhaust fumes, and lorries are there loading and unloading all day long, making it impossible to push a pram down the pavement.

But the paediatrician was very clear: the baby needs to be outdoors. In this phase of her development, spending too much time shut up indoors can make her more susceptible to viruses and germs.

Roberta suspects that the doctor thinks she's too apprehensive. I'd like to see you, she wanted to tell her, if you'd had to fight for ten years, if this angel had flown down from heaven just when you were on the verge of giving up. She's too precious to me, my little jewel.

She buttons the baby's one-piece right up to her neck and adjusts her knit cap. Stella looks up at her, recognises her and smiles. She reaches out her tiny hand, and Mamma pretends to eat it. Stella laughs happily; she likes this game. On the facing wall is the sketch of her imaginary daughter's face, the sketch she did while she was pregnant. Roberta congratulates herself: she wanted her, she dreamed of her, and she finally had her. That face is exactly how Stella will look in a few months.

Roberta is very careful as she walks down the stairs, the baby in her arms. She uses them a thousand times a day, those stairs, going from the kitchen to the upper storey, as she doesn't place a lot of faith in the baby monitor, even though she's adjusted it so that she can even hear Stella breathing. She's read terrible things, of babies dying in their sleep, inexplicable occurrences, babies suffocating in their bedclothes. She realises that she won't be able to spend her whole life with her eyes wide open, checking on the baby day and night, but deep in her heart there is a never-fading fear of losing her.

She thinks of Orlando, who makes fun of her for all her phobias; but deep down she knows that he shares many of them. He really is an outstanding father. When she first met him, that's the first thing she thought: he'd make a great father. And yet he seemed anything but, with his devil-may-care attitude and his love of nice clothes and sports cars. He might have seemed superficial, but she knew how to look under the surface, and her reward was the wonderful family she now has.

Having secured the baby in the pram, she opens the door and emerges into the fresh air outside. Yes, the weather is acceptable, at least now, at the warmest time of the day. She's put off the walk to give the pallid sun time to heat up the air somewhat, and now she has only a short while to get her grocery shopping done before the shops close for the midday break. She accelerates her step, imitating the sound of a roaring engine for the baby's amusement. The little girl laughs and claps her hands.

Roberta emerges from the gate, looking around cautiously before crossing the street, but there's no one around at that time of day.

No one but an old man sitting on a bench, reading a newspaper.

Chapter 62

Less than an hour later Piras's telephone rang again. Brigadier Mariani sounded mortified.

'Dottoressa, I'm sorry. Signore De Falco is gone.'

Piras and Lojacono looked at each other.

'What do you mean he's gone? He's gone out?'

'No, he seems to have left town. Let me explain: the De Falcos live in Contrada Spicchio, a part of town a little way out of the centre, in a terrace house built in the eighties. The house is all shut up, the blinds are down, it looks like no one's been there for a while. I asked some of the neighbours and they agreed that no one had seen Signore De Falco for at least a couple of weeks, if not longer.'

Lojacono asked,

'He didn't say goodbye to anyone? He didn't tell anyone where he'd be going?'

The brigadier replied,

'No, and that's the odd thing. He didn't leave keys with anyone, or a forwarding address. He didn't tell anyone anything. Very simply, one night he was there and the next morning he was gone. A woman who lives next door told me that she was worried about him so she went and knocked on his door but no one answered.'

Piras nervously twirled a lock of her hair.

'All right, Brigadier, listen closely: I'm going to fax you a warrant to search that residence. Give me the complete address so I can fill out the warrant. Get out there and search the place immediately, and report back right away by phone. I don't want you to waste any time writing up a report. In the meantime, whatever information you dig up on De Falco or anyone else with ties to the family, any strange developments, or anything else, call me immediately. Is that clear?'

'Certainly, dottoressa. Let me give you the exact address of the house.'

After hanging up the phone, Piras turned to Lojacono.

'Well, what do you think of that? This could be the jack-pot, no?'

Lojacono shook his head.

'Maybe, maybe not. Maybe in the aftermath of his wife's death he decided to take a trip somewhere. Or else he killed himself too, and they're going to find a dead body in the house. Anyway, what matters most right now is that we find out one thing: who was the father of Eleonora's unborn child? If you think about it, it's the one piece of the puzzle that's still missing. This friend of mine, a woman I was talk-ing to last night, opened my eyes to it. If I were out to take revenge for the death of a girl I cared about, who had done to herself what Eleonora did, the first person I'd be eager to settle scores with would be whoever got her pregnant and then abandoned her to her fate.'

Piras stared at him wide-eyed.

'A friend of yours? A woman you were talking to? Who is this? And why on earth would you be talking to other people about such a top-secret investigation?'

Lojacono raised both palms in a gesture of self-defence.

'Hold on, hold on! I didn't name any names, and my friend is the owner of the trattoria where I have dinner every night. She doesn't know anything about anything. Still, you have to admit that her suggestion is valid. He's the only one who's still missing.'

Piras thought it over.

'As a matter of fact, it's true. The classmate who told her where to get the abortion, the nurse, the doctor – all of them are basically secondary figures. The chief culprit is still missing – the one who triggered the whole affair. But how can we figure out who he is unless we at least track down De Falco's father?'

Just then an officer stuck his head round the door and said,

'Forgive me, dottoressa, but there's someone outside who wants to speak with you. A certain Doctor Rinaldi.'

The man who walked into the small conference room was a completely different person from the one they'd met a few days earlier. The vast torment filling his reddened eyes might have been the same, but this time his demeanour was humble and confused.

His face was lined from lack of sleep, a heavy five o'clock shadow darkened his jaw and his hair was in disarray. He was tieless and a tuft of grey chest hair protruded from his open collar. He looked years older.

In one hand he held a large green notebook, what looked like a school ledger book.

He stood there until Piras waved him to a chair. He drew a deep breath and started talking.

'Dottoressa, I've given a lot of thought to the conversation we had the other day. To tell the truth, I also received a phone call from Signora De Matteis, whom you saw again, from what I gather. She made me ... helped me to rethink a few things. She made me stop and consider. In a certain sense, I could say that she opened my eyes. And I realised that ... You know that my son meant everything to me. Everything. Without him, nothing has any meaning for me now: my career, my practice, my work. Nothing. And if in some way I've been the cause of this ... my god, this is madness ... then I must do something to make amends. I need to try to make amends. To the extent that I can. You see, he wanted to be a doctor, but not the way I've done it. He wanted to help others. He talked to me about Africa, about volunteering ... I can't allow him just to have died without trying to do something.'

Lojacono and Piras exchanged a fleeting glance. They understood that the man needed to talk. He went on, addressing them both.

'I knew Lorusso, but you already know that. When you're young, you understand, you have a goal in mind and that's the only thing that matters. I wanted to open my clinic … Well, it was perfectly legal, I only did it in a way that anyone who wanted greater secrecy, the absence of any official records … Anyway, luckily nothing bad happened as a result.'

Lojacono murmured through clenched teeth,

'Maybe not on the operating table. But afterwards it did.'

Rinaldi ran his hand through his tousled hair.

'Yes, afterwards it did. But I couldn't know that, could I? What could I know about what my patients did after? I read about the De Falco woman in the newspaper and for weeks I expected to be subpoenaed. I was afraid that they'd find some trace of me, my address, my phone number. Then, as time passed, I forgot about her. Until De Matteis mentioned her name on the phone.'

Piras broke in, her voice gentle. Lojacono admired her approach, designed to keep Rinaldi from feeling he was on the defensive again.

'Doctor, no one is interested in putting you on trial here. These are old stories, and right now the last thing we want to do is dig them over. What we need to know, and urgently, is anything you can tell us about Eleonora De Falco. Is there anything you remember about her?'

Rinaldi had clutched the green ledger book to his chest the whole time he'd been in the conference room. Now he lay it down on the table, opening it more or less midway through.

'I don't remember her as a person. You understand, it was in the interests of discretion. I'd talk about anything affecting the clinical picture, symptoms and tests if necessary, but if there wasn't anything physiological to discuss then I basically wouldn't open my mouth. But, to be on the safe side, I jotted down certain basic information in this book. Nothing much: last name, first name, address and nature of the treatment. Here she is: De Falco, Eleonora, Via dei Cristallini, number sixteen. Dilation and aspiration. In other words, a surgical abortion. Eighth week of pregnancy. From the article in the newspaper I found out that she had a bad infection. Evidently she hadn't taken the antibiotics I prescribed for her. Nothing odd about that, poor girl; when you've made up your mind to die, you're not likely to take your medicine.'

Lojacono jumped in,

'And you didn't see her again afterwards? She didn't come in for a follow-up?'

Rinaldi shook his head decisively.

'No, she didn't come back. They didn't usually come back.'

Piras nodded her head wearily. Rinaldi's confession added nothing to the information they already possessed.

All the same, she asked,

'And you don't remember whether, when she came to your clinic, she might have mentioned any names, a next of kin or anything?'

Rinaldi nodded.

'Of course. I always asked for a reference, a contact, in case something went wrong. After all, these were operations performed under anaesthesia; I'd never have run the risk of having no one to contact.'

Lojacono leaned forward, his eyes narrowed to two slits.

'What's the name of the contact that she gave you?'

Rinaldi checked the ledger.

'Masi, Orlando. Care of the administrator of the polytechnic.'

Chapter 63

The old man becomes the Crocodile.

Methodically he readies himself, with the curtains drawn, the bedside lamp dimly lighting the room.

He's cold, calm and composed. Every so often a tear drips out from behind the lens and he wipes it away with an abrupt dab.

He knows that his long wait is about to come to an end. He knows – from under the water's surface, from his place of hiding, from where he's watching – that his immense hunger is about to be sated.

He polishes his shoes. Then he moves on to his trousers, checking the crease, his shirt, his tie, his jacket. He knows that this time there will be no repeat performance, this time things will be different, from start to finish.

He understands that he no longer has the luxury of time, the way he did with the other killings. That it won't be enough to lurk in the shallow swamp waters, mixing his own scent with the smell of rot and decay, camouflaging himself in his drab armour, a log among logs, water in the water, vegetation amid vegetation. This time he'll have to pounce suddenly, clamp his jaws shut on his prey's throat and take a single, furious death-dealing bite. This time his jaws won't have a chance to gnaw quietly, crushing bones as part of his meal.

And he'll have to drag his victim into the abyss, on a one-way journey to death, in search of a peace that he has left behind in the impenetrable darkness of his perennial hunger.

His ravenous hunger has solidified over the years, in the wheeze of an endless death rattle, in the memory of a long-lost tenderness. His hunger has obliterated any and all memories of friendship, sentiment, joy or love. His hunger is inextinguishable, and it has devoured every feeling in his heart, and in the end, it has actually devoured the heart itself.

Now he removes the plastic tub from the bottom of the armoire, opens it and lays a cloth out on the bed. He dismantles his weapon, checks it, cleans it and oils it.

The old man is the powerful, implacable jaws; he is the pitiless clawed feet; he is the formidable clamping strength. He is the poison without an antidote.

The old man is the Crocodile.

In his icy soul, no winds of human pity blow.

Because he is the Crocodile.

Born to kill.

Chapter 64

That name had been something like an electric shock. Now they had someone to look for, and they had to find him right away. Afternoon had given way to night, and suddenly the clock had started racing at supersonic speed.

Orlando Masi, care of the administrator of the polytechnic: a message from the past. It seemed to Lojacono as if Eleonora had decided to save an innocent life, one among the many dead that had been murdered on her account: as if she were turning her back, fifteen years after her death, on the vigilante who was distributing rough justice and death sentences according to his own lights.

It wouldn't be easy though. A sleepy clerk, irritated at having been caught up in a live police investigation as he was heading out the door for the night, told them after a lengthy search that there was no employee of that name, either current or retired, in the records of the polytechnic's administrator.

Piras ran a hand over her face.

'Do you think she gave a random name? Just to put one down?'

Lojacono shook his head vigorously.

'No, I'd rule that out. Rinaldi wasn't a public health facility. All she would have had to do was state that she had no one to contact. No, this is our man; this is the Crocodile's last victim. The problem is that he could be anywhere after all these years; maybe he only worked here and now he lives somewhere outside of the country. Who the hell knows?'

Piras had been busy obtaining a warrant to search the De Falco residence. Lojacono's theory – that the man might have killed himself or left some trace of his destination – struck her as one of the more plausible lines to pursue.

The phone call from Warrant Officer Giaquinto, in San Gerardo, came in a little before nine o'clock that night. They'd had relatively little trouble getting into the house, where everything was neat and tidy, as if De Falco had just left the place. There was no evidence of preparations for a trip or an extended absence. There was nothing that pointed to the man's destination, nor was there much clothing missing from his armoire: there were only two empty hangers.

But they'd really had to do some work to force open the garage door: it was armour-plated and bolted shut from within. Once inside, they'd found what looked like a metal-working shop, with precision instruments and a computer with a high-speed connection. No evidence of any illegal activities, the warrant officer concluded with perfect bureaucratic diction.

But the man was wrong, Lojacono mused. There was

clearly evidence of the Crocodile's activities. Evidence of a lengthy, painstaking process of preparation, and of a conscientious elimination of any and all traces that might help to find him. He felt certain, and he said so to Piras, that the computer's hard drive had been removed. The warrant officer confirmed that in fact the computer wouldn't boot up.

Lojacono pulled a handful of ballistics reports out of the folder full of documents in front of him. The report on the last murder read:

EVIDENCE FROM THE MURDER OF RINALDI, DONATO, AND COMPARISON WITH PREVIOUS MURDERS

The projectile in question is a .22 LR cal. bullet, weighing 2.4 g., diameter 5.6 mm, with six right-hand striations, whose class characteristics are compatible with a Beretta 70 series semi-automatic pistol. There is the presence of typical deformations impressed by the projectile's passage through a silencing device, as well as the presence of deformations due to traces of smoking and scorching. To establish comparison between this projectile and those previously analysed, it can clearly be ascertained that in this third case the weapon used was the same one employed in the murders of Lorusso, Mirko and De Matteis, Giada.

So that's what the metalworking tools and the precision instruments were for, thought Lojacono. In Italy, you can always get hold of a handgun, and the same is true for a box of bullets. But a silencer is a whole different thing, not something you can find on the open market. You have to make it yourself.

The clock was ticking. It was almost ten o'clock already.

It was Piras who had the inspiration.

Her eyes opened wide and she said,

'Damn. Why on earth didn't I think of this before? If she was forced to do this thing on her own, it means that she was no longer in touch with him, that they had broken up. And it explains why afterwards she did what she did. So she wouldn't have wanted to have any more contact with him, much less with his family, right?'

Lojacono wasn't following her.

'So?'

'So she wouldn't have given his home number, and it is unlikely he would have had a mobile phone back then. You know why? Because he was a student. Just an ordinary student, and the best way to get in touch with him was by leaving a message with the administrator.'

Lojacono lit up.

'An engineering student. Who was working hard on classwork and coursework, and who spent all his time at the university. Which is why . . .'

Piras clapped her hands happily.

'The Engineers' Guild! Immediately!'

This time, things were anything but straightforward. At the Engineers' Guild, given the late hour, there was no answer. And when they looked up Orlando Masi on their website, all it listed was the name of the company where he worked.

'At least Masi hasn't gone to work in the north of Italy, or abroad somewhere. He's still right here in the city, and he works for Gallardo Construction, which is one of the region's largest public-sector construction companies. Or at least that was where he worked the last time he renewed his membership a year ago. We have the phone number, and a nice little message on the answering machine telling us that the offices are open from nine to one in the afternoon, and then again after lunch from three to five. There's no one in the phone book by that name. That's all we've got.'

Lojacono nodded. They were both exhausted.

'Let's hope we get to him in time. Tomorrow we'll track down this engineer of ours, and we'll ask him a question or two about his past.'

They agreed to meet very early the following morning and start by calling the construction company.

Neither of them got a wink of sleep, worn out though they both were.

Chapter 65

Sweetheart, my darling,

You know, there are nights that aren't made for sleeping.

Not that there's anxiety, or a fear of not being up to a given challenge or task. It's simpler than that: it's that you're about to get something you've wanted for a long time, so it tends to keep you up.

It's sort of the way it is for little children the night before Christmas. A mix of anxiety and anticipation.

I must have gone over the things I'll need to do a million times by now. This one is different from the others, because it won't be enough to sit still like a good boy and wait for them to come to me, heads down, like little lambs at Easter. This time, I'm going to have to arrange to have the proper time and space, and I'll have to take concrete steps to gain those opportunities.

Of course, I could have waited. If I'd patiently monitored, observed and watched, sooner or later a situation would have arisen that allowed me to act in greater safety and ease. But I have the sensation, and it's growing stronger all the time, that my chances are about to run out.

You know, my darling, now I'm in all the newspapers. The Crocodile. Every day they revisit all three murders, word by word, step by step, coming up with ridiculously elaborate theories. They don't see how simple reality can be, how easy it is to understand what's happened. What's happening.

So the best idea is to get moving and put an end to this thing, the sooner the better.

Don't worry though; I've still got everything worked out to the last detail. The last thing we want is to let them catch us now, at the last second, right? Just when it's all about to come to an end. Can you imagine how ironic that would be, my darling, to be caught and locked up before I could finish my work, without being able finally to hold you in my arms? It would be so laughable.

But it's going to be different this time. I'll have to be careful, and I'll have to be fast.

I've made all the necessary preparations. I've rehearsed every act, every movement hundreds of times. I've found the place, the situation, the logistics.

I've prepared the tool.

Two shots. Just to be safe, I've loaded three bullets;

you always want to have a safety margin. But I'm only going to pull the trigger twice.

You know how it will be: only the guilty, never the innocent.

I'm certainly no killer: I'm here to bring justice.

And there are only two guilty parties left to punish.

Chapter 66

Anna Criscuolo, the secretary at Gallardo Construction, would happily have slept for another couple of hours.

Last night, she let herself get sucked into watching an idiotic TV programme, a reality show so beastly and vulgar that she was unable to turn off the set and go to sleep. She'd once read in a women's magazine that hypnotic subtexts are inserted into certain shows to keep the viewers watching, placidly absorbing every minute of advertising. At the time she'd dismissed it as utter nonsense, but now she wasn't so sure.

But there's one point on which the boss is absolutely intractable: starting time at the office. When he gets there in the morning, he'd better find everyone at their desks, ready to take his instructions for the day before he heads out to the various construction sites.

Anna has been assigned the task of raising the shutters, as the engineer puts it. She has the keys to the office, so she has to open up, bring fresh air into the premises by opening the windows for a few minutes while the air conditioning system gets going, turn on the computers and photocopiers, start the coffee, turn off the answering service. The engineer has told her that these are crucial tasks, necessary to ensure that as the staff come into work, they all have the impression of a machine already humming along and they'll get right to work without wasting time.

Therefore, even though the firm's offices aren't officially open for business until 9 a.m., Anna makes sure she's there every morning at 8.30 a.m. to present that picture of efficiency. It's an important responsibility, the engineer always says. That may be so, but this morning she'd have happily slept in. Goddamn stupid reality show, she thinks to herself as she rummages through her bag for her keys.

From the interior, through the door, she can hear the phone ringing. Who the hell could that be, at this hour of the morning?

She takes her time getting the door open, waiting until the phone stops ringing. Teach them to call at the right time, she thinks with a hint of annoyance.

Piras looks up at Lojacono and shakes her head. Still no answer. They started calling at 8 a.m., trying every five minutes, hoping that at least one of the employees might be more of an early riser than the rest.

Piras says, perhaps more to persuade herself than for any other reason,

'Maybe this is a different engineer who happens to be

called Orlando Masi; or maybe he was nothing more than a friend, the only one Eleonora could think of, and that's why she gave his name to Rinaldi as a reference; maybe the father of the baby was the old boyfriend from her hometown, the one whose name the brigadier couldn't remember.'

Lojacono, inscrutable, sits with his arms folded across his chest.

'Maybe not. What with all the mistaken theories we've pursued, all the times we've ignored the most obvious lead, we've done nothing but waste time so far. We have this name and the only way we can make any progress is to pursue it. Come on, let's keep trying to reach someone.'

Piras shoots him a magnificent glare of hatred, then dials Gallardo Construction. On the third ring, someone at last picks up.

As he waits, standing in the shelter of a niche in the wall, the Crocodile listens intently for sounds from the villa. After thinking it over, he selected a space in the wall around a neighbouring home, because at that hour the slanting sunlight leaves that side in the shade, making it practically invisible, while still giving him a view of the garage door.

He's been there for an hour already, even though he knows with precision the time that the man will get his car and drive out of the gate. For the past few days the variations on his departure time have never been more than five minutes.

The sky is leaden grey. Maybe it will rain later on, thinks the Crocodile. But later on, it will all be over.

*

The conversation between Piras and the secretary at Gallardo Construction was surreal in a way. The woman obstinately refuses to provide any information about the chief engineer: neither his home address nor his mobile number. She keeps telling Piras to try calling back later, that Engineer Masi will be in the office at nine.

Piras does her best to keep her cool, but after a little while she starts to raise her voice. Lojacono notices that as she loses her temper, her Sardinian accent becomes much stronger and more distinct. At a certain point, seeing that the conversation has reached a stalemate, Lojacono has an idea and takes the phone out of her hand.

'Good morning, signorina, this is Inspector Lojacono of the police department. I fully understand the need to protect the privacy of your employers, you're quite right. But let's try this: why don't you call back, through the main switchboard number here at police headquarters? You can look it up yourself in the phone book. I could offer to give it to you myself but that would defeat the purpose, wouldn't it? Ask to speak to Dottoressa Laura Piras, Assistant Public Prosecutor of the Italian Republic. That way you'll know for certain who you're talking to. Just one thing: let me ask you to please make that call immediately. Otherwise you'll force us to begin lengthy and unpleasant legal proceedings, and at that point it will be painful for everyone involved.'

Piras stares at him open-mouthed.

'Since when have you become such a diplomat?'

Lojacono shrugs.

'It's just that I know women. As soon as she calls back, get the address and ask her to call the engineer. Tell her to tell him he has to get back to his house, lock himself in, and wait for us to get there. And in the meantime, tell him to open the door to no one. Absolutely no one.'

Not two minutes later, the phone rings.

Chapter 67

He watches the man leave the house. Three minutes: right on time.

He closes the door behind him and heads for the garage. He stops halfway there and looks up at the window of Stella's room. This too is part of the ritual, the same thing every time it's not raining.

At the window Roberta looks down, with the baby in her arms. The Crocodile sees that the woman is already dressed. Excellent. The mother waves her baby's tiny hand: *Ciao, Papà, buona giornata*. Have a good day. He blows a kiss in return.

Now he's in the garage. The black Mercedes starts up and emerges, as slow and sinuous as a panther emerging from its lair. He honks the horn: one last farewell.

The very last one, the Crocodile thinks.

The gate opens automatically and the car exits. The woman and the baby recede into the shadow of the nursery.

The Crocodile breathes slowly, watching.

*

Now they have the address; in the end the secretary relented.

Piras's efforts to control herself when the woman called back were plain. Lojacono even detected a vein pulsating away in her temple, something he hadn't seen even during the memorable plenary session with the station captains.

She even gave them Masi's mobile phone number, but apparently he has it turned off. So they told the woman to keep trying to call him and not to stop, and once she finally manages to reach the engineer, to ask him to return home immediately where he'd find them waiting. They had some questions to ask him.

Once that conversation is over, they look each other in the eye for a second. With that glance, Piras is asking: Is this necessary? He, with his glance, replies: I can't say. But what if it is?

They rush down into the courtyard, summoning a police car with two officers as they gallop down the stairs.

The Crocodile watches as the Mercedes reaches the bottom of the little hill. He can predict the exact instant when the red brake lights will flash on, yielding to cross traffic before turning on to the main thoroughfare.

He counts to fifteen and then he goes over to the buzzer. It's exactly ten steps from where he was hiding.

He waits another fraction of a second and then he looks around to make sure that no one is watching. He pushes the button. A few seconds later, Roberta's voice emerges, sounding vaguely surprised.

'Yes?'

The Crocodile replies in a low, slightly agitated voice,

'Signora, was that your husband who just left the house? Driving a black Mercedes?'

The woman replies immediately,

'Yes, that was my husband. Why, what is it?'

The Crocodile, turning his face away from the microphone to give the impression he's looking down the street, says,

'Didn't you hear the noise? There was an accident with a lorry, right at the end of this street. The lorry went past the stop sign. He's trapped in the car. Hurry down!'

Roberta emits a little scream and he can hear her slam the intercom receiver down into its cradle. The Crocodile retreats to his hiding place and waits. It all depends on this moment. It all depends on what the woman does right now.

A few seconds later the front door is thrown open and Roberta emerges from the house at a run.

Orlando turns into the traffic along the waterfront, his mind already focused on the problems that will face him during his workday. Today he's going to have to go into the local government headquarters to talk with officials there about a construction project that's behind schedule. He hates local government.

Almost immediately he stops in a queue of cars at a red light. He takes advantage of the stop to turn on the radio. Then, as he's about to switch on his mobile phone, the light turns green and the cars start moving again.

The mobile phone will have to wait for the next stoplight.

*

Traffic. The usual traffic.

Lojacono has grown used to thinking of the city as a wall. Mistrust, indifference, and the constant noise that drowns out words and makes a whispered conversation impossible. The traffic, the silent crowd, the hate-filled glares. A wall.

The parents of the murdered children, Lojacono decides, have chiselled a crack into the wall. They've been willing to remember and to speak, even though it ran counter to their own self-interest. A crack in the wall that's been keeping him at a distance, the wall that protects the Crocodile. But the wall is capable of closing itself back up, and one tactic it uses in order to paper over the crack is that it produces traffic.

As if Piras were reading his mind, she says to the officer at the wheel,

'Put on the siren. And step on it.'

The Crocodile moves quickly. He knows that he has only a few seconds, less than twenty if Roberta realises halfway down the short lane that there hasn't been any accident.

He walks quickly, keeping close to the wall, and slips through the pedestrian gate, which Roberta left swinging open behind her. He runs up the driveway and enters the house.

He shuts the door behind him. And he locks the deadbolt from inside.

Orlando stops at the second traffic light. Never once is this light green, he thinks. They're supposed to be timed to move traffic faster, but instead every single one is always red.

He turns on his mobile and it immediately starts ringing. The word 'Office' flashes insistently on the display. Damn it, thinks Orlando, I haven't even got in and they're already busting my balls.

He rummages around in the glove compartment for his headset. The last thing he needs is a fine from a traffic cop because that idiot of a secretary decided he needed to know some nonsense or other.

Roberta runs up the street, more and more puzzled. She's caught between a sense of relief at the fact that there is no accident and annoyance at having been made the object of a stupid prank.

She looks around to see if there is some little kid laughing behind her back. If she catches him she'll teach him a lesson he won't forget in a hurry. She remembers that a few months ago local kids started pulling the prank of ringing doorbells late at night on their way home from nightclubs, startling her out of a slumber that was already fitful, what with her enormous belly.

The memory of her pregnancy makes her remember Stella, and with a stab of worry she speeds up her pace.

The traffic parts like a choppy sea before the wail of the siren. Now they're moving quickly, but it's a long way from police headquarters to the address that the engineer's secretary gave them.

Lojacono clenches and unclenches his fist without realising

it. He's anxious to talk to this man. He wonders if he remembers the past, if he ever met Eleonora's father. If in all these years he ever thought about her again.

More than anything else, he wants to know if the man has a family. If he has children.

His heart throbs painfully in his chest, and he thinks about Marinella again: the curve of her neck, bent over as she writes, the two yellow eyes in the darkness.

Unexpectedly, delicately, Piras's hand comes to rest on his.

Orlando's turned his car around and is heading back home now.

He's perplexed, and he's worried too. An assistant public prosecutor, no less. And a police inspector.

The secretary had seemed cautious and circumspect to him. What can possibly have happened? If it was work-related, they would have been waiting for him at the office. Any legal proceedings would have had to be based on documents, blueprints, surveys and floor plans. Why ask to meet him at home?

Orlando starts to delve into the past, trying to remember anything that might have attracted the attention of the police, and no matter how hard he tries, he can't come up with a thing. Nothing.

He accelerates, honking his horn repeatedly.

Roberta wails in desperation. The door is bolted shut from inside, and her fear for her husband made her rush out of the house, leaving her keys behind her.

People start crowding around the windows, their attention summoned by the screaming and shouting. Roberta pounds on the door and the sound carries. But no sound comes from within.

The policeman at the wheel says, 'Here we are, dottore, this should be the address, at the end of this little lane.'

No sooner are the words out of his mouth than they see the woman pounding flat-handed on the door, screaming.

Piras looks at Lojacono and sees desperation, rage and helplessness in his eyes.

Lojacono hurls himself out of the car before it's fully come to a stop, his hand already groping for the gun in his shoulder holster.

At the same instant, the Mercedes pulls up with a screech of its brakes.

Chapter 68

Orlando glances quickly at the police car, parked with two wheels on the pavement, and runs to his wife's side.

The woman, babbling incoherently, is talking about an accident that never happened, someone at the intercom, and finding the door locked behind her. Lojacono runs up to them, badge in hand, followed by Piras and the two uniformed police officers.

'Are you Engineer Orlando Masi?'

The man does his best to understand what's going on. He's disoriented and can't seem to work out what to deal with first. He looks up anxiously at one of the windows on the second floor. He rattles his key in the lock but the door seems to be bolted from within and refuses to budge.

'It's my daughter, my baby girl. She's six months old and she's locked inside all by herself. The door won't open. Can you help us to get inside?'

Lojacono thinks fast. He's certain the little girl isn't alone at all. He's never been one to believe in coincidence. He looks around, trying to find evidence of someone passing by, or watching them from a distance. He realises that there's at least one person peering down from every window. Despair and panic always make an especially intriguing show.

He waves the couple aside and calls the officers over. They try the door. The bigger of the two takes a step back and delivers a stomping kick to the door, right next to the handle, followed by another, and another. Finally the wood begins to give with a crack and the door creaks open slightly.

The other officer has pulled a crowbar out of the car and is starting to prise the opening wider.

Meanwhile, Piras is with Masi's wife, trying to comfort her and at the same time find out what has happened. She glances at Lojacono over the woman's shoulders, which are racked with sobs. They were right. But that's not much consolation.

The door swings open, banging against the wall. Masi tries to run inside but Lojacono stops him.

'Stay out of the way. Stay back here with your wife. Let us go in first.'

In a single fluid gesture he draws his Beretta out of its holster. The two officers step forward and he summons one of them, asking the other one to wait there. But the engineer is driven by fury. He wriggles out of the policeman's grip and runs into the house, followed by his wife and Piras.

Lojacono signals to them to be absolutely silent. They stop in the small front hall, at the foot of a flight of stairs. At the top, Lojacono can glimpse two doors, one of them half open.

Everyone holds their breath. Outside, a bird assays a few

notes. From the top of the stairs, as faint as a whisper, they hear a voice.

'Hush a bye baby, oh, I'll give you a star.'

The sheer incongruity of the chant, the hoarse, scratchy male voice, the implicit menace in his very presence, cause everyone's flesh to crawl.

The baby's mother falls to her knees with a desperate wail. The father tries to climb the stairs, but Lojacono throws out his arm to block him, gesturing for silence. The man looks the inspector in the eyes and glimpses an expression of absolute determination. He stops, frozen to the spot.

From the baby's room the chant continues.

'Sleep pretty baby, it's the brightest by far.'

It is possible to detect a tender smile in the tone of the voice, something that makes it even more chilling. Lojacono starts climbing the stairs, trying to make no noise, his handgun levelled, the other hand pressing against the wall to help him balance. Behind him, equally silent, come Masi and the police officer.

The mother is still on her knees at the foot of the stairs, both hands covering her face. Piras is kneeling beside her, her arms wrapped around her, but her large dark eyes follow Lojacono's back as he climbs. She's terrified.

Not again, she thinks. Please, not again.

'Hush a bye, hush a bye; Now do you want the world?'

Lojacono is at the top of the stairs, next to the half-open door. He leans against the doorjamb and slowly pushes the door open with one foot, without allowing himself to be seen from within.

The voice seems to pay no attention to the opening of the door, even though it creaks slightly.

'*For the sweet love of God, go to sleep, darling girl.*'

Encouraged, Lojacono takes a step sideways to get a better view.

The room is immersed in a half-light; a milky, uncertain light filters in through the window. In the corner, Lojacono glimpses a silhouette, standing next to the cot. The singsong voice comes from there.

The policeman swings his gun around, aiming it as he blinks rapidly to accustom his sight to the partial darkness.

'Freeze. Don't move.'

The silhouette becomes a short man, with a bundle in his arms, swaying gently, rocking, lulling. He's old, or at least he's no longer young. He raises one hand to his eye and dabs at a tear. Lojacono realises he's in the presence of the Crocodile.

At the same time, he sees that the bundle in the man's arms is the baby.

There they stand, face to face. Lojacono, legs apart, duty revolver held at arm's length, one hand bracing the other, aims at the old man while he continues to rock the baby gently while mumbling the lullaby. Lojacono's eyes, by now accustomed to the half-light, spot the long barrel of a pistol with a silencer in the hand holding the bundle.

Behind him comes the father's dull lament, bemoaning his child like the sigh of the wind.

The seconds go by and nothing happens. Lojacono knows that he can't fire without the risk of hitting the baby, but if the man were to do anything dangerous, he'd still have to pull the trigger. He shifts the sight at the end of his gun's barrel imperceptibly towards the man's head, the vital point that's farthest from the bundle that his target is holding in his arms. He breathes deeply, trying to instil in himself the requisite cool calm.

The man speaks in a low voice.

'Silence. It's time for a moment of silence, don't you think? There's really no need to say anything more.'

Lojacono frantically scans the room, hunting for some way of getting the baby out of the grip of that man's arms. Out of the Crocodile's jaws. Behind him, the baby's father keeps up his dull lament.

At that moment, Lojacono's eyes are attracted by a faint reflection on the floor, against the wall across from the old man. He wonders what it is, looks up and sees a picture frame with broken glass; inside the frame is a drawing, the face of a child.

With a stain in the middle of it.

He works backwards, reconstructing the trajectory: he reaches the bundle in the murderer's arms; he understands the path the bullet followed from the gun to the drawing; what it passed through to get there.

Lojacono murmurs,

'No. Fuck, no. No.'

While the father says, his voice breaking into sobs,

'Let her go, I beg you. Let my daughter go.'

And the old man says solemnly,

'I'll let her go. The way you let mine go. Only my daughter was older when she died.'

And he gradually turns the baby girl to face them, displaying the hole in the middle of the tiny forehead.

Then he lets her drop.

Murmuring 'Sweetheart, my darling', he points the pistol at his own head.

And then pulls the trigger.

Chapter 69

Sweetheart, my darling,

These are the last words I'll write to you. Tonight I'll be with you in heaven, I'll look into your sweet eyes, I'll hold your hands in mine. I'll hold you in my arms, the way I did when you were small, and I'll sing you the lullaby that you used to love so much.

Hush a bye baby, oh, I'll give you a star.

And I'll give you a star – a Stella. Isn't it a wonderful coincidence that the baby girl – his girl – is named Stella, the star?

You never did know what kind of child you would have had, my darling. Whether it would be a boy or a girl. Maybe you would have had her, this same baby; after all, it's the same father. Maybe I'll give you back your daughter, sending her straight to heaven, to stay with you. She's yours by right, after all.

Your letter, the last one you wrote, the one they gave me after I got the news you were dead. The desperate account of the last days of your life, of what they had done to you, the names and the places: the classmate who recommended the best place to get an abortion, the nurse and the doctor who were bantering light-heartedly while rummaging around in your viscera, laughing at some idiotic joke.

And him, the guiltiest of them all, the one who seduced you and deceived you and then abandoned you, to go off and build himself a wonderful new life on the smoking ruins of your grief.

I found them all. I found them with their children, with their happiness that hadn't been amputated the way ours was.

While I was hunting them down, your mother was dying, consumed from within by your death. Death rattle after death rattle, gasp after wheeze. She spent fifteen years dying, dying a thousand times every day, every time with your name on her lips.

Not me. I lived so that I could do what I had to do. So I could dream of seeing you again.

I don't believe in the things they tell us, you know. The good, the bad, heaven and hell. I believe in love and I believe in hell on earth. I've experienced hell on earth, and I am experiencing love right now. No one can keep me away from you any longer, my darling. No one can keep me away from my wonderful, sweet baby girl.

Once I've finished with the baby, the only one left to punish will be the last guilty party, the worst of them all.

The man who collapsed under the pressure of shame.

The man who refused to take you back under his roof, baby or no baby. The man who immediately sent you the money you needed to avail yourself of the services of that butcher, telling you not to show your face again until you had done what you needed to do.

Me. Myself. The worst of them all. The first murderer.

My eye won't stop welling up. It seems right, you know. I never cried when I should have, and now I have to weep for all eternity.

Sweetheart, my darling. The time has come.

My darling, I'm coming to see you.

Chapter 70

Death is a dance, Lojacono thinks. A dance choreographed by a second-rate artist.

By now darkness has fallen. Many hours have gone by and people are still looking out of every window in the neighbourhood, in thrall to an insatiable curiosity. He watches the dance of death: medical examiners, mortuary officers, coroners and assistant coroners, forensics teams, the ambulance that came to cart off the baby's mother, in a catatonic state, and the father who seems to have turned into an old man all at once.

While the dance was playing out, he asked around. It didn't take him long to find out that the hotel across the way had a guest named De Falco, Felice, and this guest – whose room, it so happens, overlooked the Masi villa – had everything in it that he had used in his identity as a killer: binoculars, bullets, paper tissues.

The same tissues they'd found on the ground, in the nook in the external wall of the neighbouring property. The Crocodile's last stakeout.

Lojacono looks at the floodlights that now illuminate the scene of the crime for the final inspections. All that time, all that effort for something that's already happened. For a tragedy that can no longer be averted.

He can feel the scorching burden of defeat. He knows that he has lost. The Crocodile was victorious, even though he is dead and Lojacono is still alive. He took what he wanted and left nothing behind him but a long letter on the desk of his hotel room: the ravings of a soul led astray by grief and sorrow.

Leaning against the low wall overlooking the bay of Naples, Lojacono watches the city gradually light up in the falling darkness. He thinks about a short, elderly man moving through that city, from one end to the other, thirsting for innocent blood. And no one could see him. You were invisible, Crocodile; like me. And when we caught sight of each other, it was too late. Too late for everything.

A few minutes ago Giuffrè had called him. '*Bravo*, my colleague. You see? You were right all along. They've stopped calling you Montalbano, you know. Now they call you the Crocodile. After all, you're the one who caught him in the end.'

So I'm the Crocodile now, Lojacono muses. Maybe that's right. I'm alone, I'm desperate, and I'm invisible. With an insatiable hunger for love.

From a distance, Laura Piras watches Lojacono. Behind him, the city lies spread out like a sleeping beast.

Piras knows what the police inspector is thinking: that was

certainly no victory. She thinks the same thing. No victory ever ended with a dead six-month-old baby.

Paradoxically enough, though, it was the death of that baby girl that reawakened a gnawing hunger for life inside her. She's gone too long without life. She's spent too long suffering, grieving.

And the terror that swept over her as she watched him walk into the face of danger, climbing those stairs with a gun in his hand, made it clear to her that the time had come to return to the world.

Through the tears that well up in her eyes, she glimpses behind Lojacono the outline of a tall, gangly young man, bespectacled, with a turtleneck sweater and a messy mop of hair on his head, turning one last time to wave goodbye to her. *Ciao*, Carlo, she thinks. *Addio*. So long, God be with you.

And she wonders when it will occur to the inspector to invite her out to dinner, or whether she ought to make the first move.

About thirty feet away, Lojacono shakes himself out of his reverie and summons his courage. He pulls out his mobile phone, scrolls through the contacts list, and finds the name he's looking for.

With a deep sigh, he pushes the green button. He waits, with his heart in his mouth: one ring, two rings, five.

Just as he's about to push the red button resignedly, a girl's voice says uncertainly,

'Hello?'

Acknowledgements

Lojacono's gratitude goes out to: Luigi Merolla, Fabiola Mancone, Valeria Moffa, Luigi Bonagura, Paolo Ferradino; angels who watch over this unfortunate city.

To Giulio Di Mizio, and to his eyes that survey death. To Maria Pia Salerno, and her eyes that survey life.

To Giulia, Maria Paola, and Antonio, that night in Milan. To the wonderful Corpi Freddi, that night in Mantua.

The author's gratitude goes, as always, for as long as he can remember, and for ever: to Paola.

Maurizio de Giovanni, 2012

THE DARK HEART OF FLORENCE

Michele Giuttari

After enduring years at the mercy of an infamous serial killer, the people of Florence rejoice at news of his death – until a senator is found brutally murdered.

To Chief Superintendent Michele Ferrara the case is very much alive. But, with a powerful adversary conspiring against him, he is trapped in a spiral of corruption and deadly speculation. As the truth comes to light, Ferrara is left standing face-to-face with something truly rotten at the heart of the city …

The Dark Heart of Florence is an evocative, gripping work of detective fiction, and a major bestseller across Europe.

'A crime author with impeccable credentials: Giuttari is no less than the former head of the Florence police force, where he was on the case of the notorious serial killer The Monster of Florence. Who better to write about the dark undercurrents beneath the surface of the city?' *Booklist*

Abacus
978 0 349 13933 3

THE VANISHED ONES

Michele Giuttari

Everyone forgets the 'Disappeared': the hundreds of eyes that stare out from the missing person board of Italy's dark-hearted city, Rome. No one has the time or energy to find them – no one but Mila Vasquez, a fiery young officer struggling with a damaged past. Finding the people that everyone else has forgotten is what she lives for.

But what if some of these people wanted to disappear? To be swallowed into the darkness so that everyone forgets they were ever here. And now they have started to return, with strange and horrifying intentions. They seem identical at first, but something has changed them: they are an army of shadows.

The Vanished Ones is the gripping new thriller from Italian literary sensation Donato Carrisi, author of the bestselling, prize-winning novel *The Whisperer.*

Abacus
978 0 349 14005 6

ABACUS